Also by Jennifer L. Schiff

Sanibel Island Mysteries

A Shell of a Problem

Something Fishy

In the Market for Murder

Bye Bye Birdy

Shell Shocked

Trouble in Paradise

A Perilous Proposal

For Whom the Shell Tolls

The Crisis Before Christmas

Novels

Tinder Fella

Something's Cooking in Chianti

Framed in Naples

A Sanibel Island Mystery

Jennifer Lonoff Schiff

Shovel & Pail Press

FRAMED IN NAPLES: A SANIBEL ISLAND MYSTERY
by Jennifer Lonoff Schiff

Book 10 in the Sanibel Island Mystery series

https://SanibelIslandMysteries.com

Cover design by Rita Sri Harningsih

Formatting by Polgarus Studio

ISBN: 979-8-218-23764-6

Library of Congress Control Number: 2023913621

AUTHOR'S NOTE

As many of you know, Hurricane Ian hit Sanibel on September 28, 2022, sending approximately nine feet of water—more in some places, a bit less in others—across the island, damaging or destroying homes (including mine) and businesses.

However, this book takes place before the hurricane was on anyone's radar. For that reason, I have included places on Sanibel that existed then. Sadly, some of these beloved places have since closed. Though others, like Bailey's General Store, are rebuilding and hope to reopen in the not-too-distant future.

Also, while there is a Baker Museum—it's part of Artis-Naples in North Naples, Florida—the version of the Baker I describe in the book and the people I have working there are entirely fictional. That said, the museum does have a lovely outdoor terrace on the third floor, which I highly recommend, especially for viewing the sunset. And there is a hidden staircase.

PROLOGUE

Guin looked out the window of the airplane and watched as Paris grew smaller.

"You okay?" Glen asked.

"I'm fine," Guin replied. "I just…"

Glen waited for her to go on.

"You just what?" he said when she didn't continue.

"I just wish we didn't have to go back to Sanibel just yet."

Glen smiled.

"And to think you didn't want to go to Paris."

"I know."

"We can always come back, you know. Paris will still be here."

"I know," Guin said. "It's just…" She paused and looked out the window again. But clouds obscured her view.

"It's just what?" Glen asked.

Guin continued to gaze out the window.

"It's just…" She stopped again, trying to organize her thoughts. "You know that I love Sanibel."

"I do."

"And I love you."

"And I love you."

Guin smiled.

"And I love working at the paper." The paper being the *Sanibel-Captiva Sun-Times*, the paper of record for the islands of Sanibel and Captiva in Florida, where Guin worked as a reporter and Glen was a photographer.

Glen gave her a questioning look.

"Okay, maybe *love* is a bit strong. But I've enjoyed working there. And if it weren't for the paper, we wouldn't have met."

"True."

"But some days," Guin continued. She paused. "Some days, I wonder if I'm just treading water."

"Treading water?"

"You know what I mean."

"I'm not sure I do."

"I mean that while I like living on Sanibel and writing for the paper, sometimes I feel like I'm just playing it safe, that I should be doing more than writing about store openings and wealthy people who give money to charity and reviewing restaurants."

"What about solving murders?"

Guin made a face. Since coming to Sanibel, she had been involved in several murder cases. And while playing amateur sleuth had had its moments—of excitement and danger—she would be very happy to never encounter another dead body. As she told Glen.

"So what do you want to write about?"

"I don't know. Just something different. Maybe even take a break from writing and try something else."

"Like?"

"I don't know."

"What about taking some kind of class? You liked that cooking class we took in Italy."*

"True."

"Or maybe take an art class. BIG ARTS has lots of classes you could try."

"Aren't they mostly during the day?"

"I'm sure there are classes at night too. Or you could do

---

* Read *Something's Cooking in Chianti.*

one during the day. It's not like you have a nine-to-five office job."

"True." Guin worked from home, as did most of the people who worked for the paper, only going into the office once or twice a week to chat with her boss and whoever was there.

"And you could always take a freelance assignment."

"Like Ginny [their boss at the paper] would allow that."

"You don't know that. Have you ever asked her? She lets me freelance."

"That's because you came to her as a freelancer. And unless something's changed, you're still technically freelance and can take other jobs."

"Technically, I'm an independent contractor. But that's not the point. The point is, how do you know what Ginny will say unless you ask her?"

"Well, I doubt she'd allow me to freelance during the season." The season on Sanibel and Captiva running from November through April.

"There's always summer."

Guin looked thoughtful. Things on Sanibel and Captiva were much slower during the summer months. But she still had to file a story or two every week. As Ginny loved to remind everyone, even with fewer people on the islands and fewer things to do, they still had a paper to put out.

"I'll think about it."

The flight attendant came by with the drink cart and asked if they wanted something. Guin thought about getting a coffee, but she had had two large cups at the hotel that morning and asked for a glass of water instead. She took a sip and then placed the glass on Glen's tray table.

"Speaking of Ginny, I should get to work on the Paris article." She let out a yawn.

"Take a nap and work on it when we get back."

"I should really…" She was interrupted by another yawn.

"Get some sleep. Not like we got a lot last night."

Guin felt her face grow warm thinking about it. It had been their last night in Paris. They had gone to the Eiffel Tower for a romantic dinner as part of the article Guin was writing—and Glen was photographing—for the paper on how to spend a romantic Valentine's Day weekend in Paris. Afterwards, they had gone back to their hotel and hadn't fallen asleep until after midnight.

"As tempting as a nap sounds," Guin replied. "Ginny's going to want the article five minutes after we get back. And as I have all of my notes on my computer and don't have anything else to do…"

"Suit yourself," he said and reached for his book.

Guin looked at him.

"What?"

"Aren't you going to edit your pictures?"

"I'll edit them when I get home."

Guin continued to look at him.

"What?" he said again.

"You know Ginny's going to want you to send them to her as soon as…"

"Fine," he said, putting away his book and reaching for his laptop.

"Sorry," said Guin. But they both knew she was right.

"Ladies and gentlemen," came the announcement over the sound system some seven hours later. "We have begun our descent into Miami International Airport. Please stow your electronic devices and store your tray tables."

"Done!" said Guin, quickly saving her document.

"You finished the article already?"

"Just the first draft."

"Still, I'm impressed."

"Don't be. It still needs a lot of work. But I think I made

a good start. How are the photos coming?"

"Okay."

"Just okay?"

"I would prefer to edit them in my studio, on my big monitor."

Guin ignored his accusatory tone.

"Can I see them?"

"You heard what the flight attendant said. Time to put away all electronic devices."

"Just a quick peek."

"I'll show them to you later, when we get to my place."

"I should go home and check on the cats."

"I'm sure Fauna and Spot are fine. Sadie can watch them for a few more hours." Sadie was Guin's elderly, cat-loving neighbor. "Besides, it'll be late by the time we get back to my place. And you're already tired. You should just stay over. I'll show you my pictures in the morning. Then you can drive to Sanibel."

"I'll think about it," said Guin.

CHAPTER 1

"So, tell me all about Paris!"

"I already told you, Shell."

Guin was having lunch with her best friend Shelly at one of their favorite restaurants.

"No, you just texted that you were busy but having a good time and would tell me all about it when you got back. So, spill!"

Guin told her about the hotel they had stayed at on the Left Bank, which she said was very nice. And that they took long walks along the Seine.

"Did you go to the top of the Eiffel Tower?" said Shelly, interrupting her.

"We did."

"And…?"

"We had dinner there our last night."

"Ooh! How romantic! And…?"

"And what?"

Shelly gave her a look, a look that said, "You know what."

"And did he propose?! Don't think I didn't notice that ring on your finger."

Guin looked down at the sapphire and diamond ring on her left ring finger, which Glen had given her at Christmas. She had been reluctant to wear it around Sanibel, fearing people would get the wrong idea and think it was an engagement ring. However, she had worn it every day while she and Glen were in Paris and had forgotten to take it off when she got back. Or maybe she hadn't forgotten.

"It's not what you think, Shelly. It's a promise ring."

"A promise ring? What's a promise ring? Sure looks like an engagement ring to me. Did Glen give it to you?"

"He did. It belonged to his grandmother."

"Definitely an engagement ring."

"I told you…"

Shelly held up a hand to silence Guin.

"Call it whatever you want, but take it from someone who makes jewelry for a living: It's an engagement ring. So did he propose to you or not?"

"He did not."

Shelly frowned.

"But he gave you a ring. His grandmother's ring."

"I told you, it's a promise ring. And he gave me the ring at Christmas."

"You've had it since Christmas, and you didn't tell me?!" Shelly shook her head.

"I wanted to keep it a secret."

"Why?"

"I didn't want people to get the wrong idea," Guin replied, looking directly at Shelly.

"So he really didn't propose while you were in Paris?"

"Sorry to disappoint you, but no."

"Did something happen?"

"Nothing happened."

"And he's told you he loves you."

"Many times."

"And you love him."

"I do."

"So what's the problem?!"

"There is no problem. We're good with the way things are. Not everyone needs to be married."

Shelly had been married to her college sweetheart for over 30 years and thought everyone should be married. Or people who loved each other and had been dating for over a year.

"I know not everyone needs to be married. But you two are perfect for each other!"

"You said that about me and Ris and Detective O'Loughlin too. And neither of those relationships worked out."

"I don't recall saying either of them was perfect for you."

"Uh-huh."

"Okay, maybe I did. But I know for sure that Glen is the one. You even said so."

"When?"

"Just before you left on your trip."

"I don't remember that."

"Well, to be fair, you had had a margarita when you said it. So if he had asked you to marry him, would you have said yes?"

Guin mulled it over. She had been married before, to a man who cheated on her. And she had sworn she'd think long and hard about ever marrying again, although she was only in her early forties. But Glen was different than the other men she had dated since the divorce. He was kind and thoughtful and patient and good at communicating, in addition to being handsome. And they had been colleagues and friends before becoming lovers.

"Maybe."

"I knew it!" Shelly crowed. Then she turned serious. "So why didn't he pop the question while you two were in Paris?"

Guin desperately wanted to change the subject.

"Maybe he doesn't want to get married. I'm not the only one whose spouse cheated on them."

Glen's wife had also had an affair—with her tennis instructor.

"Now can we please change the subject?"

"Fine. I just hate having to pay up."

"Pay up?" Guin looked at her friend. "Did you make a bet with someone that Glen would propose while we were in Paris?"

"Maybe," said Shelly, not meeting Guin's eyes.

"Who did you make a bet with? Wait. Don't tell me."

Guin could tell that Shelly felt guilty and took pity on her.

"So, do you want to hear about the rest of the trip or not?"

Shelly immediately perked up.

"I do. Tell me everything."

And Guin did.

"Well, if it isn't Guinivere Jones, world traveler," said Ginny, sitting back in her chair.

"Here," said Guin, handing Ginny a pastry box. "These are for you."

"They from Paris?"

"No, they're from Jean-Luc's." Guin had stopped at the bakery café after lunch. "But they're just as good as the ones we had in Paris."

"You tell Jean-Luc that?"

"And inflate his already inflated ego?"

They both smiled.

"Go on, take a load off," said Ginny.

Guin glanced at the two visitor chairs. As usual, they were covered with newspapers, magazines, and folders. And on one of the piles sat a shoe box.

"I need to return those," said Ginny.

Guin removed the pile without the shoebox and sat.

"So, how was Paris?"

"Good."

Ginny gave her a look.

"Was that the wrong answer?"

"I was hoping for a little bit more than just *good.* After all, the paper did pay for your trip." Though technically, the paper had given Guin and Glen a stipend, which covered their meals and not a lot more. Glen had paid for their airfare and hotel using his points. But Guin wasn't going to quibble.

"What is it you want to know?"

"Everything."

"Now? You don't want to wait for my article? I'm almost done with it."

"Almost?"

"I wrote the first draft on the airplane. I just need to fine-tune it. I should have it to you tomorrow."

"Fine. I suppose I can wait. What about the pictures? Is Glen working on them?"

"He is."

"Good. Have him send them to me when you send me the article. I need to get everything to the printer *tout de suite.*"

"I'll let him know."

"Do that. Though I may write to him myself. I have a big story that I want the two of you to cover."

"Oh?"

"What do you know about Farley Bishop?"

"Farley Bishop?" The name sounded vaguely familiar, but Guin couldn't place it.

"Please tell me you've heard of Farley Bishop."

Guin racked her brain but wasn't coming up with anything.

"Sorry. The name sounds familiar. But I have no idea who he is."

Ginny sighed and shook her head.

"He's only one of the most important American contemporary artists."

"You know I'm not a big fan of contemporary art, Gin. So, is he having an exhibit at BIG ARTS?" BIG ARTS was the local performing and fine arts center.

"No, much bigger than that. The Baker Museum in Naples is hosting a retrospective of his work. It's sure to be covered by all of the art publications and major papers."

"And I take it you want me and Glen to be there."

"I do. And I'd like you to interview Farley beforehand."

"Fine. Give me his contact info and I'll shoot him an email."

"I don't think you understand, Guinivere. Farley Bishop hasn't allowed a museum or gallery to exhibit his work or given an interview in over twenty years."

"How come?"

"During his last exhibit, held at the Museum of Modern Art in New York back in 1998, there was a controversy surrounding some of the paintings."

"What kind of controversy?"

"He was accused of copying another artist's work."

"Did he?"

"He vehemently denied it. But not everyone believed him. Shortly after that, he left New York, never to be heard from again."

"Did he die? Wait, you said you wanted me to interview him, so I presume he's not dead. Where'd he go?"

"I was about to tell you."

"Sorry. Go on."

"He's here."

"Here on Sanibel?"

Ginny nodded.

"Bought a little place near Captiva sometime in the eighties and was a snowbird. Then he moved here permanently around twenty years ago."

"And no one knows he's here?" Guin found that hard to believe. "How do you know?"

Ginny gave her a look. *Of course*, thought Guin. Silly question. Ginny knew everything of importance that happened on Sanibel and Captiva, or almost everything, as well as everyone of importance.

"Farley and Joel play chess together. Have been for years."

Joel was Ginny's common-law husband.

"And no one else knows he lives here?"

"Some people know. But it's a well-kept secret."

"So if he's such a recluse, why is he allowing the Baker to host a retrospective of his work?"

"That's what I want you to find out."

"Joel doesn't know?"

"They don't talk much when they're playing chess. Anyway, the exhibit opens in a couple of weeks, and I want you to interview him beforehand."

"Okay. But if Bishop hasn't given an interview to anyone in twenty years, what makes you think he'll give one to me?"

"How could he resist you? Also, I told him we wouldn't publish anything without his approval."

"You promised him approval? That's very unlike you. What if he doesn't approve of what I have to say about him?"

"Then I'll twist his arm. Hopefully, it won't come to that. But it was the only way I could get him to agree to even the possibility of an interview."

"Okay. Fine. Give me his email address."

"He doesn't have one."

"What?"

"He doesn't like email. Or computers."

"Okay. What's his cell phone number?"

"He doesn't own a cell phone. Or if he does, it's a secret."

Guin stared at her boss.

"Land line?"

"That he has, but he rarely answers it."

"How are people supposed to reach him, carrier pigeon?"

Ginny smiled.

"Just come to our place tomorrow evening for drinks. Farley'll be there, and he can interview you then."

"Wait, I thought I was to interview him."

"He wants to interview you first. He's a bit suspicious of reporters."

Guin frowned.

"Just humor him. Farley comes across as a bit gruff. But I'm sure that deep down inside he's a teddy bear."

"Really?"

"Probably not. Just do your best to win him over."

"I'll do what I can."

"And do some research. I wouldn't want you to embarrass yourself or the paper when you meet him."

Ginny knew that Guin didn't have a background in Art History. Yet as the paper didn't currently have an Arts reporter, it was up to Guin as the general assignment reporter to cover the arts.

"Of course."

Guin would look into the mysterious Farley Bishop when she got home and would also ask Glen what he knew, Glen knowing much more about contemporary art than she did.

"What time should I get to your place?"

"Five-thirty. And bring Glen."

"I'm not sure he's free tomorrow evening."

"Tell him to make himself free."

"Okay. Any other orders?"

They were interrupted by the ringing of Ginny's phone, which Ginny immediately answered.

"Virginia Prescott."

Guin mouthed that she would see herself out and left.

CHAPTER 2

As soon as Guin got home, she did a search for Farley Bishop online. Yet she wondered as she typed his name into the search box how useful the internet would be if he hadn't had an exhibit since 1998. However, as soon as she hit "Enter," the screen began to populate.

Of course, Farley Bishop, the man who didn't like email or computers, didn't have a website. But there were dozens of articles about him and his artwork. Guin clicked on one from 2000, titled "Artists Settle Plagiarism Case," and began to read.

Per the article, Bishop had been accused by another artist, a painter named Willem Budge, of copying his paintings. The case had been about to go to trial when the two artists had decided to settle. The terms of the settlement were not disclosed.

The article contained pictures of the two artists—Bishop was a good deal older than Budge—as well as photographs of the paintings in question side by side. Guin studied the paintings. They were similar, but that didn't mean that Bishop had plagiarized Budge's work. Many artists painted in a similar style, even emulated artists they admired. But unless you were literally forging another artist's work and calling it your own, Guin imagined it would be hard to make a plagiarism charge stick.

Moreover, Bishop claimed that he had never seen

Budge's work or knew the man. Though Budge claimed that wasn't true, that they had had exhibits at the same gallery, albeit at different times, and that Bishop had visited his show, an accusation Bishop denied.

Guin closed the article and searched for examples of Bishop's work. She eventually found a site that featured over a dozen of his paintings. Like Picasso and some other Modern and Contemporary painters, Bishop had started his career doing realistic portraits and still lifes. However, over the years, his work had taken on a more abstract or surrealistic quality.

During one period, in the nineties, he had taken some of his older paintings, cut them into jigsaw-style puzzle pieces, and then rearranged them to create something entirely new. Guin liked these pieces much less than Bishop's earlier work, but she admired his creativity, his ability to reinvent himself.

Indeed, Bishop seemed to reinvent himself quite often. And each time he did, he received both praise and criticism. Guin studied his later works. She found some of them interesting. But she liked his earlier, realistic work best.

She clicked on a few more articles about Bishop. Critics had plenty to say about his art, but there was little about his personal life. All she could gather was that he had been married at one time and had a child, a daughter, and that his wife had left him after accusing him of having an affair with his muse, an artist's model named Amalia.

She also discovered that he had been mentored by Robert Rauschenberg and had been a frequent visitor to Rauschenberg's studio on Captiva. But that was all she was able to find about Bishop. He was a bit of an enigma. Or perhaps a chameleon, changing himself or his art to suit the time.

Guin got up at five the next morning, still suffering from jet lag. She thought about going for a beach walk, but she didn't like going out before sunrise. Instead, she worked on her Paris piece.

At three o'clock, her Paris article finished and her eyelids drooping, she went to take a nap. She needed to be fresh for her meeting with Farley Bishop at Ginny and Joel's.

She set her alarm for four o'clock and lay down, the cats immediately joining her on the bed. When she got up, she still felt a bit sleepy, but some cold water on her face and a little iced coffee fixed that.

A little after five, Glen arrived to take Guin to their boss's house. Guin had been to Ginny and Joel's place a few times. It was on Dinkins Bayou, not far from the bridge to Captiva, and charming.

While Ginny loved to entertain, Joel, an avowed introvert, did not. So Ginny did most of her socializing outside of their home, typically solo. But they would occasionally host friends for brunch or dinner.

"So tell me what you know about Farley Bishop," Guin asked Glen as they drove. "I did some research online. But I couldn't find out a whole lot about him. Just that he liked to change his style, had been married at one time, supposedly had an affair with his muse, and had been accused of plagiarizing another artist's work."

"That's pretty much what I know," said Glen. "Bishop came to prominence in the late sixties and was right up there with Roy Lichtenstein, James Rosenquist, and Robert Rauschenberg. In fact, Rauschenberg was a mentor of his."

"I read that."

"There was even a rumor that the two were lovers."

"That I didn't see. Anything else?"

"You said you read about the lawsuit."

"I did. Seemed a bit frivolous to me. You think that's why Bishop left New York for Sanibel?"

"Maybe. Maybe he was just tired of the New York art scene."

A few minutes later, they arrived at Ginny and Joel's house. It was an average-size house by Sanibel standards. Nothing fancy. Yet it had a cozy feel, with comfortable furniture, artwork by local artists, and a small chef's kitchen. It also had a good-sized screened lanai and a boat dock.

They climbed the steps to the front door and rang the doorbell.

"It's open!" Ginny called.

They let themselves in and were greeted by their boss.

"Glad you two could make it. Can I get you something to drink? I have wine, beer, single malt Scotch…"

"I'll take a beer," said Glen.

"And I'll just have a glass of water," said Guin.

"I was just on my way to the kitchen to get beers for the boys. They're out on the lanai. Come."

They followed her to the kitchen.

Ginny reached into the refrigerator and grabbed three beers, placing them on the counter. Then she poured some ice water into a glass for Guin.

"Here," she said, handing the glass to Guin and then handing Glen a beer.

"Bottle opener?"

"Right." Ginny got it out and handed it to Glen. "You mind taking these out to the lanai?" she asked Guin, holding up the two beers. "I'll be along in a minute."

"Sure," Guin replied.

They headed to the lanai. Joel and Bishop—for who else could it be?—stopped talking as soon as Guin and Glen appeared.

"Here are your beers," Guin said, placing them on the table. "Ginny will be out in a minute."

"Thanks," said Joel.

Guin looked from Joel to the man seated across from

him, waiting to be introduced. Joel finally got the hint.

"Right. Guin, this is our neighbor, Farley Bishop. Farley, this is Guin. She works with Ginny."

"And this is Glen," said Guin. "He's a photographer."

She saw Bishop studying Glen. Then he turned his gaze on her.

As he contemplated her, Guin contemplated him. He was tall and lean with an angular face, dark brown eyes, and bushy eyebrows. His face was lined, but he didn't look like he spent much time out in the sun. And although he was around eighty, he didn't seem old. He was also wearing a scowl.

"I'm a big fan of your work, Mr. Bishop," said Glen, breaking the silence.

Bishop didn't respond.

Fortunately, Ginny reappeared at that moment, bearing a charcuterie board. She placed it on the table and looked at the group.

"You introduce everyone?" she asked Joel.

"He did," said Guin.

Guin could feel Bishop still studying her.

"Where are you from?" he asked her.

"Originally? New York City."

"I meant, where's your family from?"

"All over. But we're mostly Northern and Eastern European, if that's what you mean."

"You ever model?"

"Excuse me?" Was he serious? Guin was maybe five-foot-four, five-six in heels. Though even if she had been taller, she couldn't imagine anyone thinking she'd been a model. Not that she was unattractive but… "I'm a bit short to be a model."

"Not that kind of model. I meant an artist's model."

"Oh. Well, back in high school, we used to model for each other in art class. With our clothes on," she quickly added.

Guin wondered if scowling was Bishop's default expression.

"Ginny wants me to let you interview me."

Guin wasn't sure how to reply. She could feel Bishop's eyes on her.

"I'll do it on one condition," he continued.

"What's the condition?"

"Sit for me."

"Excuse me?"

"You sit for me, and I'll sit for you."

Guin was trying not to stare.

"You want me to sit for you?"

"She hard of hearing?" Bishop asked Ginny.

"No, I think she's just overwhelmed by your generous offer," Ginny replied. "I'm sure Guin would love to sit for you. Wouldn't you, Guin?"

Guin knew that look and knew better than to contradict her boss. Yet… She turned to Farley Bishop.

"I'm flattered by your offer, Mr. Bishop. But I don't think I'm model material."

"That's for me to decide. The deal stands: You pose for me, and I'll let you interview me after."

"I…" Guin saw Ginny looking at her.

"Fine. But I'm keeping my clothes on."

Bishop snorted, clearly amused.

"Well, that's settled then!" said Ginny. "Charcuterie anyone?"

They helped themselves. As they ate, Ginny made small talk, trying to engage everyone. Suddenly, Bishop got up.

"Leaving so soon?" Ginny asked him.

"I need to work."

He made to go, but Guin stopped him.

"When can we talk?"

"Be at my studio tomorrow at ten."

"A.m. or p.m.?"

Was that a smile on Bishop's face?

"A.m.," he replied.

"Got it. I'll be there!"

Joel got up and walked Bishop out.

Guin watched them go. It was only after she saw Joel returning that she realized she forgot to ask Bishop where his studio was.

"Something wrong?" said Ginny.

"I forgot to ask him where his studio was."

"End of the road," said Ginny. "You can't miss it. Look for a big red box on stilts. There's an old red Jeep parked underneath."

"You've been there?"

"Once or twice."

"What's it like?"

"Like you'd imagine a painter's studio to look."

"And does he often ask total strangers to pose for him?"

"I wouldn't know."

"I thought he'd stopped painting."

"Farley could no more stop painting than breathe." It was Joel.

"You've been to his studio too?"

Joel nodded.

"Enough about Farley!" said Ginny. "Tell me all about Paris."

"You didn't read my article?" Guin had sent it to her that afternoon.

"Not yet. I've been busy."

Guin exchanged a look with Glen who shrugged.

"Fine. What do you want to know?"

"Tell me everything," said Ginny.

□

"I can't believe you're going to pose for Farley Bishop," Glen said as he drove Guin home.

Guin frowned.

"You're not excited?"

"Hardly. I'm only doing it so that he'll let me interview him."

Glen shook his head.

"Maybe you should pose for him."

"I wasn't the one he asked."

Neither said anything more until they pulled into Guin's driveway.

"Thanks for driving," said Guin, making to get out.

"That's it? You're not going to invite me in?"

"I'm tired."

"It's not even eight."

"I know, but I got up early and still have a touch of jet lag. And I need to be at Bishop's studio tomorrow at ten."

"Okay. Let me know how it goes."

"I will."

"Good. Now come here and give me a kiss."

They kissed for several minutes.

"You sure I can't come in?" he said.

Guin was tempted. But she knew she wouldn't get much sleep if she gave in.

"You should go. I'll talk to you tomorrow."

CHAPTER 3

Guin heard her phone buzzing. It was her mother. She thought about letting the call go to voicemail but swiped to answer instead. Might as well get it over with.

"Hi, Mom."

"Oh good, you're alive."

Guin rolled her eyes.

"Yes, Mom."

"I was worried when I didn't hear from you."

"I did text you when we landed and when I got home. Did you not get my messages?" Yet Guin knew that she had.

"I was hoping to hear your voice."

"Well, you're hearing it now. What's up?"

"I just wanted to know how your trip was."

"It was good."

"That's it, just good?"

"I'm a little jet-lagged, Mom. Could I tell you about the trip this weekend?"

"Fine. Call me tomorrow."

"What time?"

"Anytime is fine. Just not before ten. I have a yoga class. Oh, and then I have a lunch. And Philip and I have plans in the evening." Guin rolled her eyes. "Call me between three and five."

"I'll call you at four."

"Fine. Though I don't understand why you can't just tell me about Paris now."

Guin sighed.

"I told you, I'm tired. I was actually about to get ready to go to bed."

"At eight o'clock?"

"It's two Paris time."

"Very well. Just answer one question." Guin waited. "Did Glen propose?"

Seriously? First Shelly, now her mom?

"No, Mom. Glen didn't propose."

"Why not? Did you two have a fight?"

"No, Mom. We had a very nice time." Guin let out a loud yawn, hoping her mother would get the hint.

"Fine, I'll let you go. Call me tomorrow."

Guin said that she would and ended the call. She looked at the time. She should really try to stay up a bit longer. She went into the living room and took a seat on the couch. Less than a minute later, she was joined by Fauna, her black cat, who had moved with her to Florida. Right after, Spot, a big white cat with a large back spot on his back who had belonged to a neighbor of Glen's who could no longer take care of him, jumped up and curled up next to her.

"What's up guys?" she said, looking down at the two felines. "What do you think we should watch? Perhaps a little *Shark Tank*?"

Guin picked up the remote and turned on the TV. She put on *Shark Tank*, one of her favorite shows, all about entrepreneurs looking for a shark, or wealthy investor, to invest in their company, and settled back on the couch.

Despite her love of the show, Guin nodded off, waking up just before the end of the episode. Well, she could find out what she had missed tomorrow.

She got up, dislodging the two felines, who had fallen asleep on either side of her, and headed to the bedroom. She put on her nightshirt and went to brush her teeth. Then she got into bed. She was ready to turn out the light. But it was only nine-fifteen. She glanced at the stack of books she kept on her nightstand.

She picked up the book she'd been reading, a work of historical fiction by one of her favorite authors. She started to read but couldn't focus. The words kept blurring. After trying to read the same page multiple times, she gave up and turned off the light.

Guin woke up a little before five-thirty to find Spot and Fauna nestled on either side of her. She didn't want to disturb them, but she needed to pee. She went to the bathroom, turning on the faucet so that the cats could drink—they had followed her to the bathroom—and then returned to bed. She tried to go back to sleep. But it was useless. She was up.

She went to the kitchen and made coffee in her French press. As she drank, she thought about going to the beach. It wouldn't be light out for another hour. However, that didn't stop serious beachcombers or shell collectors. They would be out already, searching for seashells and sea glass in the dark, using a flashlight to guide them. Guin, however, preferred to wait until it was light out. Or at least until the sun poked over the horizon.

She finished her coffee and looked out the window. It was still dark out. She retrieved her phone and unlocked it. She checked her email and her messages. Then she played Wordle. It didn't take very long. She scrolled through her social media feeds. That took maybe five minutes. She looked out the window again. It was still dark.

"Screw it," she said. "I'm going to the beach."

Guin stood on the beach, staring up at the sky. Normally, by the time she headed out to the beach, the only heavenly body she could see, other than the sun, was the moon. But even though the sun would be rising soon, the sky was filled with stars and planets.

She tried to identify the different constellations. However, the only ones she could recognize were Orion's Belt and the Big and Little Dippers. Fortunately, she had recently installed an app on her phone that would tell you what you were looking at. You just opened the app and then held your phone up to the sky.

Guin was so intent on identifying what she was seeing that at first she didn't hear someone calling her name.

"Guin?"

This time she heard it. She turned to see her friend Lenny.

Lenny was a retired middle school science teacher from Brooklyn who strolled the beaches of Sanibel helping people (mainly children) identify the shells they found and lecturing them about beach ecology.

"Whatcha doing?" he asked her.

"Trying to identify the different stars and constellations."

"Back in my day, you didn't need some app to tell you what was above your head."

"You could see stars in Brooklyn?"

Lenny scowled.

"Maybe not now, but back in the day you could. Not like you can here, of course. But when we'd go to the Catskills in the summer, there were so many stars, you'd fall asleep trying to count them."

"Mm," said Guin. "So, what are you doing out so early?"

"I'm often out before dawn. And there's a northwest wind and a low tide. Perfect conditions for finding shells. What are you doing up? Thought you didn't like to go shelling before sunup."

"I don't. But I've got a case of jet lag and figured might as well."

"Ah."

"You find anything good?"

"Not yet. Just the usual stuff: some small horse conchs, a bunch of banded tulips, some lettered olives. But I did find an alphabet cone. Nothing to brag about though."

Guin had samples of all of those shells at home.

"Figured I'd donate them to the museum," Lenny continued, the museum being the Bailey-Mathews National Shell Museum, where Lenny volunteered.

"That's nice of you. So, which way you walking?"

"West. You?"

"Same. Shall we?"

Lenny nodded and they headed west together.

"How was your trip?" Lenny asked as they hunted for shells.

"Good."

"Did Anderson propose?"

Guin stopped and turned to her friend.

"Why is everyone asking me that?! No, he did not propose. It was a work trip." Not that that had anything to do with it.

"Do I need to have a talk with him?"

"No!" Guin practically yelled. She told herself to calm down. "Everything's fine between me and Glen. We had a very nice time in Paris."

"You two have a fight or something?"

Guin silently counted to ten.

"No. Everything's good," she repeated. "Now, can we please change the subject?"

"You know, you could always ask him."

Guin sighed.

"I'm not ready to get married again, Len." However, that wasn't entirely true.

"Why not?"

"I'm fine with the way things are." Which wasn't untrue.

But now that everyone was asking her why Glen hadn't proposed, she was starting to wonder if something was wrong.

"I don't understand you young people," said Lenny. "Being married to Ina was one of the greatest joys of my life. I only wish we had had longer together."

Guin placed a hand gently on Lenny's arm.

"I know," she said in a soft voice. "Ina sounds like an amazing woman."

"She was. And she would have loved you."

Guin didn't know what to say, so she said nothing.

They walked in silence for several minutes. Then Lenny grabbed Guin's arm and told her to look up. It was a shooting star.

"Make a wish," he instructed her.

"You believe that stuff?" she asked him, thinking he wasn't the type.

He frowned and told her to hurry up.

Guin quickly closed her eyes and made a wish. When she opened them, the shooting star was gone, and Guin wondered if her wish would come true.

CHAPTER 4

Guin arrived at Farley Bishop's studio promptly at ten. It was just as Ginny had described it, a big red box on stilts with a red Jeep parked underneath. Guin climbed the rickety stairs and looked for a doorbell but couldn't find one. So she knocked. There was no reply, but she could hear jazz music. She knocked again, a bit louder this time, and called out.

"Mr. Bishop? It's Guin Jones. You there?"

Still no reply. She was about to knock again when she decided to try the doorknob. It turned. And she let herself inside.

Guin entered the studio and looked around. There were canvases stacked against the walls and an easel set up on the far side of the room, but there was no sign of the painter. Had he stepped out? She paused to look at a canvas. It looked like a work in progress. Or maybe it was done. It was hard for Guin to tell.

"What do you think?" came a voice. Guin turned to see Farley Bishop standing a couple of feet away. Where had he come from?

"Is it finished?"

Bishop frowned and turned the canvas around, so it was facing the wall.

"Come," he said, heading to the back of the studio.

Guin followed him to where the easel was set up, in a kind of sitting area.

"You can go change in there," he said, pointing to a curtain.

"Uh, I didn't bring a change of clothes with me." Guin had been unsure what to wear, so she had put on one of her favorite sundresses.

"You'll find what you need back there."

Guin didn't move. Bishop looked annoyed.

"You want an interview? Go change."

Guin hesitated. Then she walked to the curtain and stepped through it. On the other side was a large room with a bed and a nightstand, a makeshift closet, a full-length mirror, what looked to be a dressing table or vanity, and a tired-looking couch. On the couch was a diaphanous white gown that reminded Guin of the nightgowns her mother used to wear, that Guin would dress up in and pretend she was a fairy princess.

Guin held up the gown. It was exquisite and looked to be old.

"You want me to put on this nightgown?" Guin called out.

"That *nightgown*, as you call it, was worn by the actress who played Titania in the Royal Shakespeare Company production of *A Midsummer Night's Dream*."

"Oh," said Guin, feeling chastised.

She held the gown up to the light. It was quite sheer.

"Put it on," Bishop commanded.

"Just do it, Guin," she told herself.

She removed her clothes, keeping on her underwear and bra, which were flesh-colored, and gingerly got into the costume. She was surprised by how well it fit her. She went over to the full-length mirror, turning from side to side. The gown swirled around her as she turned. She could almost imagine she was a fairy princess again.

She stepped back through the curtain to find Bishop waiting for her.

"You forgot the crown," he said.

"Crown?"

"It's on the dressing table."

Guin returned to the other room and saw a wreath of flowers. Could that be the crown he was referring to?

"You mean the wreath of dried flowers?"

"Put it on," called Bishop.

Guin placed the wreath on her head and looked in the mirror again. She had to admit, the wreath looked nice atop her strawberry-blonde curls.

She stepped back through the curtain.

"Go over there," he commanded, pointing to a green velvet divan.

Guin went over to the divan and sat.

"No, no, no," he said. "Lie down on it."

"Lie down?"

Bishop made a face and went over to the divan, arranging Guin.

"Like that," he said.

"Okay," said Guin, feeling awkward.

Bishop frowned.

"Relax."

"Sorry, but I've never done this before."

"Obviously. Look, imagine you're Titania, Queen of the Fairies."

"From *A Midsummer Night's Dream*."

Bishop nodded. Guin closed her eyes and tried to imagine herself as Titania. She had read the book, of course, a long time ago. Wasn't Titania made to fall in love with a donkey? Guin frowned.

"No, no, no," said Bishop, sounding exasperated. "Imagine you've just had sex, the best sex of your life, and now you're about to fall blissfully asleep."

Guin immediately thought about her and Glen's last night in Paris. She could feel herself blushing. The music grew louder. Guin thought it sounded familiar, but she couldn't place it. Whatever it was, she found herself starting to relax.

"Better," said Bishop. "Now just stay like that until I tell you you can move."

The next thing Guin knew, Bishop was nudging her.

She opened her eyes, momentarily forgetting where she was. Her eyes darted around the room. That's right, she was in Bishop's studio.

"Did I fall asleep?"

"Yup."

Well, at least he didn't look annoyed.

"How long was I out for?"

"A while."

Guin glanced over at the easel.

"Did you get what you needed?"

"Mm."

"Can I see?"

"No."

"Well, if you're done with me, I'll just go change and then we can do the interview."

Guin waited for him to say something. When he didn't, she got up and went to change. She returned a few minutes later to find him cleaning some brushes.

"Mr. Bishop?"

He turned to look at her.

"Where should we conduct the interview?"

"Makes no difference to me."

"How about we sit over there?" she said, gesturing to the sitting area.

He didn't move.

"Or you can pick a spot."

"Over there is fine. Just need to finish cleaning my brushes."

Guin waited for him to finish. Then they went to the

sitting area. Guin took a seat on the couch. Bishop sat on the loveseat. Guin fished her phone out of her bag and opened the recording app.

"Do I have your permission to record this interview?" she asked him.

He looked at her phone and frowned.

"Is that really necessary?"

"If you want this to go faster it is."

He continued to frown.

"Fine. Go ahead."

Guin waited.

"You have my permission."

"Thank you." Guin pressed "record" and began. "So…" She had prepared a list of questions, but she suddenly wasn't sure where to begin. *Just get on with it, Guin,* she told herself. "So, this retrospective at the Baker… Was it your idea?"

"Hardly," said Bishop.

"So the Baker Museum approached you?"

Bishop gave her a look, one that said, "What do you think?"

"And you agreed. Why?"

"I had my reasons."

"Can you tell me what they were? I thought you had sworn to never show your work at a museum or gallery again after…"

"They made me an offer I couldn't refuse."

Guin knew the reference. It was from *The Godfather.* However, she doubted anyone from the Baker Museum had put the head of a racehorse in Bishop's bed. Though maybe they had bribed him with something else? She would leave it for now.

"I understand that in addition to some of your older work, the Baker will be showcasing some new pieces. Is that correct?"

"It is."

"I'd love to see them. Are they here?"

"They are, but I'm still working on them."

"But the exhibit's less than two weeks away."

"I am aware."

"Is there a theme to your new work?"

"A theme?"

"How would you categorize the new pieces? Would you describe them as Impressionistic? Realistic? Abstract?"

"I don't like to put labels on my work."

"Yet others have."

Bishop frowned.

"Can you at least show me one or two of the new pieces? I don't care if they're not finished." Though Guin had to imagine at least some of them were.

"So you can put a label on them?"

Guin opened her mouth to object. But she realized Bishop was probably right. She would probably label it.

"You'll see them soon enough."

Why was he being so stubborn? Maybe if she changed the subject, came back to the paintings later…

"Will your family be attending the preview?"

"I have no family," he replied.

"What about your wife and daughter?"

"My wife left me years ago and took our daughter with her."

"I'm sorry."

"Don't be. It was for the best."

"How can you say that?"

Guin had always wanted to have children, but she and her ex-husband, Arthur, hadn't been able to. However, she knew that if she and Art had had a child and he had taken her away, she would have been devastated.

"I had neither the time nor the inclination to be a father. Judith knew that when she got pregnant."

"Judith is—was—your wife?"

He nodded.

"She was a model. And she knew better than most that my art came first."

"But if she knew you didn't want to be a father, why did she get pregnant?"

He gave Guin a look. Guin suspected the pregnancy had either been an accident or Judith had wanted the child and didn't care what Bishop had thought.

"What about Amalia?"

"I assume you are referring to the rumor that I was having an affair with her?"

Guin nodded.

"You really shouldn't believe everything you read."

"So you weren't having an affair with her? She was your muse though."

"She worked with me after Judith had Sasha. And unlike Judith, she understood her role."

"So you didn't sleep with her?"

"Judith was the only model I ever slept with. A mistake I have always regretted."

"And what was your relationship with Robert Rauschenberg?"

"He was a mentor and a friend."

"Did you ever…"

"Sleep with him? No. As I said, he was a mentor and friend."

"So why did your wife leave?"

"She was jealous of my art."

"So there was no affair?"

"I've never liked that word."

"But there was someone?"

Guin sensed that there was.

"He came to my studio with a friend, a fellow artist. He was young and green and had never seen my work. He told me that he had wanted to be an artist, but his parents didn't approve. I asked him to draw me something. It was clear he had some talent. I told him that if he ever decided to take up art, to look me up."

"I take it he did."

Bishop nodded.

"Less than a month later, he showed up at my studio. He had dropped out of school to pursue his dream. He asked me to mentor him. Said he'd be my assistant, clean the studio, fetch me coffee, whatever I wanted him to do, if only I would teach him.

"He didn't have a place to stay, and his parents had cut him off. So I let him stay at the studio. And I taught him about art."

Guin was amazed that Bishop was telling her this, confiding in her. Then again, Ginny had promised him that the paper wouldn't publish anything without his approval. And no way would he approve an article mentioning his personal life. Still, Guin was fascinated and wanted to hear more.

"What happened?"

"Judith didn't approve."

"Did she think you were having an affair?"

"Judith thought I was having an affair with everyone. But art was my only mistress."

"So she left?"

"She said either my apprentice left or she did."

"And she took your daughter?"

"She did."

"Where did they go?"

"To California."

"Why California?"

"Judith had a sister there."

"How old was your daughter when they left?"

"Sasha was six."

"You didn't try to stop them?"

"There was no point."

"And your daughter, did you ever see her again?"

"Judith remarried. Her new husband adopted Sasha."

"That must have been hard."

"It was for the best."

Guin wondered how he could say that. Did he really not care about his daughter?

"And the young man, your apprentice?"

"He left me too. And now, Ms. Jones, I need to get back to work. I have an exhibit to prepare for."

"I just have a couple more questions."

Bishop waited for her to go on.

"Why Sanibel?"

"I like it here."

"Was it because of Rauschenberg?"

"He was part of the reason. But as I said, it wasn't because we were having an affair. He believed in me, in the work I was doing. And he defended me."

"Are you referring to the plagiarism case?"

Bishop frowned.

"About that," said Guin. "Why did you end up settling? Did you not think you could have won?"

Bishop's frown deepened.

"I was tired of giving money to those bloodsuckers."

"You mean the lawyers?"

Bishop didn't reply, but his expression confirmed that was who he meant.

"And the other artist, Budge, what happened to him?"

"I don't know, and I don't care."

"You weren't curious?"

"Not in the least. The man tried to ruin my life. The idea of accusing me of copying him! If anything, it was the other way around. Good riddance to bad rubbish."

"Did you think his paintings were rubbish?"

"Have you seen them?"

"Just a couple. There were photos of them in one of the articles I read."

"Then you know there was no reason why I would have copied them. How he even got a show at a gallery… And now, Ms. Jones," he said, getting up.

Guin knew that was her cue to leave. She got up too.

"Thank you for your time."

Bishop was looking at her again, and Guin wondered what he saw.

She turned to go. As she reached the door, she took a final look at the studio. She wished that Bishop had shown her some of his new work. Frankly, she would have preferred seeing it to hearing about his personal life.

She let herself out, closing the door behind her, and made her way down the stairs.

CHAPTER 5

Guin was about to put her key in the ignition when she heard her phone buzzing. It was Ginny, texting to see how the interview had gone. Guin was about to text her back when her stomach let out a loud growl. She needed food. She started the car and headed off in search of lunch.

The Sunset Grill and the Lazy Flamingo were close by, right next to each other just before you crossed the bridge to Captiva. She parked the Mini in the lot by the Lazy Flamingo and went in.

She eyed the menu and ordered conch fritters and an Arnold Palmer. Then she went to look for a table on the deck. The place was busy, but she managed to snag a seat. She was just replying to Ginny when she heard her name being called and went inside to pick up her order.

She returned to her table with her conch fritters and Arnold Palmer and immediately dipped a fritter in the cocktail sauce. She took a bite. So good. The fritters were warm, crunchy, and just a bit spicy, just the way she liked them. She stared out towards the Gulf. The beach was just across the street. Maybe she'd walk over to Blind Pass when she was done. She hadn't been there in ages.

As she ate, she wondered what Farley Bishop's new paintings were like. Would they be similar in style to his other paintings? She guessed not. And how had the Baker Museum convinced him to show them?

Guin finished her conch fritters and her Arnold Palmer and returned her tray. Then she walked to the parking lot. She looked across the street. The Gulf was calling to her. But she had work to do. Still, it was Saturday. And Blind Pass was just over there. Maybe just a quick walk.

Guin's phone was buzzing as she walked through the door. It was Ginny again, asking if everything was okay. Guin realized she hadn't texted Ginny back. She speed-dialed Ginny's number and waited as the phone rang. She didn't have to wait long.

"Finally!" said Ginny. "How did the interview go?"

"Okay."

"Just okay?"

"I asked to see the new paintings, but he wouldn't show them to me or talk about them."

"That's disappointing but not unexpected. Did you pose for him?"

"I did."

"And?"

"And what?"

"How'd it go?"

"He had me dress up as a fairy."

"Excuse me?"

"He insisted I put on this costume from a Royal Shakespeare production of *A Midsummer Night's Dream* and pretend I was Titania, Queen of the Fairies."

"You're kidding."

"I wish I was."

She heard Ginny snort.

"It's not funny."

"I disagree. So, did he paint you?"

"I have no idea. He wouldn't show me."

Guin was too embarrassed to say she had fallen asleep.

"And he wouldn't show you the paintings he was planning on exhibiting?"

"He said he was still working on them. But I'm not sure I believe him. Maybe Joel could have a word with him, get him to change his mind?"

"Doubtful. I suppose we'll just have to wait until the preview. You learn anything useful?"

"Useful? Not really. He talked a bit about his wife and the rumors, but I doubt he'd let us print anything he told me."

"Knowing Farley, absolutely not. I'm surprised he even mentioned her."

"I asked if his family would be attending the preview."

"Ah. By the way, I read your Paris piece. Good stuff."

"Thanks. Anything else?"

"Nope. Was just checking to see how the modeling session and interview went."

Ten minutes before four, Guin received a reminder to call her mother. She deleted the notification and thought about not calling. But that would be a mistake. Instead, she picked up her phone and entered her mother's number. The phone rang several times before her mother answered.

"Guin?"

As if someone else might be calling her from Guin's cell phone.

"Yes, Mother. It's me. I said I'd call you at four, and here I am."

"Would you like a medal? Most children don't need to be told to call their mothers. Your brother doesn't. We talk nearly every day." *Talk about earning a medal*, thought Guin. "Speaking of Lance, did you know that his advertising agency just signed another new client? Some new health food chain. I've never heard of them. But Lance says they're very big on the West Coast and are planning to open stores on the East Coast."

"Well, bully for Lance."

"You needn't be snide, Guinivere."

Guin didn't begrudge her brother his success. He worked hard. And she admired him. He was also her mother's favorite, despite her mother claiming that she loved her children equally. That didn't bother Guin. At least not too much.

What irked her about Lance was that she felt he made her look bad in their mother's eyes. He had a successful advertising agency while Guin toiled for a small-town paper. He was happily married—to his husband Owen, who ran a gallery in Chelsea—while Guin was divorced. He always remembered to call their mother while… Wait! Owen. He owned a gallery that specialized in contemporary art. She should ask him about Farley Bishop.

"Did you hear me?" said her mother. "I asked you a question."

Guin hadn't heard. She had been thinking about Owen.

"Sorry. I just realized that I should talk to Owen. He may be able to help me with an article I'm working on."

"Oh? What does Owen know about Sanibel?"

"The article's not about Sanibel. It's about Farley Bishop. He's an artist. He's having a big exhibit at the Baker Museum. You ever hear of him?"

"Of course I've heard of Farley Bishop, Guinivere. I may not run a gallery like Owen does, but I'm not a philistine."

"You ever see his work?"

"As a matter of fact, I have. I was at that big exhibit of his at the Museum of Modern Art back in… When was it again?"

"It was in 1998," Guin supplied.

"That sounds about right."

"And? What did you think?"

"It wasn't my taste. Then again, I'm not a fan of what passes for art these days. Yet all of the art publications and the *Times* raved about it, as I recall."

"Do you remember anything about another artist suing him?"

Her mother thought.

"I don't think so. Why was someone suing him?"

"The artist claimed Bishop copied his work."

"Doesn't ring a bell. And you say Farley Bishop's having an exhibit at the Baker Museum?"

"Yes, it's a retrospective. However, they'll also be showing some of his new work. Glen and I are covering it for the paper."

"But isn't the Baker Museum in Naples?"

"It is. But we often cover important events close to Sanibel and Captiva. And Bishop—"

Guin was about to say that Bishop lived and worked on Sanibel, but she stopped herself. She didn't want her mother blabbing to her friends.

"And Bishop what?"

"And Bishop will be at the preview." Though she didn't know that for sure.

"Speaking of Naples, we won't be coming down when we originally planned."

"Oh? How come?"

Guin's mother and stepfather had rented a condo in downtown Naples for a couple of months, starting on the first of February, mainly so that her stepfather could play pickleball. Guin hadn't been thrilled to have her parents living so close, even though it had kind of been her idea.

"You remember my friend Betsy?"

"Betsy your old college roommate?"

"That's the one. And she's not that old." Guin rolled her eyes. "Her younger daughter's getting married."

"Helena? Who's she marrying?"

Helena was six years younger than Guin, and Guin didn't know her that well. She had been friendlier with Helena's older sister Ashley.

"Some doctor she's been dating. Betsy's thrilled. I think she thought they would never get married."

"I'm happy for her. Helena too. So did you not know about the wedding when you booked the condo?"

"No. Betsy just told us. Apparently, they just sprang it on her. My guess is Helena's pregnant." Again, Guin rolled her eyes. "They're getting married in Philadelphia. That's where they live. And Betsy's throwing them a reception. It's on the sixth. And, of course, I wouldn't dream of not going, Betsy being one of my oldest and dearest friends."

"Where's the reception?"

"At some restaurant."

"Well, at least it's close. And you and Philip like Philadelphia. You going to spend the weekend there?"

"That's the plan."

"So when do you think you'll come to Naples?"

"We're planning on flying down the morning of the ninth."

"Okay. I'll be here. Anything else I should know?"

"As a matter of fact… I was playing mahjong with the ladies the other day. And Beryl—I've told you about Beryl, yes? Her husband Bill works at the *New York Times*. Anyway, Beryl and I were discussing our children. Her son is a lawyer. And I was telling her how you worked for the paper there but would leap at a chance to work for the *Times* and…"

Guin closed her eyes and started counting to ten. Her mother was always trying to either a) set Guin up with one of her friend's sons or b) get her a job that would take her back to New York. Or, if possible, do both at the same time.

"That's very nice of you, Mom. But I doubt the *Times* would hire me. And I'm not interested in moving back to New York."

Her mother sniffed.

"Please, Guinivere. The *New York Times* would be lucky to have someone of your caliber. Have you read the paper recently? Your writing is ten times better than some of those reporters they've hired. And I recall a certain little girl who used to say her dream was to work there."

"That was a long time ago. And I'm on Sanibel now. And I like working for the *San-Cap Sun-Times*."

"You should at least talk to Bill."

"Does Bill want to talk to me? What does he do at the paper?"

"I forget. But why wouldn't he want to talk to you?"

"Uh, because he probably gets a zillion requests every day from people like you asking him to talk to their kid or spouse or best friend about working at the *Times*?"

"Maybe. But you're not just anyone. You're an award-winning journalist."

"Thanks for the vote of confidence. But no one's given me an award lately. And as I said, lots of people want to work at the *Times*."

Her mother huffed.

"You really need to have more confidence in yourself. That's probably why you're still toiling away at that paper that no one reads."

"Plenty of people read the paper."

"Define *plenty*."

"I don't know the current circulation numbers, but I'm guessing it's in the thousands."

Her mother scoffed.

"If you worked at the *Times*, millions would read your articles."

Just then Guin's phone began to beep. She had an incoming call. Saved by the bell—or beep!

"Hey, Mom, I need to go. I have a call I need to take. Talk to you soon. Love you!"

Before her mother could reply, Guin ended the call and picked up the new one.

"Hello?" she said.

"Everything okay?" said the caller. It was her brother. "You sound a bit frazzled."

"You got that from a single word?" Though Lance knew her better than anyone. "I was just talking to Mom."

"That explains it. What did she want?"

"Mom has a friend whose husband works for the *New York Times*. And she's hot to connect me with him."

"And would that be so bad?"

Guin didn't answer.

"Actually, I'm glad that you called. Can you ask Owen what he knows about an artist named Farley Bishop?"

"Why don't you ask him yourself?"

"Because I'm talking to you."

"He's at the gallery. You should call him."

"Won't he be busy?"

"If he is, he'll call you back. Call him."

"Fine. I'll call him. So, why'd you call?"

"Do I need a reason? I wanted to know how your trip was."

"It was good."

"Just good?"

Guin sighed. She didn't feel like talking about Paris again, but…

"It was very good. We stayed at a nice hotel, ate good food, took long walks, went to a couple of museums and galleries…"

"And?"

"And what?"

"Nothing special happened?"

Not him too, thought Guin.

"Like what?" she asked innocently. But she knew what her brother meant.

"Like, did he propose?"

"He did not. And I wish people would stop asking me that!"

"A bit sensitive, aren't we?"

Guin stuck out her tongue.

"You disappointed?"

"It was a work trip, Lance."

"If you call writing about how to spend a romantic weekend in Paris work. So nothing happened?"

"Plenty happened. He just didn't propose. Which is fine. Glen and I are good the way things are."

"If you say so."

"I do. I need to go," she lied.

"Are you mad at me?"

"Not at all. I'm just busy." Though that wasn't really true. "Oh, and congrats on the new account."

"Mom told you?"

"Yeah."

"It's a pretty big deal. We'd been working on getting it for months."

"Well, they made the right decision."

"Thanks. I'll let you go. Call me when you're in a better mood."

"I'm not—" Guin stopped herself. She *was* in a bad mood. "I will," she said.

"Good. You know you can always call me."

"I know."

"Love you."

"Love you too."

Guin stared out the window. She really should give Owen a call. She picked up her phone and entered the number for Owen's gallery. One of his assistants answered. Owen was there, but he was with a client. Would Guin like to leave a message? Guin asked the woman how late Owen would be there, but she wasn't sure.

"Tell Owen that Guin called and that I'll try him later," she told the woman.

His assistant said she'd deliver the message, and they ended the call.

Guin stared out the window again. Although she had already gone for two beach walks that day, the sun would be setting soon, and there was something special about watching the sunset from the beach.

She quickly changed, grabbed her sunglasses and a baseball cap, and headed out the door.

CHAPTER 6

There were people camped out along the beach as far as the eye could see. Some were standing. Others were sitting on foldout beach chairs. And others were holding beachside cocktail parties. Guin smiled and exchanged greetings as she passed by the various groups.

That was one of the things she loved about Sanibel, the friendliness of the people, whether residents or visitors. Everyone was happy to be there, especially for what promised to be a memorable sunset.

She glanced at the Gulf and spied a pod of dolphins. She stopped to watch them as they headed east, coming up for air every couple of minutes. There appeared to be four—or was it five?—of them. Where were they going? Guin wondered.

The sun was sinking lower in the sky as Guin headed towards Captiva. She gazed down at the sand, where the water lapped against the shore, hoping to see some shells she might want. She closed her eyes and took a deep breath, imagining a wave depositing a brown-spotted junonia shell at her feet. She knew it was unlikely. But Shelly was always going on about visualization, how if you could envision something happening, it would. And Guin, despite her skepticism, figured she had nothing to lose.

She opened her eyes and looked down at the sand. There was no junonia. But, hold on a second. Just over there. It was a cone-shaped shell with splotchy brown markings on it. She bent down and scooped it up. It was an alphabet cone. A pretty nice one too.

Huh. Maybe this visualization thing does work. I just need to fine-tune it.

She held it up, the setting sun behind it. It was as though the shell was surrounded by a halo of light. Guin pulled out her phone and took a photo. She would share it with Shelly and post it on Instagram later.

She put the shell in her pocket and looked out at the Gulf. The sky had turned a brilliant orange. And the sun was about to disappear. She watched it go, taking one last picture. Then she headed home.

The cats were there to greet her as soon as she walked through the door. Guin immediately knew what they wanted: food. She went into the kitchen and gave them some dry food. What should she have for dinner? She wasn't in the mood to cook. But she could always make herself a grilled cheese or peanut butter and jelly sandwich. First, however, she would see if Owen was around.

She glanced at the clock in the kitchen. It was nearly six-thirty. Would he still be at the gallery? Best to just call his cell phone.

"Guin?"

"Hey, Owen."

"Rebecca said that you had called. What's up? How was Paris?"

"Good!"

"Did you go to any galleries or museums? Any hot new artist I should know about?"

Guin smiled. That was Owen for you, always looking for the next great artist to feature at his gallery.

"We went to the Musée d'Orsay and the Musée de l'Orangerie. But all of the artists there are dead. However, we did go to a gallery by our hotel that had an interesting mixed-media exhibit by a young French artist named Maxine Dubonnet."

"Haven't heard of her. She any good?"

"I'm the wrong person to ask. You know me and contemporary art. But Glen liked it."

"I'll look her up."

"Do that. Speaking of contemporary art… I was wondering, what do you know about an artist named Farley Bishop? I understand he was pretty big in the late sixties and seventies and had exhibits at various museums and galleries through the nineties. And then he disappeared."

"That's right. What is it you wanted to know?"

"So you're familiar with him?"

"I am. He was kind of an idol of mine in art school."

"Really? How come?"

"I admired his ability to completely change his style every half-dozen years or so. That's not easy to do."

"Though other artists have done it. Look at Picasso."

"True. So is there a reason you're asking about him? I thought you weren't a fan of contemporary art."

"I'm not, but the Baker Museum is hosting a retrospective of Bishop's work, and Glen and I are covering it for the paper. And I thought you could maybe give me some insight."

"I heard about that. If I wasn't so busy at the gallery, I'd go."

"You can't sneak down? You know you're welcome to stay with me anytime. The Baker's going to be displaying some new paintings as well as the old stuff."

"I thought he had stopped painting."

"Well, he hasn't."

"Have you seen his new work?"

"Not yet. He wouldn't show it to me when I was at his studio." *Oops.*

"You were at his studio?"

Guin debated whether she should tell Owen about her visit to Bishop's studio.

"You promise not to repeat anything I'm about to tell you?"

"Cross my heart and…"

"He has a studio here on Sanibel."

"What's it like?"

"Like a giant tree house."

"Hm."

"And he made me sit for him."

"Excuse me? You posed for Farley Bishop?"

"I did. I didn't want to. But it was the only way he'd let me interview him."

"I can't believe it. Wow. So is there a painting?"

"I have no idea. He had me dress up like Titania from *A Midsummer Night's Dream* and lie down on this forest green divan. I actually fell asleep. And when I awoke, he wouldn't show me what he'd done. He probably didn't do anything. Just did it as a kind of power play."

"And then you interviewed him?"

"I did. But he wouldn't talk about his work or his approach. All he said was that he didn't like labels. I did read a bunch of articles about him. But his work is so all over the place. I was hoping you could enlighten me."

"Well, as you know, he came to prominence in the late sixties, though he had been active before then, doing mostly classical painting. It was when he went more avant-garde that people started to notice him. And then he kept altering his style, and people couldn't wait to see what he would do next."

"Did you go to any of his exhibits?"

"Oh yeah, several. They were a big deal."

"You see his last one at MoMA?"

"I did. Twice."

"You ever meet him?"

"I saw him, but I never spoke with him. He wasn't

comfortable around people and hated to give talks. Thought his work spoke for itself."

"What about the plagiarism case? Do you remember it?"

"A bit. As I recall, he was being sued by some young artist who accused Bishop of copying his work. Pretty sure they settled before the case went to trial though."

"That's right. Good memory."

"Did you know the artist who sued him, Willem Budge?"

"Not personally. But I'd seen his work."

"Any good?"

"I didn't think so."

"Do you know what happened to him?"

"No. He disappeared after the lawsuit. So did Bishop. Actually, I was surprised to hear that the Baker was putting on an exhibit of his work. As I recall, Bishop swore after the lawsuit that he would never show his work again."

"He did, but it's been over twenty years. And he said that the Baker made him an offer he couldn't refuse."

"Did they put a painting of a dead horse in his bed?"

"Ha! I don't think so."

"I need to go, but if you have any more questions…"

"I'm good. At least for now. Thanks for your help."

"I don't think I was that helpful."

"You confirmed what I'd read. And it was nice chatting with you."

"Same. I'll look into sneaking away so I can check out the exhibit. I'm interested in seeing his new work."

"Do. And bring Lance."

"I'll work on it."

"Good. Take care."

"You too. And let me know when you're back in the city. I'll take you to some galleries now that you're an art critic."

"I'm not an art critic. I'm just helping out until they hire one. But I'd love to go to some galleries with you when I'm in town."

"It's a date. Okay, gotta run."

They said goodbye, and Guin's thoughts turned to food. She looked in the fridge and decided to make herself a grilled cheese sandwich. She had taken two bites when her phone began to buzz. She looked down at the Caller ID. It was Glen.

"Hey," she said.

"Hey yourself," he replied.

"What's up?"

"Not much. I just miss you."

"You just saw me. And you'll see me tomorrow."

"I can still miss you."

Guin tutted.

"How are your folks?"

"Good. They asked about you."

"What did you tell them?"

"That you were good and that we had a wonderful time in Paris. Are you eating something?"

Guin had taken another bite of her grilled cheese and had been quietly chewing, or so she thought.

"Grilled cheese," she said, her mouth still full.

"Sounds good."

Guin swallowed.

"It is."

"Okay, I'll let you eat."

"Thank you."

"Speaking of eating, any special requests for dinner tomorrow?"

"Make whatever you like."

"Hm… you sure?"

Guin took another bite of grilled cheese.

"Did you just take another bite of your sandwich?"

He must have good ears.

"I did. Just no liver or meatloaf or anything with a cream sauce or deep fried."

"You on a diet?"

"I probably should be after what I ate in Paris. But no. I just don't want anything heavy."

"Got it. I'll let you go. Just one last thing."

"Yes?"

"I love you."

Guin smiled.

"I love you too."

CHAPTER 7

The week seemed to be flying by. Probably because Guin had been so busy. February was around the corner. And it was one of the busiest months on Sanibel, with lots to see and do—from art fairs and new gallery shows to lectures at the J.N. "Ding" Darling National Wildlife Refuge and the Bailey-Matthews National Shell Museum. And Ginny was constantly sending Guin new assignments.

It was now Wednesday afternoon. Guin was taking a break from work to check her messages and saw that there was an urgent text from Shelly, asking Guin to call her as soon as she got the message. Guin hoped everything was okay. With Shelly, you never knew if an urgent request to call meant she had really good news or really bad news.

She speed-dialed her friend and hoped it was the former.

"Is everything okay?" Guin asked as soon as Shelly answered.

"Everything's fine. Why?"

"You said to call as soon as I got your message."

"Sorry. I was just so excited!"

"Excited about…?"

"You're never going to believe it!" Guin waited for her to go on. "You know that reality show where they have people who make stuff compete for patches, the one with Amy Poehler and Nick Offerman from *Parks and Recreation*?"

"You mean *Making It*?"

"That's the one! Well, I applied to be on it, and guess what?! I made it!"

"That's amazing. I didn't know you had applied to be on *Making It*. Why didn't you tell me?"

"I was too nervous. But I just got an email saying I was a finalist."

"Wait. I thought you said you were going to be on the show."

"I'm sure it's just a formality."

"So what does being a finalist mean?"

"It means they want to interview me and see my work in person. I guess to make sure that I'm legit before they put me on the air. One of the producers is in Miami this week, and she's going to come to my studio before she heads back to LA. I'm so excited!"

"Well, I have no doubt that producer will take one look at your jewelry and sign you up."

"I should make something for her visit, something special. Maybe one of those jewelry boxes people really like or another shell mirror. What do you think?"

Guin had watched the show but didn't think she was the right person to advise Shelly and told her so.

"Come on, you must have some suggestions. You're a creative person. I need to make something that will knock her socks off."

"I'm sure whatever you make will be fabulous. Go with your gut."

"Right now my gut is filled with butterflies. Hey, that's an idea. Maybe I should make something with butterflies!"

"Great idea!"

"I should go," said Shelly. "I have a lot of work to do. Hey, you want to grab a drink after the producer visits? I probably can't go for a beach walk until after. Too much stuff to do."

"That's fine. I'm around. Just call or text me after you've met with her."

"Okay. Thanks, Guin. You're the best. Wish me luck!"

"You don't need it. You're going to wow her."

"I hope so. Okay, bye!"

They ended the call and Guin shook her head. Leave it to Shelly to get herself on a reality TV show. Though she was perfect for *Making It*. Guin just hoped the producer agreed. And if Shelly did make it onto the show, Guin could write about it for the paper. The thought made her smile.

Speaking of the paper, there was an email from Ginny in her inbox. No doubt another assignment. Guin opened the email and began to read. Ah, yes. The big Sanibel-Captiva Rotary Club Arts & Crafts Festival was coming up, and Ginny wanted her to interview Adele Becker, the woman in charge of the show this year, as well as a few of the local artists who'd be there.

Guin could handle that. She liked Adele, who she knew through the Shell Club. Easy-peasy. She wondered if Shelly would have a booth again this year and was about to text her but stopped. She had interviewed Shelly before. Better to let Adele suggest which artists to interview.

She sent Adele an email, letting her know she would be writing about the festival for the paper and asking when she had time to chat or meet. Then she went to get a glass of water.

"What smells so good?" Guin asked Glen upon entering his kitchen. She was having dinner at his place again.

"It's my tomato sauce," he replied.

Guin went over to the stove and closed her eyes, breathing in the rich tomatoey aroma.

"It smells heavenly. You make pasta too?"

"I thought about it, but…"

"No fresh pasta? I'm leaving," she said, pretending to go.

Glen wrapped his arms around her, stopping her.

"If it's that important to you, I'll make some right now."

Guin leaned against him.

"Mm, you smell good."

"I just showered."

They stood there for several minutes, neither moving. Finally, Glen released her.

"So, what will the tomato sauce be going on?"

"I have some homemade mushroom ravioli—made by the pasta guy at the farmers market. And I made a salad. I wound up being a bit busier today than I expected."

"Yet you had time to make tomato sauce."

"Making the sauce was easy. You just open some cans of tomatoes, throw in some herbs and wine, and let it simmer."

"Uh-huh. And to think that not that long ago you didn't like to cook."

"That's because I didn't have someone to cook for."

"Hm," said Guin. "So, when's dinner?"

"When would you like it?"

"How long does the ravioli take?"

"Just a few minutes once the water boils. I take it you're hungry."

"Starving."

"I'll start boiling some water."

Guin rolled over and gave Glen a kiss. She had stayed over, but now she needed to head home.

"I should go."

"What time is it?"

"Six-forty-five."

"Stay a little longer," he said, pulling her towards him and kissing her neck. It was one of her weak spots. And he knew it.

"But what about the cats?"

"They'll survive," he said. He kissed her neck again and

began to work his way down.

"Okay, maybe a little longer," she said.

Guin arrived home a little after nine to two pairs of accusatory feline eyes.

"I know, I know," she said, hurrying towards the kitchen. She looked down at the cat bowls. They were empty.

Immediately, both cats began to meow.

"Okay, okay. I'll give you guys some food. Sheesh."

She grabbed a can of cat food from the pantry and divided it evenly between the two bowls. The cats lunged.

"Really, you two. You'd think I didn't feed you. Maybe I should get one of those automatic cat feeders, so you can feed yourselves. Though knowing the two of you, you'd still cry for food."

She watched them eat for another minute then went to shower and change.

Before Guin knew it, it was Friday. Shelly had texted her that morning that the *Making It* producer would be stopping by that afternoon. Was Guin free to grab a drink with her afterwards?

"Sure," Guin had written her back. "Just let me know when and where."

"I'll text you after she leaves."

A little after five, Guin received another text from Shelly. The producer had gone, and Shelly needed a drink.

"You want to go to Traders?" she asked Guin.

"Sure," Guin replied. "Should I pick you up?"

"That would be great. How soon can you get here?"

"5:45?"

"Perfect. See you then."

"So, how did it go?" Guin asked Shelly as they sat at the bar.

"Good, I think. She seemed really impressed with my jewelry and the mirror I made."

"Does that mean you'll be on the show?"

"I don't know. I hope so. She asked me a bunch of questions and took photos of my work."

"When will you know?"

"She said they'd be making their final decision soon."

"Well, they'd be foolish not to pick you."

"Pick you for what?" said a familiar voice.

Guin looked up to see Sanibel's most annoying bachelor, Marty Nesbitt, hovering over them. She frowned. Had he planted a tracking device on her? It sometimes felt that way as he had a knack for appearing every time she and Shelly went out for drinks. Though Marty was a known barfly. And it wasn't as though there were a ton of places to grab a drink on Sanibel. Still, Marty's uncanny ability to materialize wherever they were was a bit alarming.

"Hey, Marty," said Shelly, who wasn't as disturbed by Marty as Guin was. Then again, Shelly wasn't single and hadn't been hit on by Marty.

"So what's the big secret?" Marty asked, his bushy eyebrows reminding Guin of two caterpillars.

"If we told you, it wouldn't be a secret now, would it?" said Shelly.

"Aw, come on. You can tell me," said Marty. "I won't tell."

Guin snorted. Marty was one of the biggest gossips on the island, second only to Suzy Seashell, who ran a popular Sanibel blog.

"Where's Sandy?" she asked him.

Sandy was the woman Marty had claimed to be dating the last time she had run into him.

Marty frowned.

"Things not work out?" Shelly asked him.

"I caught her cheating on me."

"No!" said Guin, feigning shock.

"I know," said Marty, looking serious. (He was clearly immune to sarcasm.) "Can you believe it?"

Guin had to stifle a laugh. Marty's belief that a woman would be crazy to not want him amused her. Though, to be fair, he didn't seem to have a problem finding women who would date him. At least briefly. He wasn't bad looking. If you were into skinny seventy-year-old men with thinning gray hair that they wore in a ponytail. He could be amusing. And he was generous, giving money to local charities and those in need. Indeed, Marty would probably give you the shirt off his back. That is if you didn't mind wearing a loud Hawaiian shirt. The problem with Marty was that he was really annoying.

"How do you know she was cheating on you?" asked Shelly.

"I saw her."

"With another man?" asked Guin.

Marty nodded.

"Bold as brass. I asked her to watch the sunset and have dinner with me up at the Mucky Duck on Captiva, and she said she couldn't make it. I decided to go anyway, and there she was, with another man."

"Maybe it was a relative?" said Shelly.

"They were kissing. And she hasn't returned my calls or texts."

"I'm sorry," said Shelly. "That must hurt."

"It does," said Marty.

Guin got the feeling that Marty was looking for an invitation to join them and tried to telepathically message Shelly not to ask him. But Shelly clearly wasn't on the same wavelength and was a soft touch. She had also downed half a Cosmo. And before Guin knew it, Shelly had asked Marty if he'd like to sit with them.

Marty immediately perked up at the invitation, pulled up

a barstool, and asked the bartender for a beer.

"So, Guin," he said, "you still single?" He was waggling his bushy eyebrows as he said it, and Guin wondered if Marty realized how comical it made him look.

"I'm taken," she replied, holding up her hand with Glen's sapphire and diamond ring on it.

"Nice ring," he said. "So, when's the big day?"

"They're not actually engaged," said Shelly. "It's a promise ring."

"A promise ring?" said Marty, looking confused.

"Actually," said Guin.

"Wait a minute," said Shelly. "Did you and Glen get…?"

Guin nodded.

Wait. What was she doing? She and Glen hadn't gotten engaged. She just wanted Marty to back off. Well, too late now.

Shelly hit her.

"I can't believe you didn't tell me! When?! How?!"

"Congratulations," said Marty, looking morose. "He's a lucky guy."

"Thanks," said Guin.

"Spill, woman!" said Shelly.

"I'll tell you later," said Guin, immediately regretting the lie.

"Oh, I get it," said Marty. "Girl talk." He glanced around. "That's okay. I see a buddy of mine." He turned back to Guin and placed a hand on her shoulder. Guin looked at it and then up at Marty. "You know, if things don't work out with the photographer, I'm here for you," he said solemnly.

Guin held in a laugh as she looked at Marty. He looked so serious. But the idea that she would ever go out with him was laughable.

"Thanks, Marty," she said.

He patted her shoulder. Then he turned and hailed his buddy.

As soon as he was gone, Guin breathed a sigh of relief.

"You okay?" asked Shelly.

"I'm fine," Guin replied.

Shelly hit her.

"Ow!" said Guin. "What was that for?"

"How could you not tell me you and Glen got engaged?!"

"We didn't get engaged. I just said that to get Marty to back off."

"Oh," said Shelly, looking disappointed.

"Though," said Guin. Shelly immediately perked up. "Glen did say I shouldn't make plans for Valentine's Day."

"He knows you hate Valentine's Day, right?"

"He does, but…"

"You think he's going to ask you then?"

Guin shrugged, and Shelly hit her again.

"You do!"

"Hey! Stop that! Okay, maybe I do."

"And I'm guessing from the look on your face you'd say yes."

"Maybe," said Guin, coyly.

"I knew it!" crowed Shelly.

"Down, girl. He hasn't asked yet."

"You could always ask him."

Guin gave her a look.

"What?" said Shelly. "You're a modern woman. If you want to get married, just ask him. You know he'd say yes."

"I don't know that for sure."

"Oh, please," said Shelly, rolling her eyes. "Hey, you want to order some food?"

"Sure," said Guin.

Shelly signaled to the bartender.

"Could we get a couple of menus?"

He nodded and returned a minute later with two menus. They took a quick look and ordered bang bang shrimp and crab and spinach stuffed portobello mushrooms. As they waited for the food to arrive, Shelly asked Guin what she was working on, and then Guin asked Shelly how her husband Steve and her two kids felt about their mom being on a reality TV show.

They left Traders an hour later. Though not before Marty stopped by to ask Guin when the big day was. Guin told him they hadn't set a date yet—and again wished she had kept her mouth shut. No doubt word of her engagement would be spread across the island. She asked Marty not to say anything, telling him that she and Glen were keeping it on the qt. Not that that would stop Marty from yapping but... She just hoped Glen didn't hear about her white lie. Though, would it be so bad if he did? She should probably tell him. But when she got home she decided not to.

CHAPTER 8

Guin had had another busy week. And tonight was the preview of Farley Bishop's big retrospective at the Baker Museum. For some reason Guin had been feeling anxious all day. She wasn't sure why. Glen hadn't found out about her little white lie. Thank goodness. And things were good between them. She was zipping through her work assignments. And her mother was off in Philadelphia, hopefully having a good time.

Guin just had a feeling that something bad was about to happen. And typically when she got that feeling, something bad did. She also couldn't decide what to wear.

She had been to plenty of art openings on Sanibel. But this was Naples, where people tended to dress up more. And this preview was a pretty big deal.

Guin stood in her closet, staring at her wardrobe. Why was she being so indecisive? Clearly, there was only one thing to do: call Shelly. Shelly had a great style sense and knew what looked good on Guin.

The phone only rang twice before Shelly answered.

"What's up?"

"Can you help me find something to wear to the art opening tonight?"

"I'll be right over."

Less than twenty minutes later, Guin's doorbell rang.

"That was fast," said Guin, letting Shelly in. "I hope I'm

not taking you away from anything."

"Nah. I needed a break."

"Can I get you something to drink? A glass of water or some wine?"

"What kind of wine? On second thought, better not. Let's just go to the closet."

Guin followed Shelly to the bedroom.

"Have you narrowed it down?" Shelly asked Guin on the way there.

"Not really. I've been feeling anxious all day and haven't been able to make a decision about anything."

"That's serious. Is everything okay?"

"Everything's fine. I can't explain it. I just have this feeling in my stomach."

"You're not pregnant are you?"

"What?!"

"You've been spending an awful lot of time with Glen. And you were in Paris together."

"I'm not pregnant, Shell." Though, come to think of it, her period was a bit late. But it was probably because her body was still a bit out of whack.

Guin saw Shelly looking at her.

"I'm not pregnant!" she repeated.

"If you say so."

"I do. Now help me find something to wear."

"Hmm…" said Shelly, flipping through hangers.

"What about this?" she said, pulling out a white cotton maxi dress. "I don't think I've seen it before."

"It was an impulse purchase. I've never actually worn it."

"Put it on."

"Seriously? You don't think it's a bit too boho for Naples?"

"What's wrong with a being a bit boho?"

Guin opened her mouth to reply then shut it.

"Fine," she said, taking the dress.

She slipped it on and modeled it for Shelly.

"Well?"

"It looks great on you."

Guin looked at herself in the full-length mirror. It did look good on her. It also reminded her of the gown Farley Bishop had had her wear.

"You sure it's not too casual? It's supposed to be a beach coverup. Though you can't see through it."

"Is it comfortable?"

"Very."

"Then wear it. You can dress it up with jewelry. Now about your hair…"

"What about it?"

"You're not planning on wearing it in a ponytail, are you?"

Guin had forgotten her hair was in a ponytail.

"I hadn't decided."

"Put it down."

Guin removed the ponytail holder.

"Shake your head."

Guin did as obeyed.

"Perfect. Now go put on some makeup."

Guin went into the bathroom and applied mascara and lipstick. When she returned, Shelly was holding out a necklace.

"Wear this," she said, holding up a choker.

"Where'd you find that?" asked Guin.

"It was in the bottom of your jewelry box. Where'd you get it? I don't think I've seen it before."

"Art gave it to me."

"If you don't want to wear it…"

"It's okay. Can you put it on for me? It has a tricky clasp."

"Sure," said Shelly.

Guin lifted her hair, and Shelly secured the choker.

"There!" she said.

Guin turned and looked at herself in the mirror again.

"Looks like Cinderella is ready to go to the ball," said Shelly. "We just need to find you the right pair of shoes. What about these?" she said, grabbing a pair of high-heeled sandals.

"I can barely walk in those."

"Okay, what about these?" said Shelly, holding up a pair with a slightly lower heel.

"Definitely those," said Guin, taking the sandals with the lower heel. She slipped them on her feet. "What do you think?"

"Perfect!" said Shelly.

"What time is it?"

"My phone's in my bag."

Guin hurried over to her nightstand. She looked at her alarm clock and cursed.

"I need to text Glen and tell him I'm going to be late."

She hunted for her phone and sent him a text.

"We all set here?" asked Shelly.

"Yes, thank you. Sorry to rush you out, but I need to go."

"I understand. Good luck tonight."

Shelly let herself out, and Guin went to give the cats some food and fresh water. Then she grabbed her bag and her keys and left.

She arrived at Glen's forty-five minutes later. She rang the doorbell, preparing to apologize for her tardiness.

"You look amazing," he said.

"Thank you. Sorry I'm late. So, you think this dress is okay?"

"It's more than okay. You look ethereal."

"That's what Shelly said. She picked it out."

"She did a good job."

Guin looked at Glen's outfit. He was dressed in a pair of chinos, a button-down shirt, and a jacket.

"You look very handsome yourself."

"Thank you. Shall we go?"

"Let's. We're already late."

"Don't worry. I'll get us there in time. Got my camera bag all ready to go. Shall we take the convertible or the SUV? On second thought, let's take the SUV. I don't want the wind messing up your hair."

"I doubt it will make a difference," said Guin, whose strawberry-blonde curls had a mind of their own.

"Just leave it with the valet," said Guin. The preview was about to begin, and the parking lot was full.

"I'll drop you off and see if I can find a spot across the street," Glen replied.

Guin sighed. She knew that Glen distrusted valets. But they were going to be late.

"Don't you need to get in there and take photos before it gets too crowded?"

"They're letting photographers and reporters have a look around before they let in members."

"Oh, right," said Guin. She had forgotten. "Still, we should get up there."

"You go. I'll be there soon."

He let Guin out and went in search of a spot. Guin shook her head. Then she headed to the museum. She was stopped outside by an attendant who asked for her name and a photo ID. Guin gave the woman her name and reached into her bag for her wallet, pulling out her driver's license. The attendant nodded, and Guin proceeded to a gentleman who was checking bags. Guin opened hers, and the man moved things around with what looked like a baton. Then he told her she could go in.

Was security always this tight for events at the Baker Museum?

She made her way up the main staircase, gazing up at the giant glass Chihuly sculpture, to the third floor, where the exhibit and reception were, and looked for Ginny. She didn't have to search long.

"There you are!" said Ginny. "I was starting to worry." She took in Guin's outfit.

"I couldn't decide what to wear."

"And you decided to go with that?"

Guin could sense Ginny's disapproval. But it was too late to change now.

"Shelly and Glen said I looked ethereal." Though she felt silly as soon as she said it.

"Well, you're here. That's what's important." Ginny looked around. "Where's Glen?"

"Parking the car."

"He didn't use the valet?"

"You know how he feels about valets."

A server came by with a tray of sparkling wine and asked them if they'd like a glass.

Ginny grabbed one but Guin declined. She was working.

"Where's Joel?" Guin asked her boss.

"At home."

"I thought he was going to be here."

"He changed his mind."

Ginny seemed a bit annoyed.

"And the guest of honor?"

"I haven't seen him."

"You don't think he'll bail on his own retrospective, do you?"

"You never know. For all I know, he and Joel could be at our place playing chess together."

"Really?"

Ginny downed the sparkling wine and gave the empty flute to a passing server.

Guin looked around. The area outside the exhibit space was packed, the doors leading to the exhibit closed. She glanced around to see if she recognized anyone, but she didn't. A minute later, she saw Glen coming up the stairs.

"About time," said Ginny.

"Sorry," said Glen. "I was parking the car."

"Next time use the valet."

Just then their attention was drawn to a tall, dapper-looking man who was standing outside the entrance to the exhibit, trying to get everyone's attention. He looked to be somewhere in his sixties or possibly seventy.

"Ladies and gentlemen," he said. "Thank you all for coming. I am Bennett Emerson, the director of the Baker Museum. And I am delighted to welcome you to what is sure to be a memorable evening.

"As you know, this is the first exhibition of Farley Bishop's work in over twenty years. And we are honored that Mr. Bishop has chosen the Baker to share his latest creations."

Guin heard murmuring in the crowd.

"In a moment, we will be opening the doors for the press and board members to preview the exhibit. Then the rest of you will be allowed in. Now, if members of the press and board members would be so kind as to line up over here by the door, Alexandra, who put together this wonderful exhibit, will check you in."

There was more murmuring as people went to line up.

"You're not coming?" Guin asked Ginny.

"I'll head in with the rest of the riffraff."

"Come on," said Glen, leading Guin to the entrance to the exhibit.

Ahead of them was a man in a wheelchair. Guin wondered who he worked for.

"Ludwig Belem, *Art World*," said the man when it was his turn.

"A pleasure to have you with us, Mr. Belem," said the curator.

Belem grunted and deftly rolled the wheelchair into the exhibit.

"And you are?" said the curator, looking at Glen.

"Glen Anderson. I'm a photographer with the *Sanibel-Captiva Sun-Times*. And this is my colleague, Guinivere Jones."

Guin took a step forward. The curator's eyes went wide as she looked at Guin.

"Is everything okay?" asked Guin. The woman was staring, and it was making Guin uncomfortable. Did the curator disapprove of Guin's outfit?

"It's uncanny," said the curator, continuing to stare.

"What is?" asked Guin, confused.

"I'm sorry," said the curator. "Please, go on in."

Glen led Guin into the exhibit.

"What was that about?" said Guin.

"I," he began and stopped.

"What?" said Guin, looking up at him. Then she turned her head to see what Glen was looking at and was speechless.

CHAPTER 9

There, on the wall, at the entrance to the exhibit, was a giant portrait of Guin as Titania, asleep in a verdant bower surrounded by flowers. She was wearing a flowing white gown, not that dissimilar from the dress she was wearing, her strawberry blonde hair cascading over her shoulders, just like she was wearing it, a wreath of flowers upon her head.

Guin gawped.

"I don't believe it."

"It's amazing," said Glen. "It looks just like you."

Indeed, it was as though Bishop had photographed her while she slept. It was so realistic. How had he managed to capture her in such a short period of time? Maybe he had taken a picture of her while she slept. She would have to ask him. That is, if he showed up.

Guin noticed people staring at her.

"Can I get a picture of you with the painting?" asked one of the press photographers.

"I..."

Before Guin could reply, a flash went off, momentarily blinding her. Someone—not the photographer who had asked politely—had taken a photo.

Glen whipped around to see who had taken it. It was the man in the wheelchair, the reporter from *Art World*.

"Delete it," Glen ordered him.

"Not a chance," said the man, a smirk on his face. He

turned and looked at Guin. "So you're Farley's new muse. Aren't you a bit old to be an artist's model? But I guess beggars can't be choosers."

Glen looked as though he could strangle the man.

"It's okay, Glen," said Guin, laying a hand on his arm. "Just ignore him. Let's see the rest of the exhibit."

Glen glared at the critic. Then he allowed Guin to drag him into the first room.

"You okay?" Glen asked her.

"About the painting or that critic from *Art World*?"

"Both."

"Well, I wasn't expecting to see a life-size portrait of myself. I didn't even know if Bishop had actually painted me. And as for Mr. Belem… As I said, best to ignore him."

"Well, for what it's worth, he's wrong. You make an excellent artist's model."

Guin smiled.

"Thank you. But I think you might be a bit biased."

"Maybe. But you saw that painting. You look beautiful."

"It is a remarkable painting. But we should inspect the rest of the artwork before they let the rest of the people in."

Guin was taking photos with her phone when she heard someone calling her name. She turned around and couldn't believe it.

"Pauline?" The woman smiled. "What are you doing here?"

Pauline Paulson had been Guin's boss at her first publishing job, a magazine, up in New York. She had since moved on, as had Guin, but the two had kept in touch over the years. Until Guin had moved to Sanibel.

"I'm covering the exhibit for the paper," said Pauline.

"The paper?"

Last Guin heard, Pauline was working at the *New Yorker*.

"The *New York Times*."

"You're writing for the *Times*? What happened to the *New Yorker*?"

"I left the *New Yorker* when we moved here."

"Here as in Naples?" Pauline nodded. "When did you move here? I always thought the only way you'd leave New York was in a pine box."

Pauline smiled.

"I know. But Paul wanted to live somewhere where he could play golf year round. And one gets tired of the cold after a while."

"What about the law firm? Wasn't Paul a partner?"

"He was. But he was tired of helping companies file for bankruptcy."

"Still, I can't believe he retired. When did you move?"

"In October."

So not that long ago.

"You sell the apartment?"

Pauline nodded.

"And got rid of everything. Well, nearly everything. Figured we'd get a fresh start. Also, I couldn't see our old brown antiques doing well here in Florida."

"You buy a place here?"

"In North Naples. Not that far from here. It's in a golf course community. Paul's as happy as a pig in mud."

"Is he here this evening?" Guin looked around.

"God no. You know how he feels about contemporary art. Can't stand the stuff. Frankly, I'm not a huge fan either. But I couldn't pass up the opportunity to see Farley Bishop's new work. Everyone believed he had retired—or was dead."

"Mm," said Guin. "And what about you? You happy here?"

Guin couldn't picture Pauline living in Naples, in a condo, in a golf course community. Not that there was anything wrong with living in a condo in a golf course community in Naples. But Guin had always thought of Pauline as the quintessential New Yorker. She lived to go to shows and museums, loved going out to eat. And she had written about those things for one publication or another for over thirty years.

"I like the weather. And my golf game has improved."

"I thought you hated golf."

Pauline shrugged.

"If you can't beat 'em, join 'em."

"And do you like working for the *Times*? What do you write about for them?"

"I cover arts and culture here in South Florida."

"Full time?"

"No, I'm a stringer. Which suits me just fine. I get to do what I love and get paid for it. And if I want to play golf with my husband on a Wednesday, I can."

Guin shook her head. This was not the workaholic boss she had known. But if Pauline was happy…

"And you, Ms. Jones. What have you been up to the last couple of years, other than posing for famous artists?"

Guin felt a bit guilty. She had lost touch with so many of her New York friends and colleagues after losing her job, getting divorced, and moving to Sanibel.

"Just one artist. And I had no idea he had actually painted me, let alone was planning on hanging the painting in a museum. I'm actually a reporter for a local paper here, the *Sanibel-Captiva Sun-Times*. And the man with the camera over there is my colleague, Glen Anderson. Glen!" she called.

He turned and looked at her. Guin gestured for him to come over.

"Glen, this is my old boss, Pauline Paulson."

"Who're you calling old?" said Pauline.

Glen smiled.

"Nice to meet you, Pauline."

Pauline eyed Glen appreciatively.

"Likewise. So you two work together?"

"We do," said Glen.

They made small talk for a few minutes. Then Pauline

said she needed to take in the rest of the exhibit. Guin and Glen said they should do the same.

Pauline eyed Guin before she left.

"It really is a remarkable likeness. You must tell me how you came to pose for him."

"I'll fill you in later, out on the terrace," said Guin.

"I'll look for you."

Pauline moved off, and Glen said he should go take some pictures.

"Will you be okay?" he asked Guin.

"I'll be fine," she replied. Though she saw several people glancing her way and wished she was invisible or that they had hung the painting at the end of the exhibit.

"Just yell if anyone accosts you."

"I'll be fine," she repeated.

She hurried back to the beginning of the exhibit and quickly took a photo of the portrait. She was tempted to take a selfie, but she didn't have much time until they let the rest of the people in. And she had a lot to see. She took a photo of the description of the exhibit, the title of which was Decadence. It was a play on words, and Guin thought it fitting. Below the description was a brief bio of the artist, containing information Guin knew from reading about Bishop online.

She went into the first room again. The first paintings were from the early sixties and had a realistic quality to them. Guin found them attractive. Definitely more her style. There was a mixture of still lifes, landscapes, and portraits. The next paintings were from the late sixties, and they reminded Guin a bit of Andy Warhol's work, giving the same objects he had painted earlier a Pop or Op Art spin. However, unlike Warhol, Bishop didn't appropriate brands or other people's images.

The next gallery contained samples of Bishop's work from the seventies. These works had a more surrealistic quality, and Guin wondered if Bishop had been on drugs when he painted them. Next came his work from the eighties. These works were darker and more abstract. Then came the nineties paintings.

Pauline was in there speaking with the reporter from *Art World.* They looked like they were arguing. Guin watched them from across the room, trying to be inconspicuous. She waited until they had left and then looked around.

Unlike previous eras, in the nineties, Bishop hadn't stuck to just one style. Or so it seemed to Guin. The description on the wall referred to this era as Bishop's experimental period. There were several pieces that resembled jigsaw puzzles, others that looked like graffiti, and several that Guin couldn't categorize.

Guin looked for the article that showed the paintings involved in the lawsuit, the ones that supposedly ripped off another artist's work. She found it and looked at the photos. But it was a bit hard to see them on her phone. She looked around the room. None of them were here. Not a huge surprise.

She put her phone away and entered the last room, which contained his recent work. Back to Nature was painted or stenciled on the wall, along with a brief description. Looking at the paintings, Guin could see why the curator had chosen the title.

She was looking at a picture of a little girl in a field, a butterfly on her finger, when Glen approached.

"She looks just like I imagine you looked at that age," he said.

"You think so?"

"She has your hair and coloring. You think that could be his daughter?"

There was no name on the card describing the painting.

"Maybe," said Guin. "Though she must be in her fifties now. Still, the girl in the picture looks to be around the same age his daughter was when she left."

They continued to study the painting of the little girl.

"Other than the little girl looking like me, what do you think of it?"

"It's sweet," said Glen. "A bit like his earlier work. But I prefer his later, grittier stuff."

Guin glanced around the room.

"Is it just me or do the paintings in here have a feel familiar to them? It's almost like I've seen them before, yet I know that's impossible."

"They're very Pre-Raphaelite, what with all of the naturalism, rich detail, and bright colors."

"Yes! Thank you. That's why they felt familiar. Maybe you should write the article. You're much better versed in art than I am."

"No thanks. I prefer to take photographs. You know what they say…"

"That a picture's worth a thousand words?"

"Exactly. And speaking of photographs, I should go take some of these paintings."

"Okay. I should go find the director and the curator. Shall I meet you out on the terrace?"

"Sounds like a plan."

Guin saw the director speaking with the reporter from *Art World* just outside the exhibit area. Neither looked happy. Guin wished she could read lips.

"Can I help you?" Guin turned to see the curator. She was an attractive woman, tall with large brown eyes, her brown-black hair, which had a streak of gray, pulled back into a chignon. Guin guessed she was somewhere in her fifties.

"Actually, you can. I had a few questions about the exhibit."

Guin noticed the curator studying her.

"I don't mean to stare, but you look just like the painting. That is you, isn't it?"

"It is," said Guin.

"I hope you don't mind me asking, but how did you come to pose for him?"

"It was his condition for allowing me to interview him. If I sat for him, he'd sit for me."

"Ah," said the curator. "That sounds like Farley. He always was a bit of a control freak."

"You know him well?"

"Not really. So, you didn't know your portrait would be included in the exhibit?"

"I had no idea. And it's a portrait of Titania, not me."

"Of course. So, what did you want to ask me?"

"How did you manage to convince Mr. Bishop to allow you to show his work here? I thought he had sworn off exhibiting his work in a museum or gallery."

"I'm afraid I can't take credit for that. It was Bennett's doing."

"Bennett Emerson, the director of the Baker."

The curator nodded.

"And do you know how he convinced Mr. Bishop?"

"You should ask him that."

"Did I hear someone mention my name?" It was the director. He looked at Guin and smiled. "If it isn't Titania, Queen of the Fairies, in the flesh. It really is a remarkable likeness, don't you think, Alexandra?"

"It is."

The director turned his attention back to Guin.

"I'm Bennett Emerson, the director of the Baker Museum."

"I know," said Guin.

"And you are? I'm guessing your name's not really Titania."

Guin smiled at him.

"It's Guinivere, Guinivere Jones. I'm with the *Sanibel-Captiva Sun-Times*."

"Guinivere, eh? Now there's a name you don't hear often. Right out of King Arthur and the Knights of the Round Table. It suits you."

"Thank you."

Guin regarded the director. He was tall and slender with a head of mostly gray hair that had no doubt been quite dark once. And he was dressed in a linen suit, the perfect Southern gentleman.

"Anyway, while you're both here, I'd love to ask you a few questions about the exhibit."

"Of course!" said the director. "Ask away!"

"Great. So how did you…"

But before Guin could finish her question, the room began to buzz. She looked around to see what the excitement was about. Then she saw him. Farley Bishop had arrived.

"Would you excuse me?" said the director. Without waiting for a reply, he headed towards the artist.

"Farley!" he said, smiling broadly, his arms outstretched as though he were about to hug him. "So good of you to make it. I was starting to wonder."

"I said I'd be here," Bishop groused.

"Well, you're just in time. And look who I found, your new muse!"

The director led Bishop over to Guin and the curator.

"Farley," said the curator.

Bishop looked from the curator to Guin and smiled.

"I saw the painting," she said. "You might have told me."

The smile turned into a smirk.

"What fun would that be?"

"Come," said the director, taking Bishop's arm. "There are several people who'd like to meet you."

"Wait!" said Guin.

They stopped and looked at her.

"I had a few questions I wanted to ask the two of you."

"Can it wait?" said the director. "I promised the board members I would bring Farley over as soon as he arrived."

Guin looked perturbed.

"We shouldn't be long," said the director. "Come look for us out on the terrace." He then turned to Bishop. "Come Farley."

Guin watched as the director led Bishop away.

"Perhaps I can answer some of your questions," said the curator.

"You don't need to chat up some board member?"

The curator smiled.

"That can wait. Besides, Bennett's probably talking their ears off. What did you want to ask?"

"Well," said Guin. "Whose idea was it to do a Farley Bishop retrospective?"

"Again, that was Bennett's idea. He'd been wanting to do it for years, long before I came to the Baker."

"When did you come here?"

"Just over a year ago."

"Where had you been before?"

"At the Broad in LA."

Guin wasn't familiar with the Broad, but she didn't say anything. She would Google it later.

"And was he responsible for acquiring all of the paintings?"

"The paintings are all loans. And I acquired most of them. Well, me and my staff. I have two people who work for me."

"Were you able to get everything that you wanted?" Guin wondered about the paintings from the lawsuit.

"Not everything, but we got a good sampling."

"Who wrote the descriptions on the walls? They're spot on."

"Thank you. That was my doing."

"What does Mr. Bishop think of your descriptions? He told me he hated labels."

The curator smiled.

"I am aware of that. But it's customary for curators to describe the works they are exhibiting. And if you read the exhibit brochure, you'll know that we stated that Farley is against the use of labels to describe his work."

Guin felt chastised. But she hadn't had time to read the brochure. She'd pick one up and be sure to read it later.

"And do you have a favorite work or period?"

The curator looked thoughtful.

"I've always been fond of his early pieces."

"Me too," said Guin. "Though I would have thought you would favor his later, more avant-garde works."

"I like some of them too. I just have a soft spot for his early pieces, the ones he did before he became famous. Or infamous."

"And what happens to the paintings after the exhibit closes? Will the exhibit be going on tour to other museums?"

The curator was about to answer when she was interrupted.

"Ms. Barnes, may I have a word?"

It was the man in the wheelchair, the critic from *Art World.*

"I'll be with you in a minute, Mr. Belem. I'm just finishing up with Ms. Jones."

Belem frowned as the curator directed her attention back to Guin.

"This is the only place to see Mr. Bishop's new works as well as his old. Once the exhibit closes, the paintings will be returned to the institutions and individuals who lent them to us."

"What about the new paintings? Will the Baker try to acquire some of them?"

"Of course. Though, as you can imagine, there's been a lot of interest from collectors and other institutions."

The critic from *Art World* was clearing his throat, clearly trying to get their attention. He succeeded.

"Are you quite finished?" he asked Guin.

Guin had more questions. But she sensed that Mr. Belem wouldn't leave until he got what he wanted, which was the curator.

"Do you mind?" the curator asked Guin.

"No, go ahead," she replied. "I'll look for you later."

"Thank you." The curator looked down at the man from *Art World*.

"How can I help you, Mr. Belem?"

"Let's go someplace a bit more quiet," he said and began to roll away.

The curator frowned but followed him.

Guin was tempted to follow them and eavesdrop, but she had better things to do.

CHAPTER 10

Guin headed out to the terrace, hoping to snag the director and Farley Bishop. She had just stepped outside when a server crashed into her, sending the tray of hors d'oeuvres she was carrying clattering to the ground.

"I'm so sorry!" said the young woman.

Guin looked down at her dress. Fortunately, it was okay. The finger food had missed her.

"Don't worry about it," said Guin. "Are you okay?"

"I'm so sorry!" repeated the server, who had squatted down and was picking up the hors d'oeuvres from the ground and placing them back on the tray.

"Carla! What are you doing?"

It was one of the other servers, a young man. Guin wondered if they were related. They had the same coloring and features.

"I dropped the hors d'oeuvres," said Carla.

"I can see that," said the other server. "I'll take care of them. Go get a fresh tray. And be more careful."

Carla nodded and hurried off.

"I'm sorry about that," said the male server. "Can I get you something? A glass of wine, perhaps?"

Guin was tempted. But she had a firm rule: no drinking alcohol on the job.

"Thank you, but I'm good."

"Mariano!" It was another one of the servers, or maybe

their supervisor. She looked a good deal older than Mariano and Carla and had a commanding air.

Mariano hurried over to her.

Guin was about to go in search of the director and Farley Bishop when Ginny intercepted her.

"There you are!" She took Guin's arm. "There're some people I'd like you to meet." She steered Guin over to an older couple. "Guin, this is Martha and Sid Sachs. Martha is on the board of the museum."

"Nice to meet you," Guin said.

Martha was staring at her.

"The likeness is amazing!" she said. "When Ginny told me you were a reporter, not a model, I didn't believe it."

Guin thought Martha Sachs needed her eyes checked but didn't say anything.

"Well, it's true," said Guin. "I'm a reporter."

"So if you're not a model, how'd you come to be in that painting?" asked Martha's husband Sid.

"I needed to interview Mr. Bishop about the exhibit, and the only way he'd agree to an interview was if I sat for him."

"From what I've heard about Bishop, I'm guessing he got the better deal."

"He did," said Guin.

"Ginny said you had no idea about the painting," said Martha.

"None at all. It was a complete surprise." Guin spied Bennett Emerson. "Would you mind excusing me? I need to speak with the director."

Before either Mr. or Mrs. Sachs could answer, Guin rushed off. The director was speaking with some people, either board members or patrons. Guin tried to subtly get his attention, but he was too absorbed in conversation. She looked around for Farley Bishop. But she didn't see him. Had he gone back inside? She went inside and saw Glen emerging from the nearby stairwell. He was putting his phone away.

"Hey," she said.

"Hm? he said, looking distracted. "Oh hi. You all set?"

"No. I still need to talk to Bishop and the director. What were you doing in the stairwell?"

"Taking a call."

"Everything okay?"

"It was my mother."

"Is she okay?"

"She hurt her ankle."

"Did she break it?"

"Thankfully no. It's just a sprain. But she needs to stay off it for a few days. I told her I'd swing by first thing tomorrow to check on her."

"Do you want to go see her on our way home tonight? I should be ready to go soon. I just need a few minutes with Bishop and the director. If I can corner them."

"That's fine. Take your time. Mom's at home, resting. And I should take some shots out on the terrace. Ginny promised a bunch of board members I'd take their picture."

"Okay, but the offer stands."

Guin went into the exhibit to look for Bishop. But she didn't see him in there. Where could he be? Could he have gone back out to the terrace? Could he have left? He hadn't been there that long. But maybe he had had enough.

Guin went back out to the terrace and spied Bishop talking with the director and the curator. There was something about seeing the three of them together. But Guin couldn't put her finger on it. She went over to have a word with them. As soon as they saw her approach, they stopped talking.

"Sorry to interrupt," she said. "But I was hoping to get a word with you before I left," she said to the director. "I just had a few quick questions."

"Of course!" he said. "Would you excuse us?" he said to his companions. He and Guin moved off to the side. "So, what did you want to ask me?"

"How did you manage to convince Mr. Bishop to let the Baker host an exhibit of his work?"

"It's a bit of a long story, and I'm not sure Farley would like…"

"Sorry to interrupt you, Bennett, but I need a word." It was a man in a bowtie.

"Of course, Bob. Would you excuse me, Ms. Jones?"

Guin wanted to say "no," but she just smiled and said, "of course."

Guin glanced around the terrace, looking for Farley Bishop. She saw the curator speaking with a couple. But she didn't see Bishop. Where had he gone? Maybe to the bathroom? Guin could use a bathroom herself.

She went inside and found the restroom. Then she went back out onto the terrace. The crowd was starting to thin out. However, there were still a couple of dozen people there. Guin saw Carla and Mariano with another server over by the outdoor kitchen. It looked as though they were putting things away. The party was clearly winding down.

She saw Glen with Ginny. They were chatting with Sid and Martha Sachs. She headed over to them.

"You ready?" she asked Glen.

"If you are."

Guin turned to their boss. "You okay if Glen and I head out?"

"You get what you need?" she asked Guin.

"Pretty much," Guin replied.

Ginny looked at Glen.

"What about you? You get enough pictures?"

"More than enough."

"Then you may go."

"Thanks," said Guin.

"Excuse me," said Martha Sachs.

They turned to look at her.

"Would you mind taking a picture of me and Sid?" she asked Glen.

Glen looked at Ginny.

"Go ahead," she told him.

He took several pictures of the couple, and Ginny told Mrs. Sachs that she would send them to her.

Guin and Glen were about to leave when the man in the bowtie came over.

"Ah, the woman in the painting. I don't think we've been introduced. Bob Axelrod."

"Bob's the chairman of the board of the Baker," explained Martha Sachs.

"Guin Jones," said Guin. "I'm with the *Sanibel-Captiva Sun-Times*."

"That's right. Ginny told me."

"I don't mean to be rude, but we were just leaving."

"Go, if you must," said Mr. Axelrod, a bit dramatically.

Guin wondered how much he had had to drink. She turned to Ginny.

"You staying?"

"I was hoping to have a chat with Bob here about advertising in the paper. But you go."

Guin and Glen said their goodbyes and headed inside. As they passed by the entrance to the exhibit, Guin took a last look at the portrait of Titania.

"Could I take a picture of you with it?" Glen asked.

There was no one around.

"Okay," said Guin.

She went and stood next to the painting. Glen raised his camera.

"Would you take one with my phone too?" she asked him when he was done.

Guin handed him her phone.

"Thanks," she said. "Now let's go."

When they emerged from the Baker, it was drizzling. Glen said he would get the car. Guin said he didn't have to. She would go with him. But Glen insisted that she stay there, under the awning. They started to argue.

"Fine. Go get the car," Guin said, tired of arguing.

Glen hurried off, and Guin moved under the awning to Hayes Hall, which was just across from the Baker Museum. Of course, a minute later, the rain had stopped. Guin thought about going in search of Glen, but she didn't know where he had parked his SUV.

As she waited for Glen to return, she checked her phone for messages. In the distance, she could hear sirens. The sirens grew louder, and Guin saw two vehicles with Collier County Sheriff printed on them, as well as an unmarked sedan, pull in. What were they doing there? She watched in the shadows as the vehicles parked and several police officers emerged, accompanied by a woman in a red dress. Guin wondered who she was.

Guin went to get a closer look, but they had disappeared into the Baker. Guin wanted to follow them, but she knew Glen would worry if he pulled up and she wasn't there. She waited to see if he would appear and then sent him a text, saying she had gone back into the museum. Then she headed inside. However, she was stopped from going upstairs by a uniformed officer.

Guin asked him what was going on, but he didn't explain. He just said that no one was to leave or enter the museum. Guin explained that she was a guest and had left her phone upstairs. But the officer, who looked like he had been a defensive lineman, wouldn't let her go up.

A minute later, Glen appeared. He saw Guin with the

officer and looked worried.

"Is everything okay?" he asked her.

"I don't know. I think I left my phone in the ladies room upstairs," she explained, hoping Glen wouldn't rat her out. "But this officer informed me that no one is allowed to go up."

She turned and looked at the officer.

"I'd be happy to show you my ID. And you can ask anyone upstairs. They'll tell you I'm a guest."

"Sorry, ma'am. I'm under orders."

"I really need my phone. Could you just radio upstairs? Please? I won't be long."

The officer frowned but relented, taking out a two-way radio.

"I've got a woman here claiming to be a guest. Says she left her phone in the ladies room. Says her name is…"

"Guin Jones," said Guin.

"Gwen Jones," said the officer.

She didn't correct him, just silently waited.

"Okay," the officer finally said and put his two-way radio away. "You can go up."

"Thank you," said Guin.

She headed to the stairs. Glen made to follow her, but the officer stopped him.

"I'm with her," Glen explained, as Guin said, "He's with me."

"I thought you were going to the ladies room," the officer said to Guin.

"Uh," she looked at Glen and mouthed *sorry*. "I'll be back in a minute," she told them. Then she hurried up the stairs.

Guin wondered what had happened. Had someone vandalized one of Bishop's paintings? She had read about climate change activists doing awful things to works of art. But she couldn't picture anyone in the preview crowd gluing themselves to a wall or throwing paint at a painting.

However, one of the servers could have been a protester.

She headed into the exhibit space, but no one seemed to be there. All the action seemed to be down the hall. She headed towards the terrace and saw Ginny talking on her phone. Guin went up to her, but Ginny held up a finger, indicating she should wait a minute. Guin waited, but she was impatient. Finally, Ginny was off.

"You're back," said Ginny.

"What happened here? And who were you talking to?"

"I was talking to Joel, telling him I'd be late."

"What happened?" Guin repeated. "I saw the police arrive." Just then she heard more sirens. More police?

"That must be the ambulance."

"Ambulance? What happened, Ginny? Did someone have a heart attack?" Guin immediately thought of all of the elderly people at the preview. Though many of them had left early.

"There's been an accident."

"Accident?"

"The critic from *Art World*. He fell down the stairs."

"Fell down the stairs? I didn't see anyone when I came up."

"Not those stairs, the stairs leading down to the loading dock from the terrace."

"There are stairs leading down to a loading dock from the terrace?" Guin hadn't seen any stairs.

"They're over by the outdoor kitchen. You can't really see them unless you're standing right there. They're hidden by the planters."

"What was he doing by the terrace stairs?"

"I don't know."

"You didn't see what happened?"

"I was in the ladies room."

"Is he all right?"

"I don't think so." Ginny looked around. "Where's Glen?"

"Downstairs. They wouldn't let him come up."

"Why'd they let you up?"

"I told the officer I had left my phone in the ladies room."

"And he believed you?"

"I'm here, aren't I?"

Ginny shook her head.

"I should probably text Glen, let him know what's going on."

Guin got out her phone and sent Glen a text, letting him know there had been an accident, that the critic from *Art World* had somehow fallen down the terrace stairs. She followed it with another text, asking him to see if he could find a loading dock and if he could see the terrace from there. Then she put her phone back in her bag and looked around.

"Can I go out on the terrace?"

"Be my guest."

Ginny followed her outside.

"Who's in charge?" Guin asked her boss.

"She's over there. You can't miss her."

"She?"

"Don't look so surprised. There are plenty of female detectives."

"I know. I just didn't think there were that many in Florida.

Guin looked around but didn't see a female officer.

"She's over there, speaking with that server," said Ginny, pointing to the woman in the red dress Guin had seen earlier.

Guin recognized the server. It was Carla, the young woman who had bumped into her.

"She's the detective?" said Guin, staring at the woman in the red dress.

"Got a badge and everything," said Ginny.

Guin knew sarcasm when she heard it. She looked

around the terrace. She saw the director speaking with one of the police officers. Where were Farley Bishop and the curator? There was activity by the stairs. Guin was dying to go over there. She watched as an officer went up to the detective, said something to her, saw the detective nod, and then followed him over to the stairs.

"What's going on?" Guin asked Ginny.

"I'm guessing the EMTs are here and want to speak with the detective."

Guin wanted to get a better look at the stairs, but they were being guarded by two uniformed officers. She looked back over at Carla, who was being comforted by Mariano. She again wondered if they were related.

She finally spied the curator. She was standing next to Bob Axelrod. But where was Bishop?

Several minutes went by. The detective finally emerged from the stairs.

"If I could have everyone's attention again," she said. "Please do not leave the premises without speaking to me or one of the officers."

"So we're free to go?" asked one of the guests, a man Guin had seen earlier. Though she didn't know his name.

"After you speak to me or one of the officers. We need to ask everyone a few questions and get your contact information. Then you may leave."

There was lots of mumbling and grumbling from the crowd.

"I'm going to go speak with the detective," Guin announced.

"Be my guest," said Ginny.

"Did you catch her name?"

"Romero."

Guin waited as the detective spoke with one of the officers. As soon as she was done, Guin stepped forward.

"Excuse me," said Guin.

"Yes?"

"Can you tell me what happened? Someone told me the critic from *Art World* fell down the stairs. Is that correct?"

"And you are?"

"Guin Jones. I'm a reporter with the *Sanibel-Captiva Sun-Times.* I was just leaving when I heard the police sirens."

"You attended the preview?"

"That's right."

"Did you know the deceased?"

"He's dead?"

"Did you know him?" the detective repeated.

"Not personally. Just that he worked for *Art World*."

"Do you know what he was doing by the stairs?"

"I have no idea. As I said, we had just left."

"We?"

"Me and the photographer I was here with."

"Where is he now?"

"Downstairs."

"Did anyone else leave with you?"

Guin thought.

"A few people left when we did. But we didn't know them. And before you ask, we left via the main staircase."

"What about before you left? Did you happen to notice the deceased with anyone over by the terrace stairs?"

"By the stairs? No. But I saw him talking with several people on the terrace and inside."

"Who?"

"Who did I see him talking to?"

The detective nodded.

"I saw him with Farley Bishop, the artist; the director of the museum, Bennett Emerson; and with the curator, Alexandra Barnes. But as I said, we left before the accident occurred." Though she didn't know that for sure.

"I understand. And these people the deceased spoke with. How would you describe them, their interactions with him?"

Guin thought, recalling what she had seen.

"Intense."

"Intense?"

"There appeared to be a lot of tension."

"Did you hear what they were saying?"

"No, but… the exchanges seemed heated."

The detective was studying Guin, or that's what it felt like.

An officer came over and whispered something to the detective. The detective nodded, and he moved away. When he was gone, the detective reached into her handbag and withdrew a card, handing it to Guin.

"Here's my card. If you remember anything else, let me know."

Guin looked at the card. The detective's first name was Catalina. It suited her.

"I'll do that," she said. She then reached into her bag and withdrew one of her cards. "Here's my card. So you don't think it was an accident?"

"We're investigating," said the detective.

Where had Guin heard that before? (It was a rhetorical question. Detective O'Loughlin of the Sanibel PD had always used that phrase when Guin asked him a question. Either that or "no comment.")

Guin looked at the detective's attire.

"I have to ask: Is that how you normally dress for work?"

The detective frowned.

"No. I happened to be out to dinner nearby when I got the call. I didn't have time to change."

"Gotcha."

"Now if you would excuse me?"

"Of course," said Guin. She watched as the detective went to speak with the officer who had whispered in her ear a minute ago.

"So?" It was Ginny. Guin hadn't seen her sneak up.

"What do you think of Detective Romero?"

"Interesting."

"She reveal anything?"

"Just that the critic from *Art World* was dead."

"Does she suspect foul play?"

"She wouldn't say. She just asked me who he had spoken with."

"What did you tell her?"

"I told her I had seen him with Bishop, the director, and the curator. Though not by the terrace stairs. You see anything?"

"I was in the ladies room when it must have happened. When I came out, all hell had broken loose. That server, the one who was talking to the detective before, she's the one who found him."

Poor Carla, thought Guin. It wasn't her night. She looked around for the young woman but didn't see her. Had she left?

"I'm going to go speak with one of the officers and get out of here," said Ginny. "I take it you're free to go."

"I am, but you don't want me to interview people?"

Ginny glanced around. There weren't that many people left on the terrace. And those that were left were either speaking with an officer or looked eager to leave.

"Be my guest. But I'm guessing no one will want to talk to you. Anyway, it was likely an accident."

"Okay," said Guin. However, she wasn't so sure it had been an accident. "So, should I mention what happened in my write-up?"

"Just focus on the preview, the art and who was here."

"Will do. Say, have you seen Bishop anywhere?"

"Not recently. Go. I'm going to go speak with that officer," she said, pointing to one of them.

Guin watched her go. Her phone was buzzing. She took it out. Glen had sent her another message. Guin texted him back, saying she'd be down in a minute. She turned to go but spotted Bennett Emerson. He was standing along the edge of the terrace, looking up at the night sky. She went over to him.

"You okay?" Guin asked him.

He turned and looked at her.

"Not really."

"Will you have to close the museum?"

"For a few days, while they investigate."

"Will the exhibit still open?"

"Why wouldn't it?"

"Well," said Guin.

"That man's death had nothing to do with the exhibit. It was an unfortunate accident."

"You think it was an accident?"

"Of course. What else could it be?"

Guin was going to say *murder* but held her tongue.

"Have you seen Mr. Bishop?"

"Not recently. He's probably off sulking somewhere. He wasn't thrilled to be here, as you know doubt saw, and now this."

"Bennett, could I have a word?" It was Bob Axelrod again.

"Of course," said the director. He turned back to Guin. "Would you excuse us?"

"Of course," said Guin.

She watched them huddle together not far away. No doubt they were discussing how to handle the situation. She didn't envy the museum's PR person.

Guin looked around one last time. There were only a few people left. Time for her to leave.

CHAPTER 11

Guin was surprised to see Pauline with Glen. She had assumed Pauline had left.

"There you are," said Glen.

"Sorry. I was chatting with Ginny and the director. And I spoke with the detective in charge."

"They don't make detectives like that up in New York," said Pauline. "You see what she was wearing?"

"She said she came straight from a dinner," said Guin.

"Must have been some dinner."

"I take it she's attractive," said Glen.

"Very," said Pauline. "In a Sofia Vergara or Sophia Lauren kind of way." She turned to Guin. "So what did the detective have to say?"

"Not much."

"Did she think it was an accident or…?"

"She wouldn't say. Though she asked me who I had seen Belem talking to and what they had been talking about. I didn't hear any of the conversations, but they all looked intense. Speaking of which, what were the two of you talking about? I saw you together in the exhibit."

"Probably some painting. You ever read his column in *Art World*?"

"No."

"You should. He could be quite amusing. However, I'm sure the artists and curators he criticized didn't think so. But he had a loyal following. They'll miss his acerbic wit."

"Did he say anything to you about the exhibit?"

"Not that I recall. He's notoriously cagey. Saves everything for his column. But I got the sense that he wasn't impressed. If he wasn't naturally waspish, I'd say he had a bit of a grudge against Bishop."

"What makes you say that?"

"He was mumbling something about him when I came across him."

"What did he say?"

"It wasn't so much what he said—I couldn't make it out—but how he said it."

"Hm. Speaking of Bishop, did you see him upstairs before you left?"

"No."

Guin heard a phone ringing.

"That's probably Paul, wondering where I am," said Pauline, reaching for her phone. "Would you excuse me?"

"Of course," said Guin.

Pauline moved away, and Guin turned to Glen.

"Did you get a look at those stairs?"

"I wasn't able to. The police and EMTs were there."

Guin frowned. Then she saw Alexandra Barnes near the entrance to the museum. She was on her phone.

"I'm going to have a quick word with the curator," she told Glen.

Glen followed her over.

"Ms. Barnes, do you have a minute?"

The curator was busy typing away.

"I'm rather busy," she replied, not looking at Guin.

Guin didn't move.

The curator sighed and looked up, or rather down, at Guin.

"Yes?"

"I just wanted to let you know, I enjoyed the exhibit. I

think you did a great job."

"Thank you."

"Any idea what will happen to it? Bennett Emerson thought the museum would have to close for a few days."

"Probably."

"Did you know Mr. Belem?"

"Not really."

"Yet you invited him to attend the preview."

"I issued an invitation to *Art World*. They sent Ludwig."

"You didn't like him." It was a statement, not a question.

"Not particularly. He has a reputation for being hard on certain artists."

"Were you worried when he showed up?"

"Worried?"

"Or annoyed?"

"Is there a point to these questions, Ms. Jones?"

Guin could tell that the curator was annoyed right now. But she pressed on.

"I saw the two of you together and wondered what you were talking about. The conversation looked a bit heated."

"I don't know what you're talking about," said the curator, whose phone was pinging like mad. No doubt people were frantically messaging her. Now her phone was ringing. "I need to go," she said.

Guin watched as the curator took the call and moved away. Alexandra Barnes was going to be very busy the next few days.

"I feel for her," said Glen. Guin had forgotten he was there. "Not exactly the publicity she was looking for."

"Definitely not," said Guin.

"Come, we should leave."

As they turned to go, the ambulance pulled out of the lot. Less than a minute later, the detective and some of the officers emerged from the building. Guin hurried over to them.

"Detective Romero!"

The detective stopped.

"You all done here?"

"For now."

"What was the cause of death?"

"Broken neck."

"From the fall down the stairs?"

The detective didn't answer.

"Will the medical examiner's office be conducting an autopsy?"

"It's standard procedure."

"Could I get a copy of the report when it's ready?"

"You can request one from the medical examiner's office. Now if you would excuse me?"

"Come on," said Glen, gently taking Guin's arm.

"Wait. I want to see if the caterers are still here."

Glen sighed and followed Guin around to the back of the museum. Guin could see the stairs leading up to the terrace. They were blocked off with crime scene tape.

She looked for a catering van but didn't see one. They must have left while she was in front. She should have gotten the name of the catering company. She would call the museum tomorrow and ask. Though the museum would likely be closed the next few days. She frowned.

Of course, the art critic's death could have been an accident. You did read about people in wheelchairs falling down stairs. Maybe Belem had been on the phone or talking with someone, hadn't set the brake, didn't realize how close he was to the stairs, started rolling backwards, and didn't stop until it was too late. However, that seemed unlikely.

Guin looked up at the stairs again. It would be easy to sneak under the crime scene tape.

"Don't do it, Guin." It was Glen. "I know what you're thinking. And it's not a good idea."

"I just want to take a quick look."

"Don't. Besides, we should go. It's late."

"It's not that late."

Glen waited.

"Fine," she said. She took one last look at the stairs and then followed Glen back around to the front of the museum.

CHAPTER 12

Guin had trouble falling asleep that night. She kept thinking about the exhibit and Ludwig Belem. Had someone pushed him down those stairs? Guin doubted the fall had been accidental. Had anyone seen him fall? She knew one of the servers had found him.

And where had Farley Bishop gone? She needed to have a chat with him. She would give him a call tomorrow.

She considered taking a sleeping pill, but they gave her a headache the next day. She turned on the lamp on her nightstand and grabbed her book on Florida wildlife. That always helped to put her to sleep. Not that the wildlife found in Florida was boring. Or that the author was a bad writer. Guin just found reading descriptions of birds and turtles restful.

She began to read and, sure enough, fifteen minutes later she realized she had nodded off. She put down the book and turned off the light.

It was dark when she woke up. She wondered what time it was. She looked at her alarm clock. It was six-thirty. She was normally up this early, but she had slept fitfully and felt tired. Maybe she should have stayed over at Glen's like he had suggested. At least then she would have been tired for a more pleasant reason. But she had wanted to get home and type up her notes.

She made her way to the kitchen to make herself some

coffee. The cats, who had been asleep on the bed seconds ago, were now running ahead of her. She gave them food and water and proceeded to boil water in her electric kettle. When it was ready, she poured it into her French press, where ground coffee was waiting.

As soon as it was ready, Guin poured the coffee into a mug, inhaling before she took a sip. Was there anything better than the smell of freshly made coffee? She thought, not for the first time, that someone should turn the smell into a fragrance. She took a sip. The coffee was strong, just the way she liked it, yet also soothing.

She took another sip and went to get her phone. She turned it on and saw there was a text from Shelly, asking how the preview had gone. Guin texted her back, saying it had been eventful and that she would fill her in later.

Guin had other messages, but nothing critical. She wanted to talk to the painter, but it was too early to phone him. She thought about getting to work on her article, but the beach was calling her. She took another sip of coffee and went to get changed.

Guin waved to the neighborhood dog walkers as she headed to the beach. (They were always out early and were a friendly bunch.) It was an eight-minute walk to the Gulf from her house, the main reason she had purchased it. And it was a beautiful morning, despite a slight chill in the air—a slight chill on Sanibel meaning it was around sixty degrees, which was a heck of a lot warmer than it was in New York or Connecticut.

The sun was rising as Guin stepped onto the sand. She paused to watch it, shielding her eyes. This was her favorite time of day. She had always been a morning person, but when she had lived in New York City and then Connecticut, she had never appreciated the sunrise. Probably because you could rarely see it, what with all of the tall buildings or trees blocking her view.

Here on Sanibel, however, to stand on the beach and watch the sun as it rose above the dunes and the sea, casting pink, red, orange, and gold rays across the sky, was a spiritual experience. At least for Guin. And she rarely missed a sunrise. Not if she could help it.

As the sun cast its warm glow over her, Guin closed her eyes and slowly raised her arms above her head, breathing in as she did. Then she slowly lowered her arms, breathing out. She moved her hands in front of her, as though in prayer, and asked the sea to send her some pretty shells, especially a large true tulip. She opened her eyes and looked out at the water. It was dark blue today and calm. She looked left and then right, deciding which way to go. Then she headed left.

Guin had told herself that she would only be gone for an hour at most. But she kept running into people she knew. Not that they would engage in long conversations. Mostly it would be a *hello*, or *good morning*, or *You find any good shells?* But it slowed her down. And it was nearly nine by the time Guin got back to her place.

Despite her prayer, she had not found a true tulip shell. However, she had found a shiny lettered olive, a spikey lace murex, several banded tulips, and some bright orange scallops. So the morning wasn't a total loss. But as soon as she left the shells to soak and took a shower, she would need to work on her article about the preview and ring Farley Bishop.

□

Guin had left her phone at home. Now as she checked it she saw that Ginny had texted her multiple times, telling Guin to call her ASAP. Guin rolled her eyes and called her boss.

"Where have you been?" Ginny asked, not bothering to say hello.

"It's only nine o'clock, Gin. And I was taking a walk. What's up?"

Guin thought about reminding Ginny that it was Saturday, but she knew there was no point. During the season, Ginny expected everyone to work seven days a week, especially if there was an important story.

"Well, you didn't pick up, so I called Craig."

Craig Jeffers was the paper's fishing reporter, who had had a long, illustrious career as a crime reporter in Chicago before moving with his wife to Sanibel. Ginny had convinced him to come out of retirement to cover fishing for the paper. And then coerced him into covering crime. Not that there was a lot of crime on Sanibel, which was considered one of the safest places to live in Florida. Mostly it was people going over the 35 mph speed limit or a car getting burgled because the owner forgot to lock it. Though there was the occasional murder.*

"Why'd you call Craig? Has someone been murdered?"

Guin fervently hoped no one had. At least not on Sanibel or Captiva.

"They've taken Farley in for questioning."

"Who? Why?"

"The Collier County Sheriff's Office. I assume they think he had something to do with the death of that art critic."

"The one from *Art World*?"

"Unless you know of some other art critic who died at the Baker last night."

"No, just him. How do you know the Collier County Sheriff's Office took Bishop in for questioning?"

"That's not important. What is important is for you and Craig to find out what's up."

"Did you speak to him? Craig, that is."

"Briefly. He's out fishing."

---

* See Sanibel Island Mysteries books 1 – 9.

That didn't surprise Guin. Craig was out fishing most mornings.

"What did you tell him?"

"I told him what happened and asked him if he knew anyone at the Collier County Sheriff's Office."

"Does he?"

"What do you think?"

Of course he did. Craig had contacts—people he met through fishing and his Friday night poker game—who worked in all levels of local government as well as in the police and fire departments of Lee and Collier counties. And they often provided him with information other reporters weren't privy to. Not that Craig shared or published any of it. Much of it was confidential, mentioned in confidence during fishing trips or poker games. And Craig knew better than to go blabbing without permission. Which was why his sources trusted him and would help him when they could.

"And?"

"And he said he'd get on it when he got back."

"Okay. I'll shoot him a text when I get off the phone with you, let him know we talked."

"Do that. So how's your article coming?"

"About the exhibit?"

"Yes, about the exhibit."

"I'm working on it."

"Good. Get it to me later."

"Later today?"

"No, later next week. Of course today."

Man, Ginny was in a mood. Had she not slept well either?

"I'll do my best, but I probably won't get it to you until tomorrow at the earliest. You still want me to leave out what happened?"

"Yes. Just focus on the exhibit."

"Got it," said Guin. "You communicate with Glen?"

"I sent him a message."

"Did he get back to you?"

"Not yet. If you talk to him, tell him I need those pictures."

"I'll let him know. So, do you know if they brought anyone else in for questioning?"

"No. Ask Craig."

"I'll do that. Anything else?"

"No."

They ended the call and Guin looked out the window. So much for calling Farley Bishop. She sent Craig a text, asking him to call her when he got back from fishing. Then she called Glen.

"Good morning," he said.

"For some people."

"What's up?"

"I just got off the phone with Ginny."

"What'd she want?"

"You didn't read her text?"

"Not yet."

"She wants us to send her stuff by tomorrow. Also, the Collier County Sheriff's Office took Farley Bishop in for questioning."

"Huh. Regarding that art critic's death?"

"Yes. And Ginny called Craig."

"He know someone in the Collier County Sheriff's Office?"

"Apparently. So, you able to send her photos later today or tomorrow?"

"I should be able to. You want to send me your article, so I know which photos to send?"

"Or you could send me your photos, and I can decide which ones to mention."

"See, you should have stayed over. Then we could have worked on the article together."

"If I had stayed over, I doubt that we would've gotten a lot of work done."

"Hm. Probably true. Though you could come over now. It would make life easier."

"For whom?"

"For both of us." Guin didn't respond. "You could work out on the lanai. I know you like it out there."

Guin thought about it. Glen did have a nice lanai that overlooked a canal.

"Let me try to bang out a first draft. I took some photos and can refer to them. Then I'll come over and we can go through your pictures together."

"Sounds good. What time you thinking?"

"I don't know. I'll text you later."

Guin had silenced her phone and shoved it in a drawer so she wouldn't be disturbed, only taking it out after she had finished the first draft of her article. Craig had texted her, letting her know he was back. There was also another text from Shelly, asking Guin what she meant by *eventful.* Guin wrote her back, telling her that she was on a tight deadline and would tell her all about the preview when she came up for air. Then she called Craig.

"Guin?"

"That's me. How was fishing this morning?"

"Meh."

"That good, eh? You not catch anything?"

"A couple of snook. Nothing to write home about. But I know you're not calling for the fishing report."

Guin smiled. Craig knew Guin wasn't interested in fishing.

"True. I spoke with Ginny. She told me she reached out to you."

"Did she tell you that I told her you were more than capable of handling things on your own?"

"She left that part out. But I could use your help if you're willing and able. You're the one with the contacts."

"What do you need?"

"Can you find out why the Collier County Sheriff's Office brought Farley Bishop in for questioning and if they've arrested him? I would call over there, but I doubt I'd get far. And Ginny has me on a super tight deadline for my article about the exhibit."

"I'll see what I can find out."

"Thanks. Hey, do you know a Detective Romero over there?"

"In the Collier County Sheriff's Office? The name doesn't ring a bell. Why?"

"She's the detective on the case."

"She, huh? I didn't know they had any female detectives over there."

"She may be new."

Guin thought she heard Craig's wife Betty yelling something to him in the background.

"Betty says I should ask you over for dinner. She wants to hear all about Paris."

Guin smiled. Craig and Betty had become like family to her, with Betty always asking how Guin was doing and inviting Guin over for dinner.

"Just let me know when."

"Hold on," said Craig.

Guin heard him yelling to his wife.

"You free tomorrow?"

"I think so. What time?"

"Six?"

"Six it is. Can I bring anything?"

"You got any of those chocolate chip cookies of yours lying around?"

"Did Betty say it was okay?"

Betty kept Craig on a strict low-sugar diet.

"You don't have to tell her. It can be our little secret."

"I can't lie to Betty."

Craig grunted.

"I'll see you tomorrow. And let me know if you hear anything about Farley Bishop before then."

"Will do," said Craig.

CHAPTER 13

Guin was about to head over to Glen's when she felt her phone vibrating in her back pocket. She pulled it out and saw that it was Craig.

"Hey," she said. "You hear something?"

"They released him."

"Bishop?"

"Yeah."

"When?"

"Late this morning."

"You learn anything else?"

"They were doing the autopsy today."

"Can you let me know what they find?"

"I'll see what I can do."

"You're the best, Craig."

"So they tell me."

Guin smiled.

"Okay, thanks for the call. I've got to run, but I'll see you tomorrow."

"Where're you off to?"

"Glen's."

"You two have been spending a lot of time together lately. Anything I should know?"

"No. Goodbye, Craig."

Before he could say anything, Guin ended the call. She thought about calling over to Farley Bishop's studio, but she decided it could wait until tomorrow. Then she picked up her bag and her keys and headed out the door.

□

Guin arrived at Glen's a half hour later and rang the doorbell. Glen had offered Guin a key more than once, but she had declined. However, now that they were spending so much time together, she wondered if she should take him up on the offer—and offer him a key to her place.

They exchanged a kiss and Glen asked if she'd like something to drink.

"I have some cold brew."

Guin followed him into the kitchen and watched as Glen poured them each a glass.

"You want anything in it?" Glen knew Guin preferred her coffee black, but he had seen her drink cappuccinos in Italy and France.

"Maybe a little milk."

Glen added a splash of milk to Guin's glass and handed it to her. Then he added a larger amount to his own.

"So, how goes the picture editing?" she asked him.

"I'm almost done. You want to take a look?"

"That's why I'm here."

"And here I thought you were here to see me."

"This is strictly a work visit."

Glen raised his eyebrows but didn't say anything.

Guin took another sip of the cold brew.

"Okay, show me what you've got."

"This way," said Glen, leading Guin to his office.

Glen lived in a cozy two bedroom cottage that he had renovated, turning the smaller bedroom into an office/photography studio.

"Have a seat," he said, gesturing to an empty chair.

Guin sat.

"I didn't edit every shot, just the ones I thought you

might want to include in the story."

"I'd like to see all of them."

"All of them? There's a lot."

"I don't mind. Besides, you never know what you might find."

"Like who might have pushed the critic from *Art World* down the terrace stairs?"

"Exactly."

"I didn't shoot the stairs. They were pretty well hidden."

"I know. But I'm curious to know who he spoke to. Maybe you caught something. Just humor me."

"Okay," he said, knowing not to argue with her when she had that look on her face. "But let's select which pictures I should send to Ginny first."

"Deal."

Glen opened the folder with the edited photographs. Of course, the first image was of Guin as Titania. Guin had to admit, the woman in the painting really did resemble her. Though she didn't have freckles or crow's feet or gray hairs.

"Do we have to include that one?" said Guin. But she knew if they didn't, Ginny would make Glen send it to her.

Glen looked at her. He also knew Ginny would want the photo in the article.

"Fine," Guin sighed. "What else do you think we should include?"

Glen clicked through the edited photos. For the most part, they agreed on which images to send to their boss, only disagreeing about a couple. In the end, they decided to send Ginny eight shots and let her decide which ones to include.

"I should go tweak my article," Guin said when they were done. "Then show me the rest of the photos."

"If you insist."

"I do."

Guin took her laptop out to the lanai. It was a warm afternoon, but the lanai had a roof and a ceiling fan and got a nice breeze. Guin watched as a boat cruised by and waved.

"Stop watching the boats and get to work, Guin," she told herself.

She opened her laptop and pulled up her article.

Guin was so absorbed in editing that didn't hear the sliding door open and jumped when Glen said her name.

"I didn't mean to startle you," he said.

"That's okay," Guin replied. "I'm almost done." She looked at the clock on her laptop. "Oh, wow. I didn't realize it was so late."

"It's not that late. Do you still want to look at the rest of the photos?"

"You bet I do. Just give me a minute."

"Take all the minutes you need."

Guin smiled.

"If I'm not out in ten minutes, drag me away."

Now it was Glen's turn to smile.

"I'll remind you that you said that."

Ten minutes later, Guin saved the article and closed her laptop. She would take one more look at it later before sending it to Ginny.

Guin knocked on Glen's office door, which was ajar.

"I was about to come get you," he said. "You done?"

"Pretty much. I want to take another look in the morning. So maybe hold off sending Ginny your photos until I give you the go ahead?"

"No problem. Just let me know."

"Thanks. So, let's see the rest of the photos you took. I'm mainly interested in the ones you took on the terrace. But we should probably take a look at all of them, see who interacted with Belem."

"There are a lot of photos, Guin. You sure?"

"Positive."

Just then Guin's stomach let out a low growl.

"You hungry?"

Guin thought about it. Was she? Then she remembered that she had skipped lunch.

"How about I start dinner and then we look at the photos?" Glen suggested.

Guin's stomach growled again. She told it to shush.

"What were you thinking of making?" she asked him.

He smiled.

"Coq au vin." It was one of Guin's favorites.

"Doesn't that take hours?"

"Not if you use an Instant Pot."

"When did you get an Instant Pot?"

"I just got it."

"Huh. So, how long does it take if you use an Instant Pot?"

"Around an hour including prep time."

"Huh," Guin said again.

"Why don't we go into the kitchen? You can help me prep."

They headed into the kitchen and Guin watched as Glen took out the ingredients for the coq au vin.

"You were pretty sure I'd stay for dinner, weren't you?"

"I know how you like coq au vin."

"I'm also rather fond of the chef," she said. "You want me to fry the bacon while you cut up the vegetables?"

"I was going to sauté the bacon in the Instant Pot."

"You can do that?"

Glen nodded.

"Okay, then I'll chop the carrots and mushrooms."

"What about the onions?"

"They make me cry."

"And we wouldn't want that."

While the bacon was sautéing in the Instant Pot, Glen minced the garlic and chopped the onion while Guin cut up the carrots and mushrooms. When the bacon was ready, Glen removed it from the Instant Pot and emptied most of the grease. Then he added the garlic to the pot, along with red wine, chicken broth, and a little tomato paste. When the mixture began to bubble, he added the vegetables they had chopped along with the chicken thighs and a little thyme.

"Okay, now we seal it up and let the Instant Pot do its work."

"That's it?" said Guin.

"That's it," said Glen.

"It feels like cheating."

"It does a bit. But it's a huge time saver. I'll just need to thicken the sauce up a bit when it's done. And make some egg noodles or rice. You have a preference?"

"Egg noodles."

"Egg noodles it is."

Guin helped him clean up. Then they went back to his office. Glen set a timer on his smart watch, so he wouldn't forget about the egg noodles, which took around 20 minutes to make.

"Okay," he said, taking a seat. Guin sat beside him. "You sure you want to see all of them?"

"Yes already!"

"Okay," he said. "But I warn you, there are a lot of dupes and bad ones."

"Yeah, yeah, yeah. We can skip over those. Let's get this party started."

Glen opened the file and began to click. As he had told Guin, many of the shots looked alike. And there were shots that were too dark or too light or out of focus.

"Is there something in particular you're looking for?" he asked her.

"Anything that shows Belem. I want to see who he talked to and if he was anywhere near those stairs at the back of the terrace."

"I told you, I—"

Guin cut him off.

"Just humor me. Stop," she said a few seconds later as they were clicking through the photos.

Glen stopped.

"Can you blow it up?"

Glen made the photo larger.

"There!" said Guin. "In the background. It's Bishop and Belem. They were in the exhibit together."

"So?"

Guin didn't have a rebuttal.

"Keep going," she told him.

"Stop!" Guin said again. "Zoom in." Glen zoomed in. "That's Alexandra Barnes with Belem, and she doesn't look happy. Okay, keep going."

A minute later, she had Glen stop again, on a picture showing Belem with the director of the museum. He too looked to be frowning.

"That guy sure had a way with people," said Glen. "No one looks happy to see him."

"Keep going," said Guin. "Wait," she said around a dozen photos later, as Glen was about to go to the next image. He stopped on a picture showing Pauline Paulson and Belem looking at some picture.

"Okay, keep going."

They finished going through his shots from inside the exhibit and now were going through the photos he had taken out on the terrace.

"You know, until the preview, I didn't even know there was a terrace," said Guin as Glen clicked through the photos. "But it was the perfect place for the reception. Well, until… Wait. Stop!" she said as Glen was about to go to the next photo. "Zoom in. Over there."

Glen zoomed in.

"That's definitely Ludwig Belem's wheelchair by the planters in the back. Okay, keep going."

"I should start the water for the egg noodles."

"It can wait. Keep going."

"If you insist," he said and continued.

"Stop!" Guin said when they had nearly reached the end. It was a photo of Sid and Martha Sachs. "There in the background. Zoom in." Glen zoomed in. "Isn't that Belem's wheelchair? And that looks like Alexandra Barnes heading towards him. And just over there, that looks like Bishop." Guin squinted. "Or is it Bennett Emerson? What do you think?"

"I'm pretty sure that's Bishop over there and that's Bennett Emerson."

"Huh. From a distance, they kind of look alike. But I think you're right. Okay, keep going."

"There are only a few more photos."

"Let's see them."

Glen showed her the last few photos. There were a couple more of Sid and Martha Sachs and then the photos he took of Guin with the painting of Titania. His smart watch was beeping.

"I need to check on the chicken and start the water for the egg noodles."

"Okay. You mind if I go through the pictures again?"

"Be my guest," he said. Then he headed to the kitchen.

CHAPTER 14

Guin went through Glen's photos again while he finished preparing dinner. But she didn't find anything new. Just in case she had missed something, she sent herself all of the photos from the terrace with Belem in them as well as the shots of him with the director, the curator, and Bishop. They might come in handy should his death not be ruled an accident. Though they didn't really reveal anything. Still.

Guin had just hit send when Glen called "Dinner!"

"Be right there," Guin yelled back.

□

Dinner had been delicious. It had also made Guin sleepy. Or it could have been the glass of wine she had had. She let out a yawn.

"Why don't you stay over?" Glen suggested.

"I should get back. The cats…"

"Can take of themselves," said Glen.

"But I didn't give them dinner."

Glen gave her a look.

"You wouldn't want them to starve, would you?"

"I'm sure the cats are fine. Besides, you can go home first thing."

He took her hand, running a finger over her palm. Guin shivered.

"Come," he said, leading her towards the bedroom.

"Isn't it a bit early to go to sleep?"

"Who said anything about sleeping?"

Guin felt her face (and other parts of her body) grow warm as Glen led her down the hall.

□

Guin woke up the next morning to find the bed empty. Where had Glen gone?

"Glen?" she called.

She went to turn on her phone and realized she had left it in the living room. She wondered what time it was. It was dark out. However, it could have been nearly seven as the sun didn't rise until then.

She got out of bed and went to the bathroom. Then she headed to the kitchen. No sign of Glen. Though there was fresh coffee in the coffee maker. She helped herself and went out to the lanai, where Glen was seated with a mug of coffee.

"Hey," she said, laying a hand on his shoulder.

He turned and looked up at her.

"Hey," he replied.

"You okay?"

He nodded.

"Just couldn't sleep."

"Any particular reason?"

He shook his head. But Guin got the feeling he was hiding something.

"You know if something's bothering you, you can tell me."

"I know."

Guin sat down next to him.

"I should go soon."

"I know."

"And I was thinking…" Glen turned and looked up at her. "Is that offer of a key still good?"

Glen studied her face.

"You sure?"

Guin nodded.

"I'm sure. And I'll give you a key to my place next time you're over."

Glen opened his mouth to say something and then shook his head.

"What?"

"Nothing."

"No, you were going to say something."

"It's just…" Guin waited for him to go on. He took a deep breath. "I love you." Guin smiled. "And I'm pretty sure you love me."

"I do."

"So why don't we just…"

He was interrupted by his phone, which was on the end table. He picked it up and frowned.

"I need to get this. Will you excuse me?"

"Of course," said Guin. "Is everything okay?"

He was walking swiftly to his office, and Guin wondered who could be calling him so early on a Sunday. Was it his parents? Though he would have told her.

She looked after him for several seconds, then she turned her gaze to the water. The sun was low in the sky, having just risen, and it was peaceful on the canal. Guin sipped her coffee, waiting for Glen to return. Fifteen minutes went by, and he still hadn't reappeared.

She thought about knocking on his office door but instead went to the bedroom. She should get dressed and go home. She had cats to feed and work to do.

She was just leaving the bedroom when Glen appeared.

"Sorry about that," he said. "I…" He saw that Guin was dressed and had her bag on her shoulder. "Are you leaving?"

"I have work to do."

"You weren't going to say goodbye?"

"I didn't want to disturb you."

Glen frowned.

"Can you wait a minute? I want to give you a key."

He went into the kitchen and returned less than a minute later with the key.

"Here," he said, handing it to her.

"Thank you," she said, placing the key in her bag. She would fish it out and add it to her keychain later.

"So, you going to tell me what that call was about? Your folks okay?"

"They're fine."

Guin waited for Glen to say more.

"Okay. I should go," she said when he didn't.

"If you must."

Guin tilted her head. He wasn't going to stop her? Now she was even more curious about the call. But she didn't press him. She got up on tiptoe and gave him a kiss. But he seemed distracted.

"I'll text you later when I've sent the article to Ginny."

"Sounds good," he said and walked her to the door.

Guin stood outside next to her Mini. Glen had closed the door behind her. Very unlike him. She hoped everything was okay. She stood there for a few seconds and then unlocked her car and got in.

□

The cats were waiting by the front door and immediately started meowing.

"Yes, yes," said Guin, making her way to the kitchen. "I'm a horrible mom."

She picked up the two food bowls and quickly washed them. Then she got a can of wet food from the pantry and opened it. Immediately, the cats began to meow again and rub against her legs.

"Hold on!" she told them.

She grabbed a fork and scooped the wet food into the bowls. The cats lunged.

"Slow down!" she admonished them.

But they didn't hear her, or they didn't care. She shook her head and gave them fresh water. Then she went to clean their litter box.

The cats taken care of, Guin went to take a shower and get changed. By the time she emerged from her bedroom, it was a little after nine. Time to get to work.

She went into her office, sat down in front of her computer, and opened her article about Farley Bishop and the exhibit. She read through it one last time, making a couple of minor tweaks. Then she sent it off to Ginny and texted Glen to send Ginny the photos they had selected.

She looked at the time. Was it too early to call Farley Bishop? It was after nine-thirty. Most of the people she knew on Sanibel, if not all of them, would be up. Heck, most of them had probably been up since seven, if not earlier. But she didn't think Bishop was a morning person.

"Well, the worst he can do is yell at me," she said, reaching for her phone.

She entered the number for Bishop's landline, wondering if he had an answering machine. The phone must have rung at least five times. Guin decided he must not have an answering machine and was about to hang up when he answered.

"Bishop."

"Mr. Bishop, it's Guin Jones."

"Yes?" he said. He sounded annoyed.

"I was hoping to come by your studio and have a chat with you about the exhibit."

Though what she really wanted to talk to him about was why the Collier County Sheriff's Office had wanted to speak with him. But she sensed he wouldn't let her come over if she stated her true purpose.

"I'm rather busy."

"I promise not to take long."

"I need to go," he said.

"Wait!" said Guin. "What if I agreed to sit for you again?"

She had no idea why she had blurted that when she had no desire to pose for him again.

"Fine. Be here at ten-thirty."

"Thank you," said Guin. "I'll be there." But he had already hung up.

Guin arrived at Bishop's studio at exactly ten-thirty.

She climbed the stairs and knocked on the door. As before, she heard jazz music playing. There was no answer. She knocked again, louder this time.

"Mr. Bishop?" she called. "It's Guin Jones!"

Still nothing.

She tried the door. It was unlocked. Did he always leave the door unlocked? She opened it and went inside.

"Mr. Bishop?" she called again.

"You don't need to yell," he said, emerging from behind the curtain. "I was in the john."

"Shall we go sit?" she suggested. "As I said on the phone, I had a few questions I wanted to ask you about the exhibit."

Bishop frowned. Guin was beginning to think that that was his default expression.

"You said you'd sit for me."

"After you answer a few questions."

Bishop continued to frown.

"What do you want to know?"

"Shall we sit?"

He didn't move, and his expression told Guin to just get on with it.

Guin wanted to ask him about Belem, but she knew she couldn't lead with that.

"Were you happy with the exhibit?"

"Happy?" He said it as though he was unfamiliar with the word.

"Did you enjoy it?"

No reply.

"I think the crowd enjoyed it. Ms. Barnes did a good job organizing it, I thought. What did you think?"

Still nothing. And Guin sensed he was growing impatient with her.

"Why didn't you tell me about the painting?"

Was that a hint of a smile on Farley Bishop's face?

"I thought I'd surprise you."

Well, he had certainly done that.

"Whose idea was it to put it at the beginning of the exhibit?"

"Alexandra's."

"You mean Ms. Barnes, the curator?"

He gave her a look that Guin interpreted to mean, *Are you slow? Of course I meant Ms. Barnes.*

"I understand she came up with the title of the exhibit too. Do you think it was accurate? I know you don't like people labeling your work."

"It was as good a title as any."

"How do you think the critics will receive your new work?" It was her way of segueing to Belem.

"I don't give a rat's ass what the critics think. Who are they decide what's good or what isn't?"

"Well, they…" Guin saw the look on Bishop's face and paused. Clearly, Bishop had no great love for art critics.

"So you didn't care what Ludwig Belem, the critic from *Art World*, had to say about your work?"

Bishop was scowling now.

"No," he replied.

"I saw the two of you chatting. What were you discussing?"

"Were you eavesdropping?"

"No, I just saw you together and wondered what an artist and an art critic talked about."

"None of your business."

"Did he comment on your work?"

No response.

"I understand you paid a visit to the Collier County Sheriff's Office yesterday. Did they ask you about Mr. Belem?"

"I thought you wanted to know about the exhibit."

"Did they think you had something to do with Mr. Belem's fall?"

Guin hadn't meant to say that. It just sort of popped out.

"I think you should go."

"Excuse me?"

"We're done."

"You want me to leave? But I haven't posed for you." But she could tell from the look on Bishop's face that he was done with her. She cursed herself for mentioning Belem. She should have waited until after she had posed for him. "I'm going," she said. "I apologize if I upset you."

She hoped he might say something, relent and tell her she could stay, but he didn't.

"For what it's worth, I enjoyed the retrospective, and had only glowing things to say about it in my article for the paper."

Nothing.

"I could email you a copy if you like." Then she remembered, he didn't have a computer or a cell phone. "Well, I'm sure Ginny will show it to you."

Guin knew from the stony expression on Bishop's face that her time was up. She said that she'd see herself out and left.

As she went down the stairs, Guin mentally kicked herself. She had blown it. Now she needed to figure out a way to get back into Bishop's good graces.

CHAPTER 15

Guin drove past Ginny and Joel's place, stopped, and backed up. She had no idea if they were home, but she was there. Might as well see. Their cars were there, a good sign. Guin parked the Mini and went to ring their doorbell. Ginny opened the door a minute later.

"Guin, what are you doing here?"

"I was just at Farley Bishop's place."

"Oh? How come?"

"May I come in?"

Ginny opened the door wider and gestured for Guin to enter.

"I hope I'm not disturbing you."

Guin heard classical music playing in the background.

"Joel and I were just doing the *Times* Sunday crossword."

"How's it going?"

"Joel has most of it filled in. Actually," she said, leaning in, "Joel could have finished it already. I think he just saves a few clues for me to solve to make me feel better."

Guin smiled. She could totally picture it.

They entered the living room.

"Look who's here, Hon."

Joel turned around.

"Hey, Joel," Guin said, holding up a hand in greeting.

Joel nodded. Then he turned back to the Sunday *New York Times Magazine.*

"He's in puzzle mode," said Ginny. "So, what were you doing at Farley's? Did he ask you to pose for him again? I got your article about the preview, by the way. Thank you."

"Did you read it?"

"Not yet. So what were you doing at Farley's place?"

"I wanted to ask him about his visit to the Collier County Sheriff's Office."

"And?"

"It didn't go well. He kicked me out."

"He kicked you out? What did you say to him?"

"I asked him about Belem and what the police wanted to talk to him about."

"And he kicked you out?"

"He may have thought that I thought he had something to do with Belem falling down the stairs."

Ginny shook her head.

"I know. It was a mistake to ask him about what happened right off the bat. I should have posed for him first. But I saw a photo of them by the stairs. Glen took it."

"Glen has a photo showing Farley with that critic by the terrace stairs? When did he take it?"

"Not long before we left."

"And you're sure it was Farley with him?"

Guin hesitated.

"Pretty sure. They were in the background. And it was a bit blurry. Bishop wasn't standing right next to him. But he wasn't that far away."

"Well, you should have been one hundred percent sure before you said anything. For all we know, it was an accident. And the cops just wanted to know if Farley saw anything."

"I realize that. So, can you help me to get back on Bishop's good side?"

"Why do you care about being on his good side?"

"In case…" said Guin. She let the thought trail off.

"In case he's arrested for Belem's murder? Is that what

you were going to say?"

Guin didn't deny it.

"Farley Bishop may be a lot of things, but he's not a killer. It was an accident."

"If you say so."

"I do. You talk to Craig?"

"I did."

"And?"

"He said they did the autopsy yesterday. Though you know how long autopsy reports can take."

"I do."

"So, you want me to hold off writing about what happened at the museum for now?"

"For now. I have other things for you to work on."

Of course she did.

"I'll shoot you an email tomorrow, when I'm back in the office."

Guin heard a phone ringing. Joel didn't move.

"It's probably for me," said Ginny. She went over and looked at the Caller ID. "I should get this," she said, picking up. "Hi, Terry. Can you hold a sec?" She turned to Guin. "Can you let yourself out?"

Guin said that she could and left.

Guin drove home feeling frustrated. She went into the kitchen and looked at the clock on the microwave. It was a little after noon. She hadn't eaten breakfast. Maybe that's why she was in a bad mood. She looked in her refrigerator, but she didn't see anything she felt like eating or making. What she needed was comfort food, Jean-Luc's comfort food.

Guin gave the cats some dry food. Then she picked up her bag and her keys and headed out the door.

As usual, there was a line at Jean-Luc's. But she didn't

mind waiting as the line typically moved quickly. However, things were taking a bit longer today. No doubt because part of their staff was still at the Sanibel Farmers Market, which Guin had missed that morning. Finally, it was her turn.

"Hey, Jake," she said to the young man behind the counter. "How come you're not at the farmers market?"

"We're breaking in a couple of new people."

"Oh?" said Guin.

Jean-Luc was a bit of a skinflint and had, in the past, resisted hiring more people, even during peak season.

"Things have been crazy lately," Jake explained. "And what with Jean-Luc not in the shop all the time, he finally gave in and hired more people."

"Good for him," said Guin. "And you and Jo, I suspect."

Jo was Jake's colleague and girlfriend. She had been working with Jean-Luc in the kitchen, learning to make French baguettes and macarons and all of the bakery's signature pastries.

Jake nodded.

"So, what can I get for you today?"

"Hm," said Guin, eyeing the menu, though she knew it by heart.

She was torn between the turkey, brie, and Granny Smith apple sandwich, served on a freshly baked baguette, or a savory crepe. She glanced behind her. There was a line of hungry people, so she went with the sandwich, which she figured would take less time to make.

"And a sparkling water," she added.

"Help yourself," said Jake. "No pastries today?"

Guin eyed the pastry case, which was filled with luscious looking fruit tarts, chocolate and coffee eclairs, a rainbow of macarons, and Guin's favorite, opera cake. She was tempted to get something, but she restrained herself. Though… maybe she should get a fruit tart or some macarons to bring to Craig and Betty's. Then she remembered that Craig had asked her to bring some of her famous chocolate chip cookies.

"No, that's it," said Guin.

Jake rang her up, and a couple of minutes later, her sandwich was ready. She took it outside, along with her bottle of sparkling water, and looked for a seat at one of the outdoor tables. A couple were just leaving, and she quickly went to grab the empty table. Wait a minute, she knew that couple.

"Pauline?" she said, surprised to see her former boss there.

Pauline smiled.

"Guin!"

"What are you doing here?" Guin asked her.

"I'm working on a piece for the *Times*."

"On Sanibel?" Pauline hadn't mentioned anything at the preview.

"It's one of those '36 hours in' pieces."

"On Sanibel?" Guin repeated.

"On Sanibel and Captiva."

"When did you get here?"

"Yesterday."

"You should have told me you'd be here."

"I thought I did."

Guin was sure she had not.

"The *Times* sure is keeping you busy. An art opening Friday and then Sanibel and Captiva on Saturday."

"Got to take the work when you can get it."

Wasn't that the truth, thought Guin, remembering what it had been like when she had freelanced. But it sounded like Pauline had a steady gig with the *New York Times*.

"Let me know if I can be of any help. I'm pretty familiar with the islands."

"Thanks, but I'm pretty much done. This is actually my second trip over."

"Will you be here later? I'd love to catch up." Though she was having dinner with Craig and Betty at six.

"We're about to leave. Paul has a late tee time. You ever come to Naples?"

"All the time," said Guin. A bit of an exaggeration.

"Well, let me know when you're headed my way and let's arrange something."

"I'd like that," said Guin. "How do I reach you?"

"I didn't give you my card?"

Had she? Guin couldn't remember.

"Could you give me another one? I may have misplaced it."

Pauline dug in her bag and withdrew a card.

"Here," she said. "That's my new cell phone number. Give me a call or text me whenever."

"I will," said Guin.

"We should go," said Pauline. "Nice seeing you again."

"Same." Guin looked over at Paul and smiled at him. "Nice seeing you too, Paul!"

Guin watched as Pauline and Paul made their way to the parking lot. She was a bit miffed that Pauline hadn't reached out. Then again, Pauline had said that she didn't know that Guin was living on Sanibel and probably had a packed schedule. Still, she knew on Friday that Guin was there.

Guin turned to go sit, but a family had commandeered the table while Guin had been speaking with Pauline. She frowned. All of the other tables were occupied. Should she wait for someone to get up or take her lunch to go? As she was deciding, she saw three women getting up. She quickly made a beeline for them.

"Are you leaving?" Guin asked them.

"We are," said one of the women.

Guin waited for them to gather their things and leave. Then she quickly took a seat.

CHAPTER 16

Guin stopped at Bailey's General Store on her way home from Jean-Luc's to get the ingredients for her chocolate chip cookies. She hadn't made a batch in ages and figured she'd give some to Craig and Betty, some to Glen, and keep the rest in her freezer, because you never knew when you might need a chocolate chip cookie.

She got home and immediately went to work on the cookies. Although she had memorized the recipe long ago, she took it out to double check her measurements. Around 30 minutes later, the cookies were cooling on two racks. And the kitchen had that wonderful freshly baked cookie smell.

Guin reached out to sample a cookie but stopped herself. "Screw it," she said, changing her mind. She grabbed one of the smaller cookies and took a bite. The gooey warm dark chocolate melted on her tongue, and she may have moaned.

She was tempted to take another cookie but told herself no. She could have another one after dinner.

She went to her office and opened the Sunday *Times* on her computer. She scanned the news, making her way down the Home page to the Sunday crossword. She wasn't a puzzle aficionado like Joel was. But she still enjoyed doing the Sunday *Times* crossword as well as the Spelling Bee and Wordle.

After spending over 30 minutes on the Sunday crossword, she gave up and moved on to the Spelling Bee. She had better luck there, making it to Genius. She got up and stretched. Then she headed back to the kitchen. The cookies were now cool. She put six of the best-looking ones into a small decorative tin for Craig and Betty and put the rest into a plastic container.

She glanced at the clock. She still had a little while until she needed to head over to Craig and Betty's place. Should she go for a walk? Read a book? She had a profile to do later that week, of a philanthropic couple who had just made a sizeable donation to Community Housing & Resources of Sanibel, known as CHR, which provided affordable housing to individuals and families who worked on Sanibel. But she didn't have anything to do, workwise, right now.

Guin went into her bedroom and looked at the stack of books on her nightstand. She picked up the one on top, a work of historical fiction that took place in India, and brought it to the living room. She curled up on her favorite chair and began to read. Before she knew it, she had dozed off, waking up in a panic. What time was it? Was she going to be late to Craig and Betty's? She didn't think she had slept that long. She checked her phone. She had only been asleep for half an hour. Phew.

She still had an hour before she needed to head to Craig and Betty's. She looked down at her book but wasn't really in the mood to read. Instead, she picked up her phone and scrolled through her social media feeds. She was still "friends" with many of her former colleagues from up north, though she hadn't seen most of them since moving to Sanibel. She should try to connect with some of them next time she was in the city.

Finally, it was time to go. She went to give the cats some food and fresh water. Then she picked up the tin of chocolate chip cookies she had set aside for Craig and Betty, hoping Betty wouldn't be upset with her, grabbed her bag and her keys, and left.

□

Guin was about to ring Craig and Betty's doorbell when Craig opened the door and stepped outside.

"You have the cookies?"

"Right here," said Guin, holding up the tin.

"Give that to me."

Guin held onto the tin.

"Shouldn't I give it to Betty?"

"No, give it to me," he said, reaching for the tin.

Guin moved the tin away.

"You didn't tell her, did you?"

Craig made a face.

"What she doesn't know…"

"It's not Betty I'm worried about hurting," said Guin. "I'm sure if you asked her nicely, she'd let you have a cookie. She let you have those macarons."

"Yes but…"

"Have you been cheating on your diet again?"

Guin could tell by his expression that he had.

"Let me give the cookies to Betty. I'm sure she won't object to you having one after dinner if I explain."

"You don't know Betty."

"You going to let me in?"

Craig reluctantly let her inside, looking longingly at the cookie tin.

"Is that you, Guin?" Betty called from the kitchen.

"It is!" Guin called back.

She headed to the kitchen with her tin of cookies.

"I hope you don't mind," Guin said, holding out the tin. "I was in the mood for chocolate chip cookies and made too many. And I was hoping you'd let me give you some. I know how you both like them. You don't have to eat them right away. We could each have one after dinner, and then you could keep the rest in the freezer. They keep for weeks."

Betty looked at her husband.

"Did you ask Guin to make you cookies?"

Craig was doing his best to look innocent, but Guin could see Betty wasn't buying it. Finally, he cracked.

"Maybe," he said, not looking at his wife.

Guin wanted to laugh out loud. So much for Mr. Tough Guy Reporter.

"Don't blame Craig," said Guin, feeling bad for her friend. "I hadn't made a batch in ages, and I enjoy making them. And I use dark chocolate, which is good for you."

Betty continued to look at her husband, who continued to avoid her gaze.

"All right," she said. "You can have a cookie after you eat your dinner."

"Only one?" he said.

"Don't press your luck."

Betty then turned to Guin.

"Can I get you something to drink, dear?"

"Just some water. And I can get it myself." Guin went into the kitchen. "What's for dinner?"

"Grouper."

Guin looked over at Craig.

"You catch it?"

"Yup. This morning."

"And I'm sautéing some vegetables I got at the farmers market to go with it," said Betty.

"Sounds yummy," said Guin. "Can I help with anything?"

"Thank you, but I'm good. You hungry?"

"I'll eat whenever."

"You didn't ask me," said Craig.

Betty looked at him.

"You'll eat when dinner's ready. Why don't you two go out to the lanai? I'll come get you when dinner's ready."

"You sure I can't help with anything?" Guin asked her. Though Betty always said no.

"You can help me by keeping Craig occupied. Just don't

say anything about Paris. I don't want you to have to repeat yourself."

"Okay," said Guin.

Betty sighed.

"It's been years since I've been there. Is it still lovely?"

"It is," said Guin. "Though it was a bit gray when we were there."

"Still," said Betty, a dreamy look on her face.

"Come on," said Craig, ushering Guin out of the kitchen. "Ever since she heard you and Glen were going to Paris, she's been after me to take her back."

"When were you last there?"

"On our honeymoon."

"Oh wow," said Guin. "You should definitely go back. I'm sure a lot has changed. But it's still Paris."

"Mmph," said Craig.

He opened the sliding door that led to the lanai, and they took a seat on the couch.

"So, how was it?" Craig asked her.

"I should wait for Betty."

"I won't tell her if you won't."

Guin smiled.

"Why don't you tell me what you've been up to?" she suggested. "Anything I should know? Any juicy island gossip?"

Not that Craig was one to gossip.

"Nothing I can repeat."

"Aw, come on. I promise not to tell."

"Sorry."

"Rats. Anything you can repeat?"

"Nothing that would interest you."

"Try me."

"Butchy's boat ran out of gas when we were out fishing the other day and he had to call Sea Tow. Took nearly two hours till they could tow him in."

"That sucks," said Guin, trying to sound sympathetic.

"Not really," said Craig. "Best fishing of the day. And he didn't have to lie to his wife about why he missed his doctor's appointment. Though she was pissed that he had missed it."

"She didn't accuse him of running out of gas on purpose?"

"Huh. I should ask Butchy."

"Some investigative reporter you are," said Guin, jokingly. "You hear anything more from your source at the Collier County Sheriff's Office?"

"It's Sunday."

"He doesn't work on Sundays?"

"Not if he can help it. I'll check in with him tomorrow."

"Okay. You know, I bet Betty would enjoy visiting the Baker Museum. Have you two been there?"

"I haven't. Don't know about Betty. She may have gone with one of her artsy friends."

"Well, you should take her to see the new exhibit. And I know a cute little French café not too far from there. It's not Paris but…"

Craig grunted. Time to change the subject.

"So, how are the kids and grandkids?"

"Good."

This was the problem with Craig. Ask him about fishing or sports and he could talk your ear off. Anything else, you'd be lucky to get a complete sentence out of him.

Fortunately, Guin was rescued from further attempts at conversation by Betty.

"Dinner!"

Over dinner, which had been delicious—and very healthy—Guin had told them about her trip to Paris. Betty had demanded Guin show her pictures, which she did. Betty had oohed and aahed. If Craig wanted to make his wife happy, he would take her there.

When they were through with the grouper and the roasted vegetables, Guin had insisted on helping Betty clear the table. But Betty drew the line at letting Guin do the dishes. That was Craig's job.

"Can I have a cookie now?" Craig whined—like a small child, Guin thought.

Betty had said that he could, and they each took a cookie.

"These are delicious, Guin!" she said. "Have you ever thought about selling them?"

"No. I don't have the time or interest in baking professionally."

Guin saw Craig reaching for another cookie, as did Betty, who slapped his hand.

"Why'd you put so many out if I could only have one?" he grumbled.

"I wasn't thinking."

She picked up the plate of cookies and took it into the kitchen.

"I bet if you told her you'd take her to Paris, she'd let you have another one," said Guin.

Craig grunted.

"Can I get you anything else?" Betty called out to Guin. "Some coffee or decaf?"

"I'm good. I should be getting home."

"Must you?" said Betty, returning to the table. "I'd love to hear more about Paris."

"I think I told you everything," said Guin, smiling at her. She was grateful that Betty hadn't asked her if Glen had proposed. "And it's getting late." Though it wasn't that late. "Thank you for dinner. It was delicious."

"You're very welcome."

Craig walked Guin to the door.

"So you'll call or text me if or when you hear anything?" Guin said to him.

"I will," Craig replied.

He waited until Guin was safely in her car and then closed the door.

□

Guin was sitting up in bed, talking to Glen.

"You have a good time with Craig and Betty?" he asked her.

"I did," Guin replied.

"Anything to report?"

"Betty wants Craig to take her to Paris. They haven't been since their honeymoon."

"They should definitely go."

"Try telling Craig that. Do you think people can fish in the Seine? That's probably the only way he'll go."

Glen chuckled.

"Who knows? Maybe."

"I should check."

"Craig have any more news about Belem?"

"No. But he said he'd check with his contact tomorrow. Did I tell you I went to see Bishop this morning and he kicked me out?"

"No. What did you do?"

"I asked him about his visit to the Collier County Sheriff's Office."

"And he kicked you out?"

"I may have implied that I didn't think Belem's death was an accident."

"Why'd you do that?"

"I wasn't thinking."

"You don't really think Bishop pushed Belem down those stairs, do you?"

"Then why did they bring him in for questioning?"

"Maybe they thought he had seen something."

"Or maybe they thought he pushed him."

"Did they arrest him?"

"No. But…"

"You can't go accusing people of murder, Guin. Especially without proof."

"I didn't accuse him of murder. I just wanted to know what he and Belem were discussing and what the Collier County Sheriff's Office wanted to know."

Glen sighed, and Guin made a face.

"I'm going."

"You mad at me?"

"No, I'm just tired."

"Don't go."

"So, who were you talking to this morning?"

"This morning?"

"The mysterious phone call you took in your office."

"Oh that. It wasn't mysterious."

"So, who called?"

"An old friend."

"An old male friend or an old female friend?"

"You think I'm having an affair?"

"What? No!" Though the thought had briefly crossed her mind.

"It was a male old friend, a guy I used to work with back in New York."

"What was he doing calling you early on a Sunday?"

"He lives in London now, and he knows I'm an early riser."

"Ah." Guin wanted to believe Glen was telling her the truth, but a little part of her wondered. After all, she had had no clue that her ex-husband had been having an affair with their hairdresser.

"What did he want?"

"Just to say hello."

Guin wasn't buying it.

"He called you at dawn on a Sunday just to say hello?"

"It wasn't dawn. And he was in London."

"Uh-huh."

"You don't believe me?"

"Ignore me. I'm just tired." She let out a fake yawn. "I should go, get some sleep."

"Okay, get some sleep. Talk tomorrow?"

"Sure."

"And Guin?"

"Yes?"

"I love you."

"I love you too," she said.

They said goodnight, and Guin turned off her phone.

CHAPTER 17

Spot was pawing Guin's face.

"Stop that!" she said.

She looked over to the window. Light was trickling in. What time was it?

Spot batted her face again, accompanied by a meow. Fauna was seated next to him, watching.

"Enough!" she said, tossing him off the bed. She looked over at her clock. It was after seven. She rarely slept that late.

She got up and made her way into the kitchen, turning on her phone. There was another text from Shelly, wanting to know if Guin was okay. Guin owed her an explanation. She texted Shelly back, asking if she wanted to go for a beach walk.

Shelly immediately replied.

"Shall I meet you at Beach Access #1? When can you get there?"

Beach Access #1 was roughly halfway between their two houses.

"I can be there in 15," Guin wrote back.

Shelly replied with a thumbs-up emoji.

Guin gave the cats some food and fresh water and then went to get dressed. Fifteen minutes later, she had secured the last parking spot by Beach Access #1 and was making her way onto the beach.

Shelly was already there and waved when she saw Guin.

"Hey," said Guin. "Sorry I've been incommunicado. It was a crazy weekend."

"Let's walk and you can tell me all about the craziness. So, how was the big preview?"

"Interesting."

"Can you elaborate? I need a little bit more than *interesting* and *eventful.*"

"I told you that Farley Bishop made me pose for him, yes?"

"Uh-huh."

That reminded Guin. Had Ginny posted her article about the exhibit on the paper's website? She grabbed her phone. There it was on the Home page, with the portrait of Guin.

"Here," she said, handing her phone to Shelly.

"Whoa," said Shelly, staring at the picture. She looked up at Guin. "It's you. And the dress… Wow. It's just like…"

"I know," said Guin.

"It's like you stepped out of the painting."

"I know. Good thing I didn't wear my flower crown."

"You have one?"

"It was a joke."

"Oh."

Shelly took a last look at the photo, then she handed the phone back to Guin.

"Did you know?"

"Nope. I had no idea."

"That must have been a shock."

"No kidding."

"Where was the picture?"

"Right at the start of the exhibit."

"Wow! Well, at least it's a nice picture of you."

"Mm."

Shelly grinned.

"What?" said Guin.

"I was just thinking…" Guin waited for her to go on.

"You're famous now!"

"I don't want to be famous."

"You don't?"

"Not for being in some painting. I want people to know me for my work. Though speaking of becoming famous, any news from that producer?"

"No. And they're supposed to start shooting soon. I emailed her, but I didn't hear back. Do you think I blew it?"

"How could they not want you? Your work is amazing."

"You're just saying that."

"No, I'm not. If people didn't love your work, you wouldn't always sell out on Etsy or be asked to sell your work at stores around the island."

"True. So why hasn't she called?"

"I don't know. Maybe there's a production delay? I'm sure you'll hear something soon."

"Yeah, like they don't want me."

Guin wished she could say something that would cheer Shelly up. They turned around and headed east.

"You want to grab breakfast?"

"Sure. Where do you want to go? Over Easy? The Island Cow? Rosie's?"

"You pick," said Guin.

"Let's go to Rosie's. I could go for some caramelized banana pancakes."

"So what else is going on?" Shelly asked Guin as she took a bite of a caramelized banana pancake. "How's Glen?"

"He's good," said Guin, cutting off a piece of blueberry pancake. "Though…"

"Though?" said Shelly.

Guin sighed and put down her fork.

"It's probably nothing but… He got this call Sunday morning and…"

"And?"

"I don't know. It was weird."

"Weird how?"

"First of all, who calls before nine on a Sunday? And Glen took the call in his office and was totally distracted when he finally came out."

"Huh. Did you ask him who called?"

"I did. He said it was an old friend just calling to say hello."

"But you don't believe him."

"I don't know. I want to but…"

"You're thinking about Art."

Guin nodded.

"Glen isn't Art. You know that."

"I do."

"Did he say if this old friend was a man or a woman?"

"He said it was a guy he used to work with who lives in London now."

"Well, there you go! Nothing to worry about."

"You don't think he's hiding something?"

"I don't know him well enough, but no, I don't think he'd lie to you."

Guin wanted to believe her.

They finished their breakfast and got a check. Then they headed outside.

"Don't obsess about Glen and that phone call," Shelly told her. "It's probably nothing."

"Maybe."

"So, you busy this week?"

"I have to interview a couple of philanthropists. And Ginny said she was going to email me some new assignments."

"No Valentine's Day roundup this year?"

"Mercifully no. Paris was enough."

"Like Paris was a hardship. Boo-hoo-hoo, my boss made

me and my boyfriend go to Paris."

Guin hit her.

"Ow!"

Shelly's phone was ringing. "It's Steve," she said, swiping to answer. "Can I call you back in a few? I'm just saying goodbye to Guin."

"Hi, Steve!" Guin called.

"He says 'hi' back," said Shelly. She returned to her husband. "Okay, I'll call you when I get home. I love you too."

Guin sighed. Why couldn't she have had a marriage like Shelly and Steve's? They had been college sweethearts, had had two kids, and still seemed in love.

"Gotta go!" said Shelly. "Got more pieces to make for the Sanibel-Captiva Rotary Club Arts and Crafts Festival!"

"I just interviewed Adele," said Guin.

Guin left out the part about talking to a couple of the local artists who would be at the festival. She didn't want to upset Shelly. Not that Shelly would necessarily be upset about Guin not including her this year. Still, she didn't want to risk it. Though Shelly would find out soon enough.

"How'd that go?"

"Good. I always liked her."

"She's great. So, you going to come to the show?"

"Of course! I wouldn't miss it."

"Beach walk later this week?"

"If you have time. I know you're busy."

"I could actually use more shells. Just let me know when you want to go."

They said goodbye and went their separate ways. As soon as Guin got home, she got on her computer and went to the paper's website. Her article was at the top of the page. She clicked on it. There was the portrait of her, technically Titania. She winced. It was a beautiful painting, but it made Guin feel incredibly self-conscious.

She read through the article and thought about sending the link to Bennett Emerson and Alexandra Barnes. Why not? She said to herself. True, the *San-Cap Sun-Times* wasn't the *New York Times*, but it was a nice write-up.

She copied the link and sent it to them in an email. She considered sending the link to Pauline too but hesitated. Had Pauline's review been published? It was probably too soon. She went to the *Times*'s website and searched for it, just in case. Nothing. That was good. Ginny would be pleased that their piece came out before the *Times*'s. Though what about the *Naples Daily News*? She had seen their reporter at the preview, but he had left early, before all of the drama.

Guin went to the *Naples Daily News* website and checked. Nothing there either. Maybe they were holding the article for later in the week, closer to the weekend.

She opened a new email and sent the link to the article to her mother and brother. Lance would be amused. She wasn't sure about her mother.

She had expected Ginny to email her first thing. But there was nothing from her in her inbox. Though the day was still young. She was working on the Spelling Bee on her computer when Glen's number flashed up on her phone. She immediately picked up.

"What's up?" she said.

"I just got a call from the Collier County Sheriff's Office."

"Why did the Collier County Sheriff's Office call you?"

"I assume it has something to do with what happened at the preview."

"They didn't say why they wanted to speak to you?"

"They just asked if I could come down there at my earliest convenience and bring my camera."

"Ah. Maybe they're reaching out to all of the photographers who were there. That makes sense. Who called? Was it that detective?"

"No, it was some officer, calling on her behalf."

"When are you going?"

"I'm about to head down there."

"Do you want me to go with you?"

"I'm good. I just wanted you to know."

"Wait. I'll go with you."

"You don't have to. I'll be fine."

"Do you think they know about your to-do with Belem?"

"My to-do?"

"That you got into it with him over the pictures he took of me."

"I merely asked him to delete the photos."

"You looked pretty angry."

"Guin, they're not going to arrest me. We left before he went down the stairs."

"Right. I should still go with you. I can be at your place in half an hour."

"Don't bother. I'm going."

"I'll meet you there."

"You don't have to meet me at the sheriff's office. It's a long way from Sanibel."

"I know I don't have to. I want to."

Glen sighed.

"I assume there's no way I can stop you?"

"Nope. I'll be there as soon as I can."

Guin had never been to the Collier County Sheriff's Office before and had to look up where it was. It was on Tamiami Trail East, aka Route 41, southeast of downtown Naples. She pulled in, saw Glen's SUV, and found a spot nearby. Had he been there long?

She went inside and looked around. There were people waiting but no sign of Glen. She had been hoping he'd be waiting and that he'd allow her to attend the interview with him. Was he in the men's room?

She went up to the reception desk. She was about to ask the officer on duty if Glen was there but figured either he didn't know or wouldn't tell her. Better to ask to speak with Detective Romero.

"Do you have an appointment?" asked the desk officer.

Guin thought about lying but said no, she didn't.

"Do you know if she's meeting with someone, say a man around six-feet tall, good looking with dirty blond hair?"

The desk officer gave Guin a look that said, "You don't really expect me to answer that, do you?"

"I'll just wait," said Guin.

She took a seat and sent Glen a text, letting him know she was there. Then she looked around. There were a variety of people in the waiting area, which was much bigger than the waiting area at the Sanibel Police Department, which was a small, narrow corridor. She studied them, trying to figure out why they were there. There was a Hispanic woman with a little boy sitting not too far away from her. The little boy looked at her. He had a black eye. Guin looked away.

She opened her news feed on her phone and was reading an article about a woman who had taught her dog to communicate by having him press buttons when she heard someone clear his throat. She looked up to see Glen standing before her.

"Glen! Everything okay?"

"Everything's fine. Let's go."

"Did you speak with Detective Romero?" she asked him when they got outside. "What did she want to know? Did you give her a copy of your photos?"

"Let's go grab a coffee."

CHAPTER 18

"So, what did Detective Romero want?" Guin asked Glen as they drank their coffees.

"She wanted to see my photos."

"As you thought."

"And she asked me about my altercation with Belem."

"So, I was right! What did you tell her?"

"The truth, that I saw Belem taking pictures of you without your permission, and I asked him to delete them."

"Did she believe you?"

"Why wouldn't she?"

"Anything else?"

"She wanted to know if I spoke with him again."

"Did you?"

"No. I told her I was too busy taking pictures to talk to anyone."

"And what did she say?"

"She asked me about the exhibit."

"What about the exhibit?"

"What I thought of it."

"What you thought of it? Why was she interested in knowing your thoughts about the exhibit?"

"Maybe she was wondering if she should go see it."

"Seriously? She was just there."

"I doubt she had time to take in the exhibit."

True.

"So, what did you tell her?"

"I told her I thought it was well done. And that I liked some of the paintings, others not so much, but that you had to hand it to Bishop for constantly reinventing himself."

"You tell her you had a photo showing Belem and Bishop by the terrace stairs?"

"I did not. Anyway, she has a copy of the photos now. And we don't know for sure if that was Bishop. Or that it wasn't an accident."

"If she thought it was an accident, why did she ask you to come down to the police station?"

"I got the sense they were still collecting evidence."

"Did she ask you anything else?"

"Just about my work."

"Your work? Why was she asking you about your work?"

"I don't know. Maybe she's interested in photography."

Or maybe she's interested in you, Guin thought.

"And that was it?"

"That was it."

"Did she tell you not to leave town?"

Glen looked at her.

"I'm not under suspicion, Guin. We left before Belem fell down those stairs."

"You know that for sure? She didn't ask you where you were?"

"No."

"And she didn't say anything about Belem being murdered?"

"No."

"I should reach out to Craig, see if he's heard from his contact."

"You could always speak to Detective Romero. She seemed pretty friendly."

"Pretty friendly? She's a cop, Glen."

"So? Give her a call or send her a text. You never know."

Guin looked skeptical.

"She's not O'Loughlin."

Guin was fully aware of that.

"I guess I could shoot her a text, ask for an appointment."

"You've got nothing to lose."

Guin picked up her phone and started to type.

"What are you doing?"

"Sending the detective a text." She finished typing and hit send. Glen was looking at her. "I told her I was in the neighborhood and asked if she had a few minutes to chat."

"Let me know if she texts you back."

"I will."

They got up to leave.

"So, what are you doing the rest of today?" Guin asked him as they stepped outside.

"I've got photos to edit."

Guin felt her phone vibrating. She took it out.

"Huh, it's the detective."

"What did she say?"

"She says she has a few minutes now."

"See," said Glen.

"I should get over there."

"You forgetting something?" said Glen.

Guin stopped and turned. Glen cleared his throat and pointed to his cheek. Guin went over to him and gave him a kiss. Then she hurried off to see the detective.

Guin went up to the desk officer. It was the same one as before. She told him that she had an appointment to see Detective Romero.

"Your name?" said the desk officer.

"Guinivere Jones."

He picked up the phone and spoke with the detective.

"She'll be down in a minute," he informed Guin.

"Thank you," she replied.

A few minutes later, Detective Romero appeared.

"Ms. Jones," she said.

"Thank you for seeing me."

"Shall we go to my office?"

Guin nodded and followed her.

The detective was wearing a pair of navy slacks and a white button-down blouse, her dark hair pulled back in a kind of bun, her face artfully made up. Guin followed her down a hallway, up a flight of stairs, and down another hallway to a small office.

"I think this used to be a closet," she told Guin as they entered.

The detective went to take a seat behind her desk and gestured for Guin to take the chair on the other side.

Guin sat and noticed the detective looking at her.

"Do I have something on my face?"

"Sorry. It's just… I saw that painting at the start of the exhibit. Bishop really captured you."

"So I've been told."

"You don't like it?"

"I'll admit, it's a good likeness. But it's not me."

"What, you're not the queen of a band of fairies?"

The detective was smiling, and Guin found herself smiling back at her.

"Not that I'm aware of."

"So, what can I do for you, Ms. Jones?"

Well, that was new, thought Guin, remembering how unhelpful Detective O'Loughlin had been.

"I was hoping you'd tell me whether Ludwig Belem's death has been ruled a homicide or not."

"We're still collecting evidence and waiting for the medical examiner's report."

"Do you honestly think it was an accident?"

Guin felt the detective was studying her.

"Off the record."

"Off the record?"

Guin nodded.

"Off the record."

"Off the record, no. I don't believe it was an accident." Guin opened her mouth, but the detective stopped her. "But we're still investigating."

"Understood. So, can you tell me what evidence you've collected so far? Any suspects?"

"I can't tell you that."

Guin smiled.

"It was worth a shot."

Detective Romero smiled back at her.

"Now can I ask you a question?"

"Shoot."

"Who does your hair?"

"My hair?" said Guin.

"I've been looking for someone here, but I haven't found anyone I like yet."

"Uh," said Guin. "I've been seeing someone on Sanibel lately, but there was this guy in Naples I saw not long after I moved here who was very good. Let me see if I can find his name. It's been a while." She took out her phone and scrolled through her contacts. "Here he is. Shall I send you his vCard?"

"Please."

Guin sent it to the detective.

"Done!"

"Thank you."

"So, when did you move to Naples?"

"In August."

Guin wondered if the detective had children. She didn't see any photos on the detective's desk. She was about to ask when there was a knock on the door.

"Yes?" called the detective.

A male uniformed officer poked his head in.

"The boss wants to see you."

"Tell him I'll be right there."

The officer nodded and left.

"I need to go," said Detective Romero, getting up.

"I understand," said Guin, rising from her chair. "Thank you for your time."

The detective opened the door for Guin, and they exited together.

CHAPTER 19

Guin stood outside the Collier County Sheriff's Office, thinking. Should she go back to Sanibel or…? Pauline lived in Naples. And she did say to look her up if Guin was ever out her way. Guin pulled up Pauline's phone number from her contacts and sent her a text.

She waited to see if Pauline would get back to her. No reply. She was probably working on her articles for the *Times* and not checking her phone. That's what Guin would be doing if she had articles to work on. Ginny still hadn't written to her. Guin waited another minute. Still nothing. She put her phone back in her bag and headed to her car.

As she drove back to Sanibel, she thought about Detective Catalina Romero. She didn't fit Guin's image of a detective. Yet surely there were plenty of female detectives. However, she doubted many were as attractive (though the first word that popped into her head was *sexy*) as Detective Romero or as friendly. Guin thought the detective was probably around her age, in her early forties. Or she could have been younger. Her ability to guess people's age had worsened over the years.

When she got home, Guin would see what she could find out about the detective online.

Guin didn't realize how many Catalina Romeros there were. There was an actress (who Guin had never heard of), a lawyer, an engineer, and a doctor, as well as at least a half-dozen others in the first two pages of the search results. But there was only one Detective Catalina Romero.

Guin clicked on the link to the Collier County Sheriff's Office. There was a brief bio of the detective, very brief. It merely stated that she was a detective with the Collier County Sheriff's Office. Guin frowned and returned to the search results.

"Ah," she said, finding an article from the *Miami Herald* that mentioned the detective. She clicked on it and began to read. Again, there wasn't much information about the detective, just that she had been involved in solving a child abduction case. Guin checked the date of the article. It was two years old.

So, she had worked in Miami before coming to Naples. Guin wondered why she had left.

She continued to search for information about the detective, but all she found were a handful of mentions, cases she had been involved in in Miami, nothing about her background or what she was doing in Naples.

Guin sat back in her chair. She leaned forward a minute later, picking up her phone and texting Craig.

"You hear anything from your CCSO contact?"

She waited for a reply, but none came.

"When you hear from him," she continued, "ask him what he knows about a Detective Catalina Romero."

Guin waited for the telltale dots, but her screen remained blank. Was he out fishing? He was usually back before noon. Maybe he and Betty were having lunch someplace or were running errands.

She thought about writing to Ginny but decided not to. Ginny had said she would be sending Guin new story ideas. She would just wait. Instead, she sent Glen a text, letting him know she had spoken with the detective and asking how the photo editing was going.

Glen replied a few minutes later. He was at his parents' place, fixing a leak.

"Don't they have a plumber on staff?" Guin wrote him back. Though Glen was quite handy.

"He was busy. Couldn't get here until later."

"What about the photos?"

"They're dry."

"Ha."

"So you had a good talk with Detective Romero?"

"I don't know if I'd call it good. But it was okay. Can I call you?"

"Give me a minute. I'll call you."

"OK," Guin typed.

A few minutes later, Glen's number flashed up on her phone. Guin immediately swiped to answer.

"Hey," she said. "So, where was the leak?"

"Under the kitchen sink."

"Were you able to fix it?"

"Yeah. Not a big deal. Just a loose valve."

"Well, that's good."

"So, you had an okay talk with Detective Romero?"

"I did. She at least talked to me, which was a pleasant change."

"What did she have to say?"

"Not a whole lot. They're still collecting evidence and waiting for the medical examiner's report. But she doesn't think Belem's death was an accident."

"She said that?"

"Off the record."

"Still, that's something."

"I guess."

"You don't sound happy."

"I hate not knowing."

"I know. But I'm sure we'll hear something soon."

"I hope so. I sent Craig a text, asking if he'd heard from his contact. But I haven't heard back from him. And Ginny said she was going to send me some more assignments, but I haven't heard from her either."

"You can always call her."

"I know. But I'm afraid if I do she'll think I don't have enough to do and will pile stuff on me."

"So you don't have anything going on?"

"Not right this minute. As of now, I just have the Farkases on Wednesday." They were the philanthropic couple who had made a sizeable donation to CHR.

"Well, try to enjoy your free time."

"I know I should, but it's hard when you're expecting something to happen any moment. Did I tell you I saw my old boss again?"

"Pauline?"

"That's the one. Good memory."

"Hard to forget a name like Pauline Paulson."

"True."

"Where'd you see her?"

"On Sanibel, at Jean-Luc's."

"Did you meet her there for lunch?"

"No. She was on Sanibel working on a story for the *Times*. One of those '36 hours in' pieces."

"Huh. And she didn't tell you she'd be there?"

"Nope. And she knew I lived here."

"Try not to obsess about it."

"I'm not obsessing." Though she was, a bit. "I actually texted her from the police station, but she didn't get back to me. Do you think she's avoiding me?"

"Guin."

"Yes?"

"I doubt she's avoiding you. She didn't even know you were living on Sanibel until Friday, yes?"

"That's what she said."

"And she had the article about the exhibit and another about Sanibel to write?"

"What's your point?"

"The point is, she's probably just busy, not ignoring or avoiding you. Give her a few days, then reach out to her again."

"Okay. You're probably right."

"I know I'm right."

"Very sure of yourself."

"Why would she be avoiding you? Wait. Don't answer. Forget I said it."

Guin chuckled.

"I'll try not to obsess about it. Speaking of the *New York Times*, did I tell you my mother wants me to talk to the husband of a friend of hers who works there?"

Her mother had sent her a text over the weekend, asking Guin if she had written to Bill Hendricks at the *Times* yet. But Guin had ignored the text.

"No. What does this husband of a friend do over there?"

"I'm not sure. I should probably look him up."

"You going to talk to him?"

"Maybe."

"Why maybe?"

"The *New York Times* is not going to hire me."

"You don't know that."

Guin opened her mouth and then shut it. Why wouldn't the *New York Times* hire her? She was a darn fine reporter.

"What if they say I have to move to New York?"

"Don't they have reporters all over the world?"

"They do. But I think my mother is hoping they'll make me move up there, at least initially. And chances are, she's right."

"Would that be so bad?"

Guin stared at her phone. *Did Glen want her to move to New York?*

"Just talk to the guy. You'll regret it if you don't."

"You sound like my mother."

"Well, we both love you and want the best for you."

"Yeah, yeah, yeah. Okay, I promise to reach out to the guy."

"Good. Let me know how it goes."

"So, you going to hang out with your folks for a while?"

"No, I was about to head home. I still have photos to edit. Why?"

"I was going to invite you over for dinner."

"What are you making?"

Guin hadn't really thought about it.

"Pasta?"

"I love pasta. What time?"

"You sure it's okay? What about your photos?"

"I should be able to finish editing them before dinnertime. Okay to get there around seven?"

"That's fine. Though if you get here earlier, we could go catch the sunset on the beach."

"Hm… I'll get there as soon as I can."

"No rush. So, would you prefer pasta with pesto or Bolognese?"

"You decide. I'm good with either. I'll bring wine."

"Okay. And by the way, I made chocolate chip cookies."

"You should have led with that."

Guin smiled.

"Okay, go home and edit photos. I'll see you later."

"See you later."

Guin drove to Bailey's to get the ingredients to make pesto. While she was there, she picked up some fresh pasta, salad fixings, and a loaf of Italian bread.

Guin had made pesto before but not in a while. Still, it was easy to make. You just pulsed some basil and pine nuts in a food processor. Added some garlic and Parmesan cheese. Slowly added some extra virgin olive oil. Then sprinkle it with salt and freshly ground pepper and presto! You had pesto!

"Maybe I should have made fresh pasta too," she said when the pesto was done. But she had already bought a bag of pasta.

She cleaned up and went to check her phone. Still nothing from Ginny or Craig. She thought about texting them but held off. She would wait.

She went to her bedroom to get a book. But she couldn't decide which one. She was having trouble getting into anything lately and kept switching. She picked up the new mystery she had purchased, the one her friends in the Shell Club had recommended, about a group of senior citizens in the UK who lived in an upscale retirement community and had a murder club.

She took the book into the living room and curled up on the couch. Fauna jumped up and nestled beside her. Guin smiled. Then she began to read. And this time, she didn't fall asleep.

The doorbell rang a few minutes before six. Guin opened the door to find Glen standing there.

"You're early," she said.

"You said to get here when I could. And I recall something about a sunset walk on the beach and chocolate chip cookies."

Guin smiled.

"Good to know I can bribe you with cookies. But they are for after dinner."

Guin noticed that Glen had his overnight bag with him.

"Planning on staying over?"

"It's my Boy Scout training. Always be prepared."

"You know, you could just leave some stuff here."

Glen's right eyebrow went up.

"What?" said Guin.

"First you offer to give me a key. Then you tell me I can leave stuff here. Next you'll be suggesting we move in together."

Guin felt her heart begin to race. What would it be like to live with Glen? Though some days it felt as though they were already living together. She imagined what it would be like to fall asleep and wake up next to him every day and smiled. However, they would need a bigger place if they both planned on working from home. And Guin was not hot to live in Fort Myers.

"I see your brain working. What are you thinking?"

"I'm thinking we should head to the beach. We don't want to miss the sunset."

Glen knew that hadn't been what Guin was thinking, but he didn't press her.

"What should I do with the wine?"

"Put it in the fridge. Then let's go."

Glen did as he was told. Then they headed out.

It was a cool evening, and Guin wrapped her arms around herself, trying to stay warm. She should have worn a sweatshirt.

"Here," said Glen, rubbing Guin's arms.

It felt good.

"Okay," she said a minute later. "We're going to miss the sunset."

They walked down the path to the beach. There were people spread out along the sand, some sitting, some standing, all waiting for the show that was about to begin.

"Looks to be a good sunset," said Guin, as they stood near the shoreline. The sky was dappled with clouds that had started to turn pastel colors. "You should have brought your camera."

"Sometimes it's nice to not have a lens between you and the world."

"Do you mind if I take some pictures?"

"Be my guest."

Guin pulled out her phone and took a photo. Then they headed west. They stopped as the sun neared the horizon line.

"I wonder if we'll see the green flash. I've only seen it once."

She took out her phone and took a photo of the sun just before it disappeared.

"There it goes!" she said.

They watched as the sun seemed to melt into the sea.

"Look at the sky!" she said. "It looks like it's on fire!"

Glen reached for Guin's hand and squeezed it.

They stood there for a few more seconds, then Guin said they should head back.

"That was excellent," said Glen, pushing his plate away. "Best pesto I've ever had."

"Please," said Guin.

"It's true!"

"Yeah, right. Well, I'm glad you liked it. Let's clean up a bit. Then we can have some cookies and ice cream."

Guin took out a pint of vanilla ice cream to thaw a bit and they loaded their plates into the dishwasher.

"You should sell these," said Glen, taking a second cookie.

"That's what Betty said."

"Have you ever thought about it?"

"Selling chocolate chip cookies? Where would I sell them?"

"At Bailey's or the farmers market."

He took a bite of his cookie.

"I'm serious."

"I believe you, but I'm not ready to become the next Mrs. Fields."

"What about the next Mrs. Anderson?"

Guin froze. Was Glen proposing?

"Was that a proposal?" she asked him.

Glen looked at her.

"Would you accept if it was?"

Guin felt her heart hammering against her chest again. The next thing she knew, Glen was getting off his stool, lowering himself, and… picking up a large chocolate chip cookie crumb that had fallen on the floor. He popped it in his mouth and stood up.

"What?" he said, seeing the look on Guin's face. "Should I have not eaten that? It was only on the floor a few seconds."

Was that relief Guin felt or disappointment?

"It's fine," Guin said. "Let's finish cleaning and go watch something."

"What did you have in mind?"

"I don't know. But I'm sure we can find something we'd both enjoy."

Glen smiled.

"I have no doubt."

CHAPTER 20

Guin woke up the next morning to an empty bed. Was Glen in the kitchen? She went to see. What she found instead of Glen was her old coffee pot, the one she kept for when she had guests, filled with coffee, a note beside it.

"Had to go," it said. "I'll text you later." He had signed it with an *x* and an *o*.

Where did he have to go before seven o'clock in the morning? And why hadn't he woken her?

Guin thought about texting him, but he'd written that he'd text her later. She poured herself a mug of coffee and took a sip. Not bad. Though not as strong as hers. She took a few more sips, looking out the window. The sky was a pale shade of blue. She checked the temperature. Another cool morning. But Guin didn't mind. She would bundle up and head down to the beach. She took one more sip of coffee and went to get dressed.

□

Guin came back from her beach walk with a pocket full of shells. She left them to soak in a bucket filled with water and a little dishwashing soap and was fixing herself a bowl of cereal when her phone began to vibrate. It was Ginny.

"Good morning," Guin said.

"Not for everyone," her boss replied.

"What's up?"

"Joel just phoned. He heard sirens, and he thinks Farley was arrested."

"What makes him think that?"

"He walked down to Farley's place and saw two vehicles from the Collier County Sheriff's Office there."

"Did he see Farley?"

"No. But when he went back later to check on him, Farley didn't answer."

"Maybe they just wanted to have another talk with him?" However, Guin didn't really believe that. "You call Craig?"

"He didn't pick up, and I'm about to head into a meeting."

"Okay, I'll call him. But he's probably out fishing."

"Let me know if he finds out anything."

"I will."

"You get the list of story ideas I sent you?"

"No. When did you send it?"

"Yesterday morning."

"Well, I didn't get anything."

Guin heard Ginny mumble something about *stupid internet.*

"I'll send it again. Let me know if you get it this time."

Guin said that she would. Then she called Craig, but his voicemail picked up.

"Craig, it's Guin. Give me a call when you get this. It's about Bishop."

Next she called Detective Romero. But she didn't answer either. Guin left her a message, asking if they had arrested Farley Bishop and to please give her a call. Guin wondered if she should call the Collier County Sheriff's Office too. May as well. But she was told that Detective Romero was unavailable. Would she like her voicemail? Guin said sure, even though she had already left a message for the detective on her cell phone. She wondered if she should text the detective but thought that might be overkill. She sent her a text anyway.

As she was texting, she saw that she had a new email message. It was from Ginny. Guin opened it. It was a list of articles Ginny wanted her to work on. Guin scanned the list. Then she let Ginny know she'd received her email and would get back to her about the articles later. First, she needed to eat something.

Guin was finishing her bowl of cereal when Craig called.

"Craig!" she said. "You get my message?"

"Just saw that you and Ginny had called. What's up?"

"You didn't listen to my message?"

"Not yet. I just got in."

"Ginny thinks the Collier County Sheriff's Office arrested Farley Bishop. Can you reach out to your contact and find out if it's true? I tried to reach Detective Romero, but she's not answering."

"I can try, but… Why does she think they arrested Bishop?"

"Joel heard sirens and saw two vehicles from the Collier County Sheriff's Office outside Bishop's place. And when he went to check on Bishop later, Bishop didn't answer."

"Hm."

"What does 'hm' mean?"

"*Hm* means it sounds like they arrested him. But I'll check with Pete."

"Pete's your contact in the Collier County Sheriff's Office?"

"Did I say Pete?"

"You did."

"Hm. I should go."

"So you'll call Pete, ask him about Bishop, and let me know if they've arrested him?"

"I'll do my best."

"Thanks, Craig."

The call ended, and Guin looked out the big bay window. There were four ibis nibbling on her lawn. She didn't mind.

In fact, she liked it when birds and wildlife came to visit. In addition to the ibis, she had seen anhingas, great egrets, and gallinules on the lake behind her house, as well as the occasional alligator.

As she continued to watch the birds, she felt something rub against her leg. It was Spot.

"What?" she said, looking down at the cat.

"Meow," said Spot.

Guin picked him up, and he started to purr. Then he jumped up on the counter and stuck his face in her cereal bowl.

"Hey!" she said. But it was too late.

Guin sighed and let Spot lap up the milk. When he was done, she cleaned her bowl and went to her office. She opened Ginny's email and reviewed the list of articles, wondering if Ginny would still want her to work on all of them if Farley Bishop had been arrested.

She started to type a reply but stopped. Better to wait until she had confirmation about Bishop's arrest. She stared down at her phone, but it was silent. Would Alexandra Barnes or Bennett Emerson know if something had happened to Bishop? Maybe. Was the museum even open? Well, there was only one way to find out. She called the Baker but got a recorded message, saying the museum opened at ten. It would be ten soon, so she would call back.

Guin looked at the list of articles again, but she was distracted. Hopefully, someone would call her back sooner rather than later, so she would know what to do.

□

There was still no word about Farley Bishop by lunchtime. Guin wondered what was taking so long. Either the man had been arrested or he hadn't.

She wasn't that hungry, but she decided she might as well fix herself something. It would give her something to do. As soon as she stepped into the kitchen, the cats magically appeared. She looked down at them, wondering how they always knew when she was in the kitchen. Guin gave them some more dry food and then opened the refrigerator. She pulled out a package of tortillas and a bag of shredded Mexican cheese. She would make herself a quesadilla.

She had taken a few bites when her phone began to vibrate. Why did people always call her when she was eating? She looked at the Caller ID. It was her mother. Guin thought about not answering but picked up.

"Hi, Mom," she said. "Everything okay?"

"Philip twisted his ankle playing pickleball."

"Oh no! Is he okay?"

"He's on crutches. So we're delaying our trip for a few more days."

"That's too bad," said Guin. Though she was secretly relieved. Maybe the universe was telling her parents they shouldn't come to Naples. Though she felt bad about her stepfather twisting his ankle.

"Yes, well. I told him to be careful. But does he listen to me?"

"At least it's just a sprain."

"He still wants to head down this week. But I told him we should wait. It's supposed to snow here."

"Very sensible of you. So were you able to go to Helena's wedding reception in Philly this weekend?"

"Yes. He twisted his ankle yesterday, after we got back. He was so eager be back on a pickleball court after not playing all weekend that he was a bit too aggressive and…"

"It happens," said Guin. "So how long until he can ditch the crutches?"

"Until it doesn't hurt to walk on it. Probably just a few days. Philip insists he's fine. But I saw him wince when he tried to walk on it this morning. And I told him if he wants to play pickleball anytime soon, he should take it easy for a few days."

"Well, I hope he feels better soon. So, how was the wedding reception?"

"It was fine."

"Just fine? Where was it?"

"At some Italian restaurant. Not someplace I would have chosen, but I guess it was the best Betsy could do on short notice."

"Were there a lot of people?"

"I don't know about a lot. It wasn't that big a place. Yet it was full. There must have been at least a dozen doctors. As a matter of fact…"

"Mom," Guin said warningly, knowing what was coming.

"What?" her mother replied, all innocence.

"You know what. I'm not interested in dating a doctor." *Or anyone you might want to fix me up with*, she silently added.

"I wasn't implying… Though I did chat with this very nice dermatologist, Dr. Johansson. He's Swedish. Very good looking and recently divorced. Could be handy to have a dermatologist down there in Florida. All that sun."

"I wear sunblock, and I'm not in the market for a dermatologist or a new beau. I'm quite happy with the one I've got."

Guin heard her mother sigh and desperately wanted to end the call.

"Is there something else?"

"No. I just want you to be happy, Guinivere."

"I am happy, Mom."

"If you say so."

Time to change the subject.

"So about Beryl's husband, the one who works for the *New York Times*…"

"Did you talk to him?"

Guin could hear the hope in her mother's voice.

"Not yet. Does he even know who I am?"

"Beryl knows all about you."

"But does her husband? Just make sure he does, please, before I reach out to him. Better yet, have Beryl ask him to contact me."

"He's a very important man, and I'm sure he's very busy, Guinivere. You should just pick up the phone and call him."

"I don't have his number." But it was probably easy to find.

"I'll talk to Beryl and send you his information. Just think, my daughter working for the *New York Times*!"

"Slow down there. Do you even know what he does at the *Times*? He could work in Production or Sales."

Guin had meant to Google him but had gotten distracted. Or that's what she told herself.

"Beryl said he's very important."

"Well, ask Beryl what he does and send me his contact info."

"I'll do that."

"Great. I need to go. Got a lot of work." Though that wasn't technically true. "And tell Philip I hope he feels better soon."

"I will," said her mother.

Guin said goodbye and looked down at her quesadilla. It was probably cold now. She took a bite and then threw the rest into the garbage. Ten minutes later, she received a text from her mother, containing the vCard for Bill Hendricks, Deputy Managing Editor, *The New York Times*. Well, well, well. Beryl hadn't been exaggerating.

□

Guin was reading the *New York Times* online when her phone began to buzz. It was Craig.

"You find out anything?" she asked him.

"That's why I'm calling. Joel was right. They arrested Bishop."

"What did they charge him with?"

"Voluntary manslaughter."

"Voluntary manslaughter?"

"They believe the victim provoked Bishop, and Bishop pushed him down the stairs."

"Intentionally?"

"That's for a jury to decide."

"Do you know where he is?"

"Awaiting bail."

"How much?"

"Didn't say."

"Anything else?"

"No."

"Pete have any info about Detective Romero?"

"Just what you said, that she came here from Miami a few months ago."

"He know why she moved there?"

"Word is a messy divorce."

"Does she have any kids?"

"Why are you so interested in her?"

"I don't know. Maybe it's because I haven't come across a lot of female detectives. And… she interests me."

"You should interview her."

"For the paper?"

"Why not?"

"Because she's in Naples?"

"Naples isn't that far away."

"You find out anything else?"

"That was it. I was lucky to get that much."

"Okay. Well, thanks for your help. You tell Ginny?"

"Not yet. I phoned you first."

"Thanks. I appreciate that. I'll let Ginny know."

She said goodbye and was about to call Ginny but decided she would deliver the news in person instead.

It was quiet at the *Sanibel-Captiva Sun-Times* office. Not that surprising. Many of the staff—the reporters and photographers—were freelance or part-time, only working out of or stopping by the office occasionally. And the sales staff, which consisted of two people and Ginny, was typically out of the office schmoozing advertisers.

There was no one at the front desk, but Guin saw Jasmine the art director and asked her if Ginny was around.

"She's in her office having a late lunch," Jasmine informed her.

Guin looked around.

"Where's Peanut?" Peanut was Jasmine's dog, who often accompanied Jasmine to work.

"He wasn't feeling well, so I left him at home."

"I hope he's all right."

"I'm sure he'll be fine. Probably all the pizza he ate last night. If he's not better tomorrow, I'll take him to the vet."

"He eats pizza?" Guin had never heard of a dog eating pizza.

"We had pepperoni, and Peanut loves pepperoni. We had stupidly left the box on the counter and… You can guess the rest."

Guin could.

"Well, I hope he'll be okay."

"Like I said, he should be fine by tomorrow. Stupid dog."

Guin made her way back to Ginny's office and knocked on the door.

"Go away unless it's important!" Ginny called.

"It's important," said Guin, knowing Ginny would want to hear the news if she hadn't already.

"That you, Guin?"

"It is."

"Come in!"

Guin opened the door and entered to see Ginny in front of her computer, a half-eaten container of salad and a Diet Coke in front of her.

"Close the door and take a seat."

Guin did as she was told.

"So?"

"Craig called. Joel was right. They arrested Bishop and charged him with voluntary manslaughter."

Ginny frowned.

"They set bail?"

"They did."

"How much?"

"Craig didn't know. His contact didn't say."

Ginny picked up her phone. Guin wondered who she was calling. But she didn't have to wait long to find out.

"Yeah, it's me," she said to whoever picked up. "I'm here with Guin. Find out how much Farley Bishop's bail is and get back to me." There was a pause. "I don't care if he's busy. Call and ask or find someone there who knows."

Then she hung up.

"You called Craig?" Though it had to have been Craig.

"I did. So, is that what you came over here to tell me?"

Guin nodded.

"Also, I got the list of story ideas you sent me. You still want me to work on them or should I hold off and focus on Bishop?"

Ginny frowned and looked at her monitor. She clicked on her mouse until she found what she was looking for.

"Hm," she said. "I can farm out some of these. But I'd like you to tackle at least a couple while you're looking into the museum story. Take a look and let me know which ones you want."

"Can I let you know later?"

"That's fine. Just let me know by end of day."

"Today?"

"Yes, today."

"Got it," said Guin.

Guin continued to sit.

"Well, what are you waiting for?" said Ginny. "Get going!"

Guin got up and left.

CHAPTER 21

Guin stood outside the *Sanibel-Captiva Sun-Times*. She checked her phone. Detective Romero still hadn't gotten back to her. Not a huge surprise. Should she try her again? No, too soon. She should wait. She thought about Farley Bishop being in a jail cell. Did he have a lawyer? Ginny would probably know. She turned around and went back into the office. Ginny's door was shut, and Guin could hear her on the phone. She would wait.

Several minutes went by. Guin was about to give up and send Ginny a text when Ginny's door flew open.

"Jasmine!" Ginny shouted. Then she saw Guin. "Why are you still here?"

"I forgot to ask, does Bishop have a lawyer?"

"Not that I know of. Why?"

"I was wondering who was going to bail him out."

Ginny looked thoughtful.

"Good question. I should ask Joel."

"You bellowed?" said Jasmine.

"I never bellow," said Ginny. "I need you to make room for another ad on page three."

Jasmine opened her mouth to protest but saw the look on Ginny's face.

"What size ad are we talking about?"

"Quarter page."

"You can't be serious. I'm about to send the issue to the printer."

"You have a few hours."

"Ginny, I…"

"The ad's all set to go. I just need you to slot it in."

Jasmine looked annoyed.

"Just work your magic."

"I'm not a magician. Can't it wait until the next issue?"

"No."

"Then you either need to cut down the article that's currently on page three or convince the bank to cut their ad from half a page to a quarter."

"Let me see," said Ginny, heading to Jasmine's desk.

Guin thought about following them and volunteering to help, but she decided it was probably best to stay out of it.

"I'm going," she said. However, she doubted they heard her.

As Guin drove home, she thought again about who she had seen arguing with Ludwig Belem at the preview, other than Glen and Pauline. There were three people she had personally seen with the critic: Bennett Emerson, the director; Alexandra Barnes, the curator; and Bishop. However, there could have been others.

Then she remembered: the catering staff. They had been on the terrace and just outside the exhibit serving drinks and food all evening. (Food and drinks were not allowed in the exhibit area. Though Guin could have sworn she saw a few patrons with drinks in there.) Surely one or more of the servers had seen Belem that evening—and who he had talked to. And it was one of them, Carla, who had found Belem on the stairs.

Guin wished she had gotten the name of the catering company when she had been at the Baker. An oversight. But it should be easy enough to find out who had catered the event. She would phone Alexandra Barnes at the museum as soon as she got home.

Guin phoned the museum and was put through to the curator's office. Guin hoped she was in.

"Alexandra Barnes."

"Ms. Barnes, this is Guinivere Jones with the *Sanibel-Captiva Sun-Times*. Do you have a minute?"

"That's all I have," the curator replied. "Things have been a bit crazy around here."

"I can imagine. I'm wondering, do you have the name and number for the catering company the museum used on Friday?"

"I don't know the number off the top of my head, but I'm sure you can find them. It's Catering by Caroline. Caroline Williams is the owner. Why?"

Guin quickly made up something.

"The food was delicious, and my mother, who's renting a place in Naples, is looking for a caterer."

Guin knew it sounded lame, but it was the best that she could come up with on the fly.

"Is that all?" said Ms. Barnes.

"Actually… Are you aware that Farley Bishop has been arrested?"

No response.

"Ms. Barnes?"

"Sorry, yes, I'm aware."

"Does that mean you'll have to close the exhibit?"

"Close the exhibit?"

"Because of the arrest."

"We weren't planning on it. Wait, you can't possibly think Farley killed that man."

"I don't," said Guin. Though she wasn't so sure. "But the police wouldn't have arrested him unless they had some sort of proof."

"He didn't do it. And that's all I will say about the matter. I need to go."

"I had just a couple more questions. They won't take long."

"They'll have to wait."

"Please. I want to help. If you think he didn't do it, let me help prove it."

The curator didn't reply.

"Do you have some time tomorrow? I could come to the museum."

Guin heard the curator sigh.

"Can you be here at eight-thirty?"

"Absolutely. Do you know if Bennett Emerson will also be there? I'd like to speak to him too while I'm there."

The curator let out a laugh.

"Bennett here early? Unlikely. He rarely comes in before ten. I need to go. I'll see you tomorrow at eight-thirty."

"Tomorrow it is."

Guin had hoped to speak with Bennett Emerson while she was at the museum, but she would have to interview him another time. She picked up her phone and redialed the number for the museum.

"Bennett Emerson, please," she told the operator.

"He's left for the day," the woman replied.

It wasn't yet five. Where had he gone?

"Could you transfer me to his voicemail?"

The woman said that she would, and Guin left a message, asking the director to call her. Then she looked up Catering by Caroline. As Alexandra Barnes had said, it was easy to find. She called the number and waited while the phone rang.

"Catering by Caroline!" trilled a female voice.

"Hello," said Guin. "Is this Caroline?"

"No, this is Michelle."

"Hi, Michelle. Is Caroline available?"

"Who's calling, please?"

"My name's Guinivere Jones. I'm a reporter with the *Sanibel-Captiva Sun-Times*. And I was hoping to speak with Ms. Williams for a story I'm working on."

"Caroline's busy right now. Is there something I can help you with, Ms. Jones?"

Guin hesitated.

"I had some questions regarding an event you catered at the Baker Museum on Friday."

"What kind of questions?"

Guin paused.

"Were you at the event, Michelle?"

"No, sorry. I'm in charge of scheduling."

"Is Carla there?"

"Carla?"

"One of your servers. She was working that evening." Guin described her.

"Oh, Carla! No, I'm sorry she's not here."

"Could you put me in touch with her?"

"I…"

"It's important that I speak with her. If I give you my number, could you get it to her, and ask her to call me?"

"I can give her the message, but…"

"Thank you. And could you let Caroline know I'd like to speak with her too?"

Guin heard someone talking to Michelle in the background.

"Sorry, it's a bit busy here. What was your name again?"

"It's Guinivere Jones. I'm with the—"

"Can you spell that?"

"Just tell them Guin Jones called. That's G-U-I-N. I'm a reporter with the *Sanibel-Captiva Sun-Times*. I'll give you my number."

Guin recited it.

"Got it," said Michelle. "I'll give them the message."

"Thank you. Any idea when they might be available?"

"Caroline left and won't be back until tomorrow. I'm not sure about Carla."

Guin frowned. Well, nothing she could do. She would just have to wait—and call back if they didn't get in touch with her. She thanked Michelle again and ended the call. Now what? She decided to text Glen. She hadn't heard from him all day.

"Bishop was arrested," she typed. "Charged with voluntary manslaughter. Awaiting bail." She wanted to ask him why he had left so early and why she hadn't heard from him, but she thought better of it.

She reread what she had written and pressed send.

She stared at her phone, hoping Glen would reply right away. Nothing. Where was he? Was he okay? It was rare for her not to hear from him. Maybe they should get one of those location apps, so they'd know where the other one was. Though was that really necessary?

She needed a distraction. Then she remembered Ginny's article list. She opened Ginny's email and went over the list again. As she was deciding which articles she wanted to tackle, Craig called.

"Hey," she said. "Any news?"

"That's why I'm calling."

"What's up?"

"Bishop just made bail."

"How much was it?"

"Ten K."

"Is that normal? It doesn't seem like that much."

"He must have a good lawyer."

"Is that who bailed him out?"

"Don't know."

"Did you ask?"

"What do you think?"

"Sorry. Did your source know if it was a man or a woman?"

"All he could tell me was that Bishop made bail."

"Do you know if whoever it was paid cash?"

"Didn't say."

Guin frowned.

"You know when Bishop was released?"

"Not that long ago."

She wondered if Bishop was home.

"Okay, thanks, Craig."

Guin thought about calling over to Bishop's studio. Would he even be there? And if he was, would he pick up his phone? Probably not. She wouldn't. And if he did pick up, would he even talk to her? Again, probably not. She decided to call Ginny instead.

CHAPTER 22

Guin listened as Ginny's phone rang. The call went to voicemail.

"Ginny, it's Guin. I just heard from Craig. Bishop made bail. Give me a call when you get this."

She waited to see if Ginny would call her back. When she didn't right away, Guin sent her a text. Fifteen minutes later, "Ginny" flashed up on her Caller ID.

"Hey," said Guin.

"Hay is for horses."

Guin made a face. It was something her mother used to say to her.

"You get my messages?"

"I did."

"So, do you know if Bishop's back at his studio?"

"I do not. I called Joel, but he's not answering. Craig say who paid Farley's bail?"

"No. Maybe Joel would know?"

"I'll ask him. You review the articles I sent you?"

"I was about to write you back."

"Hold on," said Ginny. Guin thought she heard Ginny speaking to someone. "I need to go. Let me know about the articles." Then she hung up.

Guin returned to Ginny's email and reviewed the list again. Most of the articles had to do with upcoming events or new restaurants or shops opening, things Guin had written about dozens of times. And none of them got her that excited.

She picked up her phone and opened the text from her mother again, the one with Bill Hendricks's vCard. She was about to Google him but stopped. Ginny first.

Guin wasn't in the mood to write about another art festival. (There was one practically every weekend, or so it seemed, during the season.) But she was okay writing about the upcoming lectures at the Shell Museum. She was also fine writing about the Sanibel Sea School. And she was interested in checking out the new Asian restaurant that had just opened. Sanibel could use an Asian place. Maybe she'd do takeout tonight.

She wrote Ginny back, telling her which articles she would tackle. Then she opened her browser and did a search for Bill Hendricks. *Well, well, well.*

Guin was eating a spring roll when she saw Ginny's name flash up on her Caller ID.

"You get my email about the articles?" Guin asked her.

"I did. Thanks. But that's not why I'm calling."

"What's up?"

"I talked to Joel."

"And?"

"Farley's not at his studio, but Joel says he's fine."

"Where is he? Does Joel know who bailed him out?"

"Slow down there, pardner. Joel spoke with him, but he claims Farley didn't tell him where he was."

"Do you believe that?"

"I haven't decided."

"Why wouldn't he tell you if he knew?"

"They're probably worried I might blab to someone."

"And he didn't say who bailed him out?"

"Correct."

"What did he say to Joel then?"

"That he didn't think he'd be able to play chess with him this week."

"That's it?"

"That's it."

"Did Farley tell him when he might be back?"

"If he did, Joel's not saying."

"Huh. Now what?"

"Now I'm going to eat my dinner."

"What did you make?"

"Joel cooked."

"What did he make?"

"Chicken something or other. I think it was a Julia Child recipe. I wasn't paying attention."

Guin smiled.

"*Bon appetit!*"

Guin was watching TV when Glen finally called.

"Hey," she said. "You okay?"

"Sorry," he said. "A photographer friend called me early this morning and asked me to cover for him."

"What was the matter with him?"

"Food poisoning."

"Ugh. Why didn't he just cancel?"

"It was an important job."

"And they were okay using someone else?"

"He told them I was his partner."

"Do I know this guy?"

"I've probably mentioned him, Sam Elliott."

"Like the actor?"

"That's the one."

"I don't recall you mentioning him."

"He mostly does corporate work. I met him at a photography meetup after I moved back down here.

Anyway, I had nothing major going on today, so I said I'd do it."

"I hope he paid you for saving his ass."

"He did."

"How much?"

Glen told her, and Guin whistled.

"I'm in the wrong line of work."

"You're a great writer."

"That's not what I meant. Writers get paid peanuts compared to photographers."

"Not all photographers make that kind of money. It's mostly corporate ones."

"What about weddings? They pay well, don't they?"

"They can. But most photographers just get by."

"Huh."

Guin wondered how much Glen made and thought about asking him. But now was not the time. She knew he had worked on Wall Street for years before moving back to Fort Myers to help his parents. And he had no doubt saved enough that he could afford to freelance. At least for a while.

"Anyway, I'm sorry I didn't call sooner. The shoot was all day, and then I checked on my folks."

"How's the leak?"

"All gone. Mom just insisted on feeding me. I just got home."

"Her ankle okay?"

"Mostly. Not much can keep her down."

Guin smiled.

"I'm glad she's doing better. So will I still see you tomorrow at the Farkases' or do you have to help Sam out again?"

"I told Sam I was busy tomorrow. So I'll be there."

"Okay. I'm going to the museum first thing to speak with Alexandra Barnes. Then I plan on stopping by the catering company."

"Catering company?"

"The people who catered the event Friday. I want to speak to the young woman who found Belem and to the owner, see what they know."

"Okay. Good luck."

"Thanks." Guin let out a yawn.

"I'll let you go. See you tomorrow. And Guin?"

"Yes?"

"I'm sorry for running out on you this morning."

"Just don't do it again."

"I promise."

Guin slept well that evening and woke up the next morning in a hopeful mood. She went to the kitchen to make herself some coffee, feeding the cats as the coffee brewed. She drank half the mug. Then she went to brush her teeth and get dressed. She eyed the clothes in her closet, deciding on a white, button-down shirt and a navy pencil skirt. Then she went back into the bathroom to apply a bit of makeup and do something with her hair.

Normally, Guin didn't dress up or put on makeup to do interviews, especially ones at eight-thirty in the morning. At least not since moving to Sanibel. But she recalled how stylish Alexandra Barnes had looked, and Guin felt obliged to look if not her best then at least professional.

She stood in front of the bathroom mirror and examined her face. She had accepted her freckles long ago. They came with her pale Northern European skin and had multiplied since Guin had moved to Florida. Though Guin religiously applied sunblock whenever she went out.

Her hair was another matter. Guin had been blessed—or cursed—with a head of curly strawberry-blonde hair that had a mind of its own and that no gel or cream could fully tame. Men claimed to adore her wild locks, but Guin had hated her hair when she was young and still wasn't sure how she felt about it.

She removed the ponytail holder and watched as her curls sprang around her face. She looked a bit wild. So she grabbed her hair and wrestled it into a mock French twist behind her head, pinning it up with a large barrette.

She slipped on a pair of peep-toe shoes, grabbed her bag and keys, and headed out, praying there wouldn't be too much traffic. Yet, of course, there was.

Guin parked by the administrative building, where the director and curator had their offices, and hurried inside. There was a security guard in the lobby. Guin gave him her name and told him that she had an appointment to see Alexandra Barnes. He asked Guin for an ID and had her sign in. Then he told her how to find the curator's office.

Guin thanked him and headed upstairs. The door to the curator's office was ajar, and there was a light on inside. Guin knocked.

"Come in," called the curator.

Guin stepped inside. Alexandra Barnes's office reminded Guin of Ginny's with its piles of magazines, folders, and other items. On the walls were posters from various museum exhibits, two from the Broad in Los Angeles, where Alexandra Barnes had worked before, and two from the Baker.

The curator was seated at her desk, her head down, reviewing some papers.

"Ms. Barnes?" said Guin, waiting for the curator to acknowledge her.

"I'll be with you in a minute," she said.

The curator finished whatever it was she was doing and looked up. She reminded Guin of a Modigliani painting with her long face, dark hair, and dark eyes. As at the preview, the curator was well put together, her hair pulled back in a chignon, her face subtly made up, and wearing a simple yet elegant white shirt that was unbuttoned at the top to reveal a large multicolored pendant that looked a bit Native American. Guin was glad she had decided to dress more formally.

"Ms. Jones," said the curator. "Please, have a seat."

Guin looked at the two chairs, one of which was occupied by a pile of magazines.

"You can put those magazines on the floor," Ms. Barnes told her.

Guin removed the pile of magazines and placed them on the floor, noticing that the magazine on top was an issue of *Art World.*

"So, remind me what you wanted," said the curator. "With everything that's been going on, I can barely remember my own name. Though I'm guessing your visit has something to with Farley."

"That's right," said Guin. "I…"

"Oh, and before I forget, thank you for sending us a link to your article. It was a nice write-up."

"You're welcome." Guin was pleased to see that the curator seemed to be in a better mood this morning—and had seemingly forgotten or gotten over her irritation with Guin. "Actually, I wanted to ask you about Ludwig Belem, what you knew about him."

"Not very much."

"Oh, I got the sense that you knew him."

"Mainly from his column," said the curator.

"But you'd met him before, yes?"

"I had. But we never exchanged more than a few words."

"Oh. I got the impression from seeing the two of you together the other night that you knew each other well."

Silence.

"Yes, well. About that evening. I saw the two of you having a chat, and I was wondering what he said to upset you."

The curator looked confused.

"I don't recall being upset."

"Sorry. Perhaps *annoyed* is a better word."

"Ah. Quite possible. Mr. Belem was an expert at annoying people."

"Do you remember what he said to you?"

"I'm afraid I don't. I spoke with so many people that evening."

"Did he say something about the exhibit?"

"Sorry. I really don't remember."

Guin didn't believe her.

"Did he say whether he liked it?"

The side of the curator's face formed a half smile.

"He would never do that. It wasn't his style. He liked to keep curators on edge."

"You mentioned his column. What did you think of it?"

"I know some people find it amusing, but I thought it mean-spirited. He seemed to delight in taking artists down a peg. Are you familiar with it?"

"I've read a few of his critiques."

"And?"

"I feel the same way you do. Had he ever written about Mr. Bishop?"

"Not that I'm aware of."

"But they knew each other."

"What makes you say that?"

"I saw them talking. And they…"

Guin was interrupted by a knock on the door. A young woman popped her head in.

"I'm sorry to disturb you, Alex, but the meeting's about to start."

"Right," said the curator. She turned to Guin. "I have to go." She turned back to the young woman. "Tell them I'll be right there."

She got up, as did Guin.

Guin wondered what the meeting was about. Did it have something to do with what happened? Probably.

"Just one more question," said Guin as they stood at the door. "Why did you leave a prestigious institution like the Broad to come to the Baker?"

The curator gave Guin a patronizing smile. No doubt she had been asked the question before.

"The Baker might be smaller than the Broad, but it's a world-class institution, and I have far more authority here than I did there. And one gets tired of LA after a while. I know I did."

"You didn't consider going to New York or Boston or Philadelphia?"

"No. And now Ms. Jones…" She held the door open.

"Thank you for your time," said Guin, stepping through it.

CHAPTER 23

Guin left the Artis-Naples campus and headed to Catering by Caroline, which was located on a quiet side street in Old Naples. She parked the Mini and wondered if she should have called first, the shops on the street looking closed. But she was there already. May as well see if anyone was in.

The small white brick building that housed the catering company had an old-fashioned striped awning, and *Catering by Caroline* was stenciled on the large plate-glass window. Guin didn't see anyone inside, but there was a light on. She tried the door. It was unlocked. She opened it and heard a bell jangle.

"Hello?" she called.

"Just a minute!" replied a female voice.

A minute or two later, a tall, attractive woman, wearing an apron over her dress, appeared. Guin thought she looked too glamorous to be a baker. But maybe that was how caterers dressed in Naples.

"Can I help you?" the woman asked Guin.

"By any chance are you Caroline?"

"I am. How can I help you, Ms. …?"

"Jones, Guinivere Jones. I'm a reporter with the *Sanibel-Captiva Sun-Times*."

"Ah yes. Michelle left me a message saying that you had called. Something about an article?"

"That's right. I wanted to ask you about the event your

company catered at the Baker Museum last Friday. It was for the opening of the Farley Bishop exhibit."

Guin felt the caterer staring at her.

"Is something wrong?" Guin asked her.

"I'm sorry. It's just that you look just like the woman in that picture, the one at the start of the exhibit. It's uncanny."

"So you were there at the Baker that evening?" Guin didn't recall seeing Caroline Williams there.

"Briefly. I had to leave early. But I saw the painting. It's you, isn't it?"

"Guilty. So you weren't there later when…" Guin didn't want to discuss the painting with the caterer.

"No. As I said, I left early. We had another private event we were catering that evening."

"But you know about the man who died."

"I do."

"I understand it was a member of your staff, a young woman named Carla, who found him."

"That's right."

"She seemed quite upset. Is she okay? It must have been quite a shock."

"You were there?"

"I was. And I was hoping to speak with Carla."

"Poor thing. She's new here, still getting the hang of things. And then to find… I told her to take a few days off."

"That was very kind of you. Do you know when she'll be back? I'd like to speak with her."

"She's scheduled to work this weekend."

"Any way I could speak with her before then?"

Caroline looked uncertain.

"I could use her help. A man's been accused of murder."

"Oh. I thought it was an accident."

"Not according to the police."

"Did they arrest someone?"

"Farley Bishop."

"The artist?"

"Yes."

"I can't believe it."

"Neither can a lot of people. I'm investigating what happened. That's why I wanted to speak with Carla. I understand you probably can't give me her phone number, but could you get in touch with her, let her know I'd like to speak with her?"

"I can let her know but…"

"You don't think she'll speak with me?"

"As I said, Carla's new here and a bit on the jumpy side."

Guin knew that firsthand.

"I'll do my best not to upset her. I just want to know what she saw."

"Have you spoken with the police?"

"I have, briefly. But… I prefer to hear what happened from an eyewitness. I'm sure you understand."

"I do. Okay. I'll let Carla know that you'd like to speak with her. But I can't promise anything."

"Understood."

"Do you have a card?"

Guin fished in her bag and pulled out her card case. She withdrew a card and handed it to the caterer.

"I'd also like to speak with anyone else who was working that evening, particularly anyone who may have interacted with Mr. Belem. He's the man who died."

"No one who was there is here right now. It's just me."

"Will any of them be in later?"

"Most of the ones who worked at the Baker only work weekends. But I'll talk to Michelle and see if any of them are working this week."

"That would be great. And you can tell them I would be willing to speak with them off the record, meaning anything they told me would be done in confidence. I won't publish their names."

A chime sounded in the kitchen.

"That's my timer," said Caroline. "Would you excuse me? I've got something in the oven that needs my attention."

"Of course," said Guin. "Thank you for your time."

"Don't go anywhere," said the caterer.

"Okay," said Guin, unsure why the caterer wanted her to stick around.

She glanced around the shop while Caroline was in the back. The walls were painted a pale pink, and there were a couple of bistro tables and chairs, no doubt for tastings. It was simple yet elegant, like Caroline Williams.

A few minutes the caterer returned bearing a small pink box.

"These are for you," she said, holding out the box to Guin.

"For me?" said Guin.

The caterer nodded.

"They're my granny's butter pecan cookies. Just made a batch this morning. Go on. Try one."

Guin opened the box and took out a cookie.

"Wow!" she said after taking a bite. "It's really moist." She wanted to ask Caroline how much butter was in there, but she didn't want to seem rude.

The caterer smiled.

"Glad you like them."

"Mm," said Guin, having taken another bite.

"I need to get back to the kitchen. I have a tea party to cater this afternoon. Good luck with your story."

Guin thanked her for the cookies and left.

She checked her phone for messages as soon as she was back outside. There was nothing that needed her immediate attention. She unlocked the Mini and got in. She had planned on heading back to Sanibel but decided to swing by the Collier County Sheriff's Office to see if Detective Romero was around instead.

As luck would have it, Detective Romero was in, but she didn't have much time. Guin said she only needed a few minutes. As the detective led Guin up to her office, Guin observed that the detective was wearing an outfit similar to the one she had on the other day. Guin wondered if it was a kind of uniform.

The detective gestured for Guin to have a seat and then went to sit behind her desk.

Guin got right down to business.

"I understand you arrested Farley Bishop."

"That is correct."

"I assume you have evidence proving he pushed Ludwig Belem down those stairs."

"We do."

"Can you tell me what you found linking him to the murder?"

"Mr. Bishop's fingerprints were found on the wheelchair."

"Anything else?"

The detective didn't reply.

"I'm not an expert," said Guin, "but typically fingerprints aren't enough to convict someone." But the fact that Bishop's fingerprints were found on the wheelchair didn't look good for the artist. "Did anyone actually see Mr. Bishop push Mr. Belem down the stairs?"

"We have several eyewitnesses who saw them together."

"But did any of them actually see Mr. Bishop push Mr. Belem?"

Again, the detective was silent.

"Were there any other prints on the wheelchair, other than Mr. Belem's and Mr. Bishop's?"

"None that we could identify."

"But there were other fingerprints."

The detective didn't comment.

"What about video footage?"

Guin tried to remember if there was a video camera on the terrace.

"As I said, we spoke with several people who saw Mr. Bishop and Mr. Belem arguing, including yourself."

"Mr. Belem argued with several people. I understand he was a bit of a provocateur."

"That may be the case, but he was seen arguing with Mr. Bishop shortly before his body was found on the terrace stairs."

"But no one actually saw Mr. Bishop push Mr. Belem down the stairs."

The detective didn't comment.

"Yet you're convinced that he did it."

"All of the evidence points to him."

"What if someone uncovers new evidence?"

The detective tilted her head and raised her eyebrows. Guin knew that look. It said, "You really think you're going to find something that the Collier County Sheriff's Office didn't?" But Guin liked a challenge.

"You know who posted his bail?"

"That information is confidential. Though you can always ask Mr. Bishop. What is your relationship to him again?"

"I interviewed him for an article."

"That's it? What about the painting? Is it typical for artists to paint portraits of the people who interview them?"

"I doubt it's typical. But Bishop isn't your typical artist. He wouldn't allow me to interview him unless I posed for him."

"How many times?"

"Just the once."

The detective looked skeptical.

"It's the truth," said Guin. "Frankly, I had no idea he was planning on painting a life-size portrait of me and hanging it in the museum."

"Truly?"

"Yup. I only found out about the painting when I got to the museum."

"That must have been quite a surprise."

"You can say that again."

The detective smiled. Guin thought she had a nice smile and wondered if it was hard being a woman detective, especially when surrounded by a bunch of men. Probably. Maybe she should talk to Ginny about doing a profile of the detective, even if the detective was in Naples. *I bet readers would be interested. Especially if Glen took some photos of her*, Guin thought.

"Getting back to Mr. Belem, I saw you talking to the young woman who found him. What did she say she saw?"

"I'm afraid I can't…"

She was interrupted by her phone. "Romero," she said, answering it. She listened and then told the caller she'd be right there. "I need to go," she told Guin, rising out of her chair.

"Of course," said Guin, getting up too.

They walked to the door, which the detective held open.

"Thank you for seeing me," Guin said.

The detective accompanied Guin to the stairs.

"I trust you can find your way out?"

Guin said that she could and watched as the detective made her way down the hall.

CHAPTER 24

Guin thought about what she had learned as she drove back to Sanibel. Though it seemed as though no one had actually seen Bishop push Ludwig Belem down the terrace stairs, things didn't look good for the artist. And if he hadn't pushed Belem, how did his fingerprints get on Belem's wheelchair? And what had Carla seen? Guin wished she could talk to the young woman—and Bishop.

She hoped that Caroline Williams would pass along the message and Carla would call her. But Guin had her doubts. Well, if she hadn't heard from Carla by tomorrow afternoon, she would call the caterer. Maybe someone else there had seen what had happened.

Guin also wanted to speak with Bennett Emerson. The museum was on her way home. But she had to interview the Farkases back on Sanibel. She would just have to return to North Naples another time.

She sighed in frustration and turned up the radio to drown out her thoughts.

Guin was waiting for Glen to pick her up when her phone rang. It was Pauline.

"Guin. Forgive me for not getting back to you sooner. I've been a bit crazed."

That seemed to be a theme.

"I understand," said Guin. "Hey, I'm actually on my way out the door. Can I call you later?"

"Actually, I was hoping you might be free for lunch tomorrow. We could meet someplace halfway if you don't want to drive to Naples."

Guin would need to write her article about the Farkases and get going on her other articles. But none of those things was urgent or would take that long. Or so she hoped. And Pauline said that she lived near the museum.

"Could we meet near the museum?"

"You planning on revisiting the scene of the crime?"

Pauline knew her too well.

"I am."

"Well, I know a darling little French place not far from the Baker. It's called Café Gourmand. You want to meet me there?"

"Sounds good. What time?"

"Twelve-thirty?"

"I'll be there."

"Wonderful. I look forward to catching up."

"Me too."

They said goodbye and Guin looked at the time. Glen would be there any minute. Should she quickly try Bennett Emerson, see if he was around before or after lunch tomorrow? Guin entered the number for the Baker and asked to be connected to the director. Lo and behold, he was in.

"Bennett Emerson."

"Mr. Emerson, this is Guin Jones with the *Sanibel-Captiva Sun-Times*. I was wondering, are you around tomorrow? I'd love to have a quick chat."

"I'm sorry, Ms. Jones, but I'm rather busy. As you can imagine, it's been all hands on deck doing damage control."

"I understand. I promise not to take up too much of your time. But it's important that I speak with you about what happened."

"As I said, Ms. Jones…"

"I know you're busy. And I'm sure you think Mr. Bishop didn't do it. I'd like to prove that he didn't. But I need your help."

Guin heard the director sigh.

"I suppose I could spare you a few minutes. Would two o'clock work?"

"Two is perfect. Thank you."

She heard a car honk. No doubt it was Glen. She hurried outside. Glen had his convertible today. She got in and handed him the box of cookies Caroline Williams had given her.

"These are for you."

"Are they your chocolate chip cookies?"

"No, they're butter pecan, made by Caroline Williams, who runs Catering by Caroline, the company that catered the event at the Baker on Friday. And they're delicious."

"You don't want them?"

"They're a bit rich for me."

Glen put the box of cookies on the back seat.

As they drove to Milton and Miriam Farkas's place on Captiva, Guin told him about her day. Fifteen minutes later, they had arrived.

The Farkas house—make that mansion—was located off of Captiva Drive, on the Pine Island Sound side of the road. There was a sign in front with the house's name, *Captivating*, and another sign warning visitors that the house was under 24-hour surveillance.

Glen drove down the driveway, parking to the side of the house, which was painted a bright yellow. Guin thought the place had to be at least 3,000 square feet. Probably more. It was not to Guin's taste, but she liked the landscaping. And she guessed it had killer views of Pine Island Sound.

They climbed the staircase leading to the large front door and rang the doorbell. The door was opened a minute later by a petite woman who was dressed like she had just hosted a luncheon for a dozen of her closest friends at the Captiva Yacht Club. Maybe she had.

"Ms. Jones?" said Mrs. Farkas.

"That's me!" said Guin cheerily. "And this is my colleague, Glen Anderson. He'll be taking the photos of you and Mr. Farkas."

Mrs. Farkas looked at him and then back at Guin.

"Please, won't you come in?"

They stepped inside, and Guin took in the place.

"You have a lovely home," she told Mrs. Farkas.

Mrs. Farkas smiled.

"Please, call me Mimi. I'll go get Mickey." She paused. "Can I get you something to drink?"

"I'm good," said Guin. "But thank you."

Mimi looked at Glen.

"I'm good too."

"Please, have a seat in the living room. I'll just be a minute."

Guin and Glen looked around. As Guin had surmised, the living area looked out onto Pine Island Sound.

"Nice view," said Glen.

"Very nice," said Guin.

A short time later, Mimi returned with her husband. He wasn't much taller than his wife and was dressed as though he had just played a round of golf.

"These are the people from the paper," Mimi explained to her husband.

"Nice to meet you," said Guin, smiling at Mr. Farkas.

Mr. Farkas didn't return the greeting or the smile.

"Why don't we chat for a few minutes and then Glen can take some pictures of the two of you?" Guin suggested.

"Would it be okay if I look around while you three chatted?" said Glen. "I'd like to find a good spot for the photographs."

"Would you like a tour?" said Mimi. "I'd be happy to show you around."

Glen looked over at Guin who shrugged.

"That would be great," said Glen.

Mimi smiled. Then she turned to her husband.

"Would you like to join us?"

"I know what the house looks like. Just get me when you're done." He headed back to his office.

"Yes, well," said Mimi. "Shall we start the tour in here? This is the living room, which, as you can see, has a marvelous view of Pine Island Sound."

Mimi led Guin and Glen around the house, giving brief descriptions of each room. The décor was eclectic, as though they couldn't decide which style to go with. There were mid-century modern touches here, a bit of coastal there, and a more masculine vibe in Mr. Farkas's office, which had a large antique wood desk, a big leather couch, and a glass-and-wood coffee table with golf magazines on it.

While it wasn't how she would have furnished the house, Guin made sure to make appreciative noises throughout the tour as Mimi clearly took pride in her home.

"Let's start by photographing the two of you in Mr. Farkas's office," Glen suggested to Mimi as they returned to the living room. "That is, if that's all right with you and Mr. Farkas."

"I'm sure he won't mind," said Mimi. "I'll just go ask him. I'll be right back."

They didn't have to wait long.

"He says it's fine," said Mimi. "Though are we dressed okay? We can go change."

"That's up to you," said Glen.

"I think you look fine," said Guin. "I like that dress, Mimi. It's almost as if you and Mr. Farkas coordinated your outfits."

Mimi laughed.

"We didn't do it on purpose. It just happens. So you really think this is okay for the paper? We can put on something more formal."

"It's really up to you," said Guin.

"How about I take a few pictures with the two of you as is, and if you don't like them, you can go change?" suggested Glen.

"Thank you," said Mimi. "Shall we?"

She led the way down the hall. Mr. Farkas looked less than thrilled. But he did what Glen told him to do, except for smiling. After taking a bunch of pictures, Glen showed them to the couple.

"What do you think?" he asked them.

"I think they're very nice, but could we take some in the living room?" said Mimi. "I just love the view in there."

"Of course," said Glen.

They returned to the living room, and Guin could see that Mimi looked more relaxed. This was clearly her favorite room. Glen took multiple shots and then showed the photos to the Farkases.

"Oh, these are very nice!" said Mimi. "Would you mind sending me some of them so I could send them to our children?"

That wasn't normal practice, but Glen said that he would.

"Shall we do the interview in here too?" said Guin.

"If that's all right," said Mimi.

Guin looked over at Mr. Farkas who shrugged. Clearly, this was his wife's show.

Guin took out her phone and opened her recording app.

"Before we begin, do I have your permission to record the interview? It's just for my playback."

Mimi said that was fine. Mr. Farkas grunted. Guin took that as a yes.

Half an hour later, Guin was done. Mimi had done most of the talking, which had been fine with Guin. She was charming and very knowledgeable about CHR and passionate about providing housing to workers and their families here on the islands.

As she walked them to the door, Mimi asked Guin when the article would be out. Guin wasn't sure but said that she would let Mimi know.

"That was relatively painless," said Glen as they drove back to Sanibel.

"Mm," said Guin. She was looking out the window.

"You okay?"

"Hm?" she said, turning towards him.

"I was saying that that went well."

"Mm," said Guin.

"Got something on your mind?"

"I was just thinking about Farley Bishop. We're about to go by his studio." The location of his studio was supposed to be a secret. But she knew Glen wouldn't tell anyone.

"You want to stop? See if he's there?"

Guin looked at him.

"You mean it?"

"You got something better to do?"

Actually, she should be getting home and transcribing her interview with Mr. and Mrs. Farkas, but she told Glen to turn left instead. A few minutes later, they arrived at Bishop's studio. His Jeep was there, but that didn't mean anything. Guin remained in the car.

"You going to get out, see if he's home?"

"I…"

"What?"

Guin didn't want to admit that she was worried that Bishop wouldn't speak to her, their last encounter having not gone well.

"Nothing."

"You want me to go with you?"

"No, stay in the car. He's probably not even there."

She got out and climbed the stairs. The door was closed, and she didn't hear any music coming from inside. She knocked on the door. No answer. She waited a few seconds and knocked again, calling Bishop's name. Still no answer. She tried the door. It was locked.

She reached into her bag and pulled out her notepad and a pen. She quickly jotted a note, asking Bishop to call her. Then she wedged the note in the door. She waited a few more seconds, to see if she heard anything. But the studio was silent. She turned and made her way back down the stairs.

"I take it he wasn't there," said Glen.

"Nope. Or else he's in the back and didn't hear me. Though I think that's unlikely. I left a note, asking him to call me."

"I'm sure he will."

"I wouldn't be."

Glen put the car into reverse, and they headed back to Guin's.

CHAPTER 25

Glen dropped Guin off and headed back to Fort Myers. They both had work to do.

Guin got herself a glass of water and headed to her office. She wanted to transcribe her interview with Mimi Farkas and bang out a first draft by that evening as she would be away most of tomorrow. Fortunately, neither took that long. She had only spoken to Mimi briefly and already knew what she wanted to say. However, she would wait until the next day to send Ginny the profile.

Proud of herself for finishing an assignment in record time, Guin treated herself to a fried chicken dinner from the Pecking Order, complete with coleslaw and cornbread. She then curled up on the couch and watched an Italian rom-com she found on Netflix.

□

The next morning Guin made herself coffee, took her mug to her office, and reviewed the profile she had written the night before. *Not bad*, she said to herself. She read it through one more time and then sent it off to Ginny.

It wasn't yet eight o'clock. She had time to go to the beach before she needed to head to North Naples, but now she was in work mode. The beach would have to wait until that evening.

Guin opened the article she had started about the Sanibel

Sea School. She was about to dive in when she stopped. She should take a shower and get dressed first. After all, she didn't want to show up for lunch or to the Baker looking like a wet poodle.

As soon as she was dressed, she returned to her office and reread what she had written about the Sea School. A couple of hours later, she had a solid first draft and her hair was nearly dry. It was time to head to North Naples.

The drive to Café Gourmand took Guin over an hour. But she had been expecting traffic and had left herself plenty of time. She found a place to park in the small lot and headed to the restaurant. Pauline was sitting at one of the outdoor tables, an iced tea in front of her. She smiled when she saw Guin.

"Have you been waiting long?" Guin asked her.

"No, I just got here a few minutes ago. Have a seat."

Guin sat in one of the metal bistro chairs and looked around. The place reminded her of Jean-Luc's. She wondered if the food was similar too. She picked up a menu and glanced at it.

"The food here is delicious," said Pauline. "You really can't go wrong. Though I recommend the crepes."

A server came over and asked Guin what she'd like to drink. Guin ordered a sparkling water with lime.

"So, how are you?" Pauline asked after the server had left.

"Good!"

"You like living on Sanibel?"

"I do, very much."

Pauline looked skeptical.

"What?"

"I just can't picture it. I always thought of you as a city girl."

"I could say the same of you. And you forget, I lived in Connecticut for years."

"Yes, but you worked in New York. And living in Fairfield County isn't the same as living on an island."

"Manhattan's an island."

Pauline made a face.

"You know what I mean."

"I do," said Guin, smiling at her old boss. "And honestly, if you had asked me five years ago where I'd be today, I would have never imagined I'd be living in Southwest Florida."

"Same. You ever think about moving back?"

"Occasionally. But then I go visit my family up north and am happy to be back on the plane to RSW," RSW being the airport code for Southwest Florida International Airport in Fort Myers.

Pauline smiled at her.

"How are your parents and your brother?"

"They're good. My mother and stepfather actually rented a place in Naples for a couple of months. They're flying down any day now. They were supposed to be here on the first, but they had a wedding up north and then my stepfather sprained his ankle."

"How do you feel about them being here?"

Pauline knew about Guin's somewhat strained relationship with her mother.

"I'm fine with it. Not like I have to see them all the time. My parents are good at keeping busy."

"So, what's it like being the general assignment reporter for a smalltown paper? I have to say, I always thought you'd wind up at someplace like *Inc.* or the *Times*."

"I used to think so too."

"So, what happened?"

"Life happened. But I enjoy working for the *San-Cap Sun-Times*. I have a great boss. Though not as great as you," Guin quickly added. "And I get to write about all sorts of different things and meet different people." However, Guin found herself increasingly writing about the same things and the same people.

"Uh-huh."

Clearly Pauline wasn't buying it.

The server came over with Guin's sparkling water and asked if they were ready to order. Guin said she needed a minute and picked up the menu again.

"What are you going to get?" she asked her friend.

"The salad Niçoise. What are you thinking of getting?"

"The *campagnarde* crepe sounds good."

"It is."

"You've had it?"

"Paul's had it, and I had a bite. I told you, everything here is good. Shall we order?"

Guin nodded, and Pauline signaled to their server.

"And what about you?" asked Guin, after they had ordered. "How do you like working for the *Times*?"

"I enjoy it. By the way, I apologize about the other day. I thought I told you I was going to be on Sanibel. Though we really didn't have time to socialize. We were on a very tight schedule."

"I understand, and I forgive you."

Pauline smiled.

"Thank you."

"So which places did you include?"

"The Shell Museum, Tarpon Bay Explorers, the Historical Village, the Bubble Room…"

The usual places guidebooks and articles recommended people visit. But Guin didn't say anything.

"When will the article run?"

"Not sure. It's up to the editor. They no doubt have a stockpile of '36 hours in' pieces."

"Speaking of editors, do you happen to know a Bill Hendricks at the *Times*? He's a deputy managing editor there."

"The name sounds familiar. Why?"

"My mother is good friends with his wife and wants me to speak with him."

"Oh? About a job?"

"She thinks I'm wasting my talents here and should work for a proper paper or magazine."

"I don't disagree."

Guin frowned.

"Tell me, how many people read the *Sanibel Sun*?"

"It's the *Sanibel-Captiva Sun-Times*, and I'm not sure. But I suspect at least a few thousand."

"If you wrote for the *New York Times*, your articles would reach a few million people."

Pauline sounded like her mother.

"In any case, you should at least talk to Bill."

Guin was saved having to reply by the arrival of their meal. As they ate, Guin asked Pauline about her husband and people they knew.

"That was delicious," said Guin as the server removed their plates.

"Do you have room for dessert?" asked Pauline. "Their sweet crepes and opera cake are to die for. And the chocolate mousse isn't bad either."

"You going to have something?" Guin asked her.

"I shouldn't. But you go ahead."

Guin was tempted. French sweets were her weakness. Especially opera cake. But it was nearly time for her meeting with Bennett Emerson.

"I need to get going. I'm meeting with the director of the Baker Museum at two, and I don't want to be late."

"You go. I'll take care of the check."

"Don't be silly."

Pauline gave Guin her best schoolmarm look.

"At least let me leave you money for the tip."

"You can pay next time. Go."

Guin knew better than to argue with her former boss.

"Okay. Thank you."

She got up and walked to her car.

Guin arrived at the administrative building at two minutes past two and made her way to Bennett Emerson's office. His door was ajar, and Guin heard him speaking to someone.

She knocked and waited for him to answer. When he didn't, she poked her head inside. He was on the phone. He held up a finger, indicating that he would be off in a minute. Guin mouthed that she would wait outside.

Several minutes later, the director opened the door.

"Sorry about that," he said. "Won't you come in?"

Guin followed him inside, gazing around his office. The shelves were crammed with books, mostly art books, as well as some framed photos. And the walls were hung with museum posters, probably exhibits he had curated or overseen.

"Please, have a seat," he said.

Guin sat.

"So, what can I do for you?"

"I wanted to ask you about Farley Bishop."

"Ask away."

"I understand you were responsible for getting Mr. Bishop to agree to the retrospective."

"Did Alexandra tell you that?"

"She did. How did you persuade him to allow you to show his work? I read that he had sworn off museum and gallery shows."

"That was a long time ago. People change."

"But surely other museum directors and curators had approached him over the years. Why the Baker?"

"Farley trusted me."

"Why? Had you worked with him before?"

"In a sense. He was an early mentor of mine."

"He mentored you?"

Had Bennett Emerson been an artist?

"I wasn't always the director of a museum," he said.

"I assume you'd been a curator."

"And before that, I was an aspiring artist. It was a long time ago but..."

His face took on a dreamy look.

"I had wanted to be an artist since I was a boy. I loved to draw and was never happier than with a crayon or pencil and a piece of paper.

In high school, I dreamed about going to art school in New York or Rhode Island. But my parents insisted I apply only to traditional colleges, and I obeyed. I wound up going where my father had gone. Probably the only reason I got in. And was deeply unhappy there.

"One of my suite mates, Andy, was from New York. One spring vacation, I went home with him, and I met his older brother, Jack. Jack was an artist, living in Tribeca. He's the one who introduced me to Farley."

"How did Farley become your mentor?"

"Jack took me to Farley's studio. His work was a revelation. I told him I had never seen anything like it. You have to understand, I had led a rather sheltered life. I told Farley that I had wanted to be an artist and go to art school. But my parents had insisted I go to college instead.

"He asked me to draw him something. I was nervous, but I did. He looked at what I had drawn and told me that I had talent. Though how he could tell that from one drawing... In any case, he told me that if I decided to take up art, he would be happy to mentor me. I thought he was just being polite. But he wasn't.

"On the way back to school, I told Andy I was going to drop out of school and go live in New York. He told me I was crazy. But my mind was made up. When the semester was over, I went back to New York and asked Farley to be my teacher.

"I didn't have much money and didn't know anyone in New York other than Farley and Jack. When I told Farley that, he said I could crash at his studio. It had a small bedroom and bathroom and there was a kitchenette as well.

"Those were some of the happiest days of my life."

Guin couldn't help feeling that the director's story sounded familiar, but she didn't know why.

"That's amazing," she said. "And very generous of Farley."

"He was very generous to young artists, mentoring them and introducing them to his famous friends."

"Like Rauschenberg?"

The director smiled.

"And others."

"So how did you go from being an artist to becoming a curator?"

The director's face turned wistful.

"Despite Farley's ministrations, I realized rather quickly that I wasn't very good. Oh, I was all right. But I was never going to achieve the kind of acclaim that people like Farley and Bob had. And Farley was experiencing some personal problems."

"Personal problems?"

"Farley's wife wasn't thrilled about all the time he was spending at his studio."

"With you?"

"Farley was rarely at home. And they had a young child. But Farley had always put his art first. Even before I entered the picture. But me living at Farley's studio was a bridge too far for Judith. She insisted Farley kick me out."

"I take it he refused."

"He did. And Judith left him, taking their daughter with her. I felt responsible and told Farley I couldn't stay. He told me I was being ridiculous. That Judith had been threatening to leave him for years. But my mind was made up."

"So you left? Where did you go?"

"I had made a few friends and stayed with one of them for a while. I couldn't go back home. And I knew I'd never make it as an artist. After some soul searching, I got a job at a gallery, went back to school, and got a degree in Art History.

"I liked working in the gallery, but it didn't pay that well. But I knew that I wanted to be around art. So after I graduated, I got a master's degree in Museum Studies. And I eventually landed a job as an assistant curator at the Art Institute of Chicago. And the rest, as they say, is history."

"And you stayed in touch with Mr. Bishop?"

"I did."

"Did you ever try to arrange an exhibit of his work at one of the museums you worked at before you came to the Baker?"

"I did, but it never happened. The timing was never right. Then came the lawsuit. And Farley swore his work would never grace the walls of a museum again."

"Yet you managed to convince him to show his work at the Baker."

"As I said, people change. I had been wanting to host a retrospective of Farley's work for years. And technically, I could have once I got to the Baker. But I didn't want to do it without his permission.

"Then one day he showed me some new pieces he had been working on. They were nothing like his previous works. But that was Farley for you. I said it was a shame no one would ever see them and convinced him to allow the Baker to show them. It was supposed to be just a small exhibit…"

"But it morphed into a retrospective."

Bennett Emerson smiled.

"It took a bit of arm bending, but Farley finally agreed. Though he got to pick which of the new paintings to include."

"What about his older paintings?"

"Alexandra was in charge of that."

"Did she leave out the paintings he was accused of copying on purpose?"

"How much do you know about the history of art, Ms. Jones?"

"I confess, not a whole lot."

"Well, if you know anything about art, you know that many artists have similar styles. Sometimes it's intentional, other times not."

"I take it you don't think Mr. Bishop intentionally copied that artist's work."

"Absolutely not. Willem Budge was a mediocre talent at best. If anyone did any copying, it would have been Budge."

Guin didn't say anything.

"So what happens to the exhibit now that Mr. Bishop has been arrested? Will it need to close?"

"Certainly not. Ticket sales have gone through the roof. The public loves nothing more than a good scandal."

"But that art critic…"

"Was an odious man who loved to take artists down a peg. I'm not saying he deserved to die, but the art world is better off without people like him."

"I take it you didn't like him."

"Let's just say I didn't find his column as amusing as some."

"Was he planning on giving the exhibit a bad review?"

"I have no idea. But I wouldn't put it past him."

"Did the two of you talk about the exhibit? I saw the two of you together."

"I don't recall what we discussed. I spoke with a lot of people that evening."

"Do you happen to know what he and Mr. Bishop talked about?"

"I have no idea."

"Do you know where Mr. Bishop is now? I heard he was released on bail, and I'd like to speak with him."

The director was stopped from replying by the ringing of his telephone.

"I should get this," he said.

Guin scowled. Why was it that a phone always rang just when she was about to get the answer to an important question?

"Bennett Emerson," said the director. "Hold on." He covered the mouthpiece with his hand and looked at Guin. "Do you mind?"

Guin got up.

"Thank you for your time. And if you hear from Mr. Bishop or know how to contact him, please ask him to call me." She quickly removed a card from her bag and placed it on Bennett Emerson's desk. "My number's on my card."

She saw the director waiting for her to leave and left.

Alexandra Barnes's office was next door. Should she see if she was in? The door was ajar, and the light was on. She knocked softly, but there was no answer. She leaned in to see if she could hear anything. She thought she heard jazz music. She knocked again, a little louder this time, and poked her head inside. The curator was at her desk, staring at her computer.

"Ms. Barnes?"

The curator turned, looked at Guin, and frowned.

"I'm sorry to disturb you. Do you have a minute?"

"I'm rather busy."

"I just had a quick question."

The curator didn't reply. Guin took that as permission to continue.

"Do you know how I can get in touch with Mr. Bishop?"

"Farley's not interested in talking to reporters."

"Does that mean you know where he is?"

No reply.

"Well, if you see or speak with him, would you ask him to call me?"

"I told you…"

"I know. He's not interested in speaking with reporters. But he knows my paper won't publish anything without his permission. Ginny, my boss, promised him." Though Guin hated that Ginny had made that promise and wasn't sure it still held. "Tell him I'm interested in hearing his side of the story."

"I'll let him know. Now if you would excuse me?"

"Of course," said Guin.

"And close the door behind you."

CHAPTER 26

Guin headed over to the Baker Museum. Might as well have a look around while she was here. She went up to the third floor and walked through the exhibit, getting looks from visitors as she did. She ignored them and headed to the terrace. It was a clear afternoon, and Guin could see for miles. It would be a great spot to watch the sun set.

She went over to the stairs. You couldn't see them unless you were standing right next to them. Most people probably didn't even know they were there. Though anyone who worked at the museum knew they were and so did the catering staff.

Guin slowly made her way down, stopping at the first landing, where Belem's body had been found. She knelt, looking for…? She wasn't sure what. But there was nothing to see other than some scuff marks. The police, no doubt, had gone over the stairs, bagging any possible evidence.

She continued down to the second floor. There was another smaller terrace and a glass-enclosed event space. She tried the door, but it was locked. Had the door been unlocked the night of the preview?

She made her way down to the first floor. In front of her were several parking spots, some filled with cars. And to her right was the loading dock. This must have been where the caterers had parked their van and staged everything.

Guin looked back up at the stairs. It would have been

easy for someone to have gone down them and disappeared into the night. Is that what whoever had pushed Ludwig Belem had done?

Guin searched the area, but she didn't find anything. She went back up the stairs to the third floor. There was no one on the terrace. She looked to see if there was a camera anywhere, but she didn't see one. However, that didn't mean there wasn't one somewhere.

She went inside, passing another stairway, a set of restrooms, and a gallery space before returning to the entrance to the exhibit and the main staircase. She looked back at the entrance to the exhibit. There were a half-dozen people looking at the portrait of her. She remembered what Bennett Emerson had said about people snapping up tickets.

She went down the main staircase to the first floor and headed outside. She walked over to the new wing, where the terrace was, and looked up. You couldn't really see the terrace from there. She walked around to the loading dock again and looked up. Then she retraced her steps and headed back to the administrative building.

Guin heard her phone buzzing on the passenger seat as she drove back to Sanibel. She glanced down and saw that it was Glen.

"Hey," she said, picking up. "I'm on the road. What's up?"

"Where are you?"

"I'm heading home from Naples. I was just at the Baker Museum."

"You find out anything?"

"I'll tell you later, after I get home. You know I don't like talking on the phone while I'm driving." Yet here she was, talking on the phone while driving.

"You want to stop at my place? There's something I want to ask you."

"Just tell me now."

"I'd rather do it in person. Where are you?"

"I'm about to hit Estero."

"Okay, I'll see you soon."

"I didn't say I'd stop by."

But Glen had already hung up.

Guin parked in Glen's driveway and walked to the front door. She had a key, but she still felt weird about using it. She rang the doorbell instead. A minute later Glen opened the door.

"Did you lose the key already?"

"No, I just… It feels weird to just let myself in."

"You'll get used to it. You want to try? I'll close the door and…"

"Just let me in," Guin said, putting her hand on the door to stop him from closing it.

She stepped inside, and Glen closed the door behind her.

"So, what did you want to ask me?"

"You want something to drink?"

"I'll take a glass of water."

She followed Glen into the kitchen and watched as he filled a glass with water.

"Here," he said, handing it to her.

Guin took a sip.

"So?" she said.

"Remember that guy I told you about, the photographer?"

"Sam Elliott?"

"That's the one."

"What about him?"

"He called me again."

"And?"

Was Glen nervous?

"He asked if I could help him out again."

"So? Did you say you'd help him out? What does he need you to do for him?"

"He wanted to know if I could shoot a party for him this weekend."

"Don't you have a wedding to shoot on Saturday?"

"I do. This was for Sunday. Specifically Sunday night. Valentine's Day."

He was looking expectantly at Guin.

"What did you tell him?"

"I told him I needed to talk to my significant other first."

Guin liked that he referred to her as his *significant other*. She wasn't a huge fan of *girlfriend*. It seemed so high school.

"You want to do it?"

"Not if you don't want me to."

"You know I'm not a fan of Valentine's Day."

"I know, but I was planning on making you a special dinner."

"You can make me a special dinner another night."

"I know, but I have that wedding to shoot on Saturday and…"

"I'll live. So, who's hosting the party?"

Glen looked decidedly uncomfortable.

"A local matchmaking service. It's a singles party. They're holding it at this new wine bar in Naples."

"Why doesn't Sam want to shoot it?"

"It's not that he doesn't want to. It's that he promised his girlfriend he'd take her away this weekend. They're not getting back until late on Sunday."

"Then why did he take the job?"

"He spaced."

"That man really needs a partner and/or an office manager."

"I know. So you're really okay with me doing it? You could come with me. It sounds like a cool place."

"Just how I want to spend Valentine's Day, with a bunch of horny singles getting drunk at a wine bar."

Glen smiled. Then he turned serious.

"You sure you're okay with it?"

"As long as he's paying you good money."

"He is. He's not even taking a commission this time."

"Awfully generous of him."

"I think he was desperate."

"Just make sure those hot single women know you're taken."

Glen smiled again.

"I'll wear a tag that says TAKEN."

Guin laughed.

"You don't have to go that far."

"Speaking of far, come here."

Guin stepped closer, and he pulled her into him.

"Thanks for being so understanding."

"So is that what you wanted to ask me?" she said, taking a step back.

"It was."

"Good. You had me worried."

"Sorry. So, how did things go at the Baker?"

Guin told him about her meeting with Bennett Emerson. Then she said she should be getting home. Glen tried to convince her to stay, but she knew what would happen if she did, and told him she had work to do. Plus the cats would be pissed if they didn't get their dinner.

However, when she got home, Guin didn't feel like working. She hadn't gone for a walk that morning, and she needed to stretch her legs. She changed and headed down to the beach.

It was breezy by the Gulf, but Guin didn't mind. She closed her eyes and took a deep breath, slowly releasing it. She did it again. Then she opened her eyes and headed west. As she walked she scanned the shore for shells. But the sand was nearly bare.

She walked for half an hour, then she turned around and headed home, stopping to watch a squadron of brown pelicans overhead.

When she got back, Guin made herself some scrambled eggs and toast for dinner. As she ate, she thought about what Bennett Emerson had told her and hoped that Farley Bishop would call. She wondered where he was. Could he be staying with the director? The director had crashed at Bishop's studio when he had needed a place to say. Seemed right somehow that Bishop would crash at the director's now.

Guin wondered if Joel had spoken with Bishop again. She should ask Ginny. She sent her boss a text and then went to get a cookie. As she bit into it, she realized she hadn't heard from Carla or the caterer. She would call over there in the morning.

The next morning, Guin sat at her computer doing research. She looked up Bennett Emerson. He had had quite the career. Even though he didn't make it as an artist, he had an impressive resume, having worked at the Art Institute of Chicago and the Massachusetts Museum of Contemporary Art, known as MASS MoCA, before coming to the Baker.

Next she went to *Art World* to read more of Ludwig Belem's columns. She had read a few before, more like skimmed them. But after speaking with Pauline, Alexandra Barnes, and Bennett Emerson, she decided she should read a few more.

She entered Belem's name into the search box on *Art World*'s website. As the screen began to fill, a headline caught her eye: "*Art World* mourns the death of one of its own." Guin immediately clicked on it.

The article was about Ludwig Belem. He had been only sixty-five but had looked much older. It made no mention of the cause of death, just stated that he had died while in

Naples, Florida, on assignment. No mention of what the assignment was.

The piece wasn't long, and Guin quickly read through it. Then she read it a second time. She had had no idea that Belem had been an artist before becoming an art critic. That was interesting. As was the fact that he had become an art critic after an accident had left him paralyzed from the waist down.

There was a photograph of Belem with the article, clearly taken many years ago, likely before he had been paralyzed or shortly after. It looked familiar. Though Guin was sure she hadn't seen a photo of Belem before.

She clicked on a recent column. No photo. She clicked on an older one. Again, no photo. She wondered if it was because he didn't wish to be recognized. But Bennett Emerson and Alexandra Barnes, as well as Pauline, had recognized him.

Guin scrolled through the search results to see when Belem's first column or article appeared in the publication. The oldest article she found—he wasn't given a column until later—was from the fall of 2000. She wondered when Belem had been injured. She would do a separate search after she read a few of his pieces.

She picked an article at random and began to read. Belem clearly knew how to write—and dish it out. It was quickly apparent that he didn't think much of the artist's work. But he wrote about it in such a clever, witty way that Guin couldn't help smiling. However, she doubted the artist had found Belem's critique amusing.

She clicked on another article. Belem hadn't thought much of this artist's work either. Guin read a few more of Belem's pieces. He didn't dislike all of the work he reviewed, but Guin had a feeling that he had disliked the majority. And it wasn't just living artists Belem panned. He was equally hard on dead artists and curators.

Guin wondered if Belem had had an axe to grind with the art world. It sounded that way from some of his critiques. The *Art World* obituary mentioned that he had started his career as an artist. Had his work been savaged by curators and other artists?

She opened a new tab and typed *Ludwig Belem artist* into the search box. But only his articles for *Art World* were listed. Nothing about his own work or an exhibit. But maybe that was because his days as an artist preceded the internet. Or maybe his artwork had been nothing to write about.

She returned to *Art World* and read more of his columns. Why, she wondered, did the magazine give a column to someone who disliked most of what he saw? Then again, newspapers hired opinion columnists with differing points of view. And she had a feeling that people enjoyed Belem's acerbic wit. She had to admit, she did. Though maybe that was because she wasn't a fan of contemporary art.

Guin sat back in her chair and stared at her monitor. The photograph of Belem was still bothering her. Where had she seen it before?

She did an image search for *Ludwig Belem*. But all she found was the photo of him in the *Art World* obit and a photo of him, really a group shot, taken at *Art World*'s fiftieth anniversary party. Guin frowned. Who else besides Bennett Emerson and Alexandra Barnes might know something about Belem? She immediately thought of Pauline and picked up her phone to call her, hoping she'd be up.

As luck would have it, she was.

"Guin! That's so funny you called. I was just about to call you!"

"You were?"

"Yes. I asked a colleague about Bill Hendricks. He said Bill was a good guy. Did you know that he manages the Business section?"

"I did." Guin had looked him up.

"You should definitely call him. With your business background, you're a shoo-in."

"The world is full of business reporters, Pauline. And I don't even know if there are any openings."

"The *Times* is always looking for good reporters."

"What if there's a hiring freeze?"

"I haven't heard of one. What are you so afraid of? The worst thing that can happen is they don't hire you and you keep doing what you're doing."

Pauline had a point.

"Just call him."

"I should email him first."

"Fine. Write to him. You've got nothing to lose."

"You sound like my mother."

"Well, she gave birth to you, so she can't be all bad."

Guin smiled.

"So, why were you calling?"

"I just came across Ludwig Belem's obit in *Art World*. I didn't know he'd been an artist. Did you?"

"No. I've only known him as an art critic."

"You know anything about his personal life?"

"No. We didn't fraternize. In fact, I got the impression he was a loner."

Guin could picture that. The man didn't seem to like people.

"Do you know anything about his accident, the one that put him in a wheelchair? It was before he became a critic."

"Again, I only know him from his time at *Art World*. Though… I think I heard someone say he had been hit by a cab. I'd say it must have been driven by an artist whose career he had ruined, but you say the accident occurred before he traded his paintbrush for a poison pen, yes?"

"That's what I read. So you don't know anything about him prior to joining *Art World*?"

"Nothing at all. Why the interest?"

"Curiosity, I guess. Do a lot of art critics start out as artists? I'm sure they must study art. Or maybe they're failed artists. Those who can't do write about it?"

"Interesting theory. Some critics may have started out as or aspired to be artists but couldn't make it. You think that's why Belem is so vicious? Failed artist lashes out at art world that spurned him? Come to think of it, Hitler wanted to be an artist. But he was rejected by the Vienna Academy of Fine Arts. Twice. And look how he turned out."

"I guess we should be glad Belem confined his wrath to artists and curators."

"Indeed."

"I'm still curious as to why I can't find anything about him prior to 2000."

"Is that when he started writing for *Art World*?"

"It is. Another thing, there's a photograph of Belem in the *Art World* obit. I think it might have been taken before his accident. He looks much younger. And I can't stop thinking I've seen it before. But I couldn't find a similar photo of Belem online. Could I send you the link to the obit and have you take a look? Maybe it will jog your memory."

"Go ahead and send it. But I doubt I'll be able to help you."

"Just take a look. You never know. Maybe you saw an exhibit of his work at some gallery way back when."

The thought made Guin think of Owen. He owned a gallery. And he'd been living in New York since the nineties. She would send him the link too, see what he knew about Belem. But first she would send the link to Pauline.

CHAPTER 27

While Guin was waiting to hear back from Pauline and Owen—and Farley Bishop—she decided to send an email to Bill Hendricks. She began to type but stopped. What should she say to him? That her mother was friendly with his wife and told her she should write to him? She frowned. Would he even know who she was? He must receive dozens of emails from people looking for a job, mentioning this person or that. Indeed, you couldn't get your foot in the door at a place like the *New York Times* without knowing someone.

She picked up her phone to call her mother and then put it back down. She wasn't in the mood to get into it with her. Then she heard Pauline in her head and picked up the phone again.

Guin was preparing to leave her mother a message when she answered.

"Guin! What a pleasant surprise. We were just talking about you."

"Who's we?"

"Beryl and I. Did you write to Bill?"

"Not yet. That's actually why I'm calling. Does Bill even know who I am?"

"Of course he knows who you are."

"I mean, other than that I'm your daughter. Does he know I'm a journalist?"

"Of course he knows you're a journalist. I made Beryl tell him all about you."

"And he said he was interested in speaking with me?"

There was silence. Just as Guin thought.

"I'm sure he'd be delighted to talk to you. You have so much in common."

"Uh-huh. I'm sure he gets tons of emails and calls from people who think he'd be delighted to talk to them. I'm just…"

Her mother interrupted.

"You're not just anyone, Guinivere. You're an award-winning reporter. And just as good as any of those people writing for the *Times*."

"Thanks for the vote of confidence, but those awards were given to me a long time ago and…"

"Just write to the man. How hard can that be? You write for a living. Or better yet, call him."

"I'm sure he's very busy."

"Beryl will make sure he knows to expect your call."

"I think I should email him first."

"Whatever. Just promise me that you'll reach out to him already."

Guin sighed.

"I promise. Though even if by some miracle the *Times* offers me a job, it doesn't mean I'm moving back to New York. They have reporters all over the world."

"Whatever you say, dear."

Time to change the subject.

"How's Philip doing?"

"Much better, and he's insisting we fly down first thing Monday."

"Monday as in this Monday?"

"Yes, dear. And I made us a reservation at Ridgway for Wednesday."

Ridgway Bar & Grill was a popular restaurant in Old

Naples, not far from where Guin's mother and stepfather had rented an apartment.

"For dinner?"

"Yes, for dinner."

"Is Glen invited?"

"Are you still seeing him?"

Did she think they had broken up in the last few days?

"Yes, I'm still seeing him."

"Then bring him along."

"Thanks."

"You're welcome."

"So, you don't need me to meet you at the airport Monday or at the apartment?"

"We have a car service getting us, and Harriet said she'd give us a hand. We're having dinner with her and her new beau Tuesday."

Harriet was a friend of her mother's who lived in Naples.

"All righty then. Glen and I'll see you Wednesday. Just let me know if anything changes."

"Of course!"

"What time?"

"Seven fifteen."

"We'll be there."

"Good. I need to run. Goodbye, dear."

"Goodbye, Mom."

Guin ended the call and checked her phone. She had heard a message come in while she and her mother were talking. It was an email from Pauline, letting Guin know that she was nearly positive that she had not seen an exhibit of Ludwig Belem's work and she couldn't check because she had chucked all of her old files before moving to Naples.

Oh well. Maybe she would have better luck with Owen. She wished he'd write back to her. But he was no doubt busy at the gallery.

She thought about calling Caroline Williams, to see if she

had had any luck reaching Carla. Or maybe now that it was Friday, Carla would be there, as would some of the other servers who had worked at the Baker event. But it was early yet. She'd call over there later, assuming she hadn't heard from anyone.

Unable to make any progress with the Belem/Bishop piece, Guin decided to work on her other articles. Though none of them were as interesting—or as frustrating. The latter a good thing.

She was working on her article about upcoming lectures at the Shell Museum when she received a text from her mother.

"I just spoke to Beryl. Bill will be on the lookout for an email from you."

"Thanks," Guin wrote back.

She thought about writing to Hendricks now, but she was in the middle of her piece on the Shell Museum. She would finish that and then write to him.

Guin was proud of herself for getting another article done. Then again, writing about the Shell Museum was easy. She had written about the place a dozen times and loved attending lectures there. She would have written her review of the new Asian restaurant too, but she would need to go there at least a couple of times before writing about the place.

She picked up her phone and called Shelly.

"How do you feel about Asian food?" Guin asked her.

"Love it. Why?"

"You want to check out the new Asian place with me?"

"Bamboo?"

"Unless there's another one."

"I'm game. When?"

"You and Steve have plans tonight?"

"Not that I'm aware of, but I'll check. Glen coming?"

"I haven't asked him, but I'm sure he will."

"By the way, Steve and I are having a special Valentine's Day-themed BBQ on Sunday if you and Glen are available."

Steve and Shelly were known for their Sunday barbeques. Steve would grill up whatever he caught fishing that weekend as well as the special brats he ordered every fall and winter from the butcher in Wisconsin where he grew up.

"Though now that I think about it, didn't you say that Glen had something special planned for Valentine's Day?"

"He was going to make me dinner, but he got a gig."

"He's not spending V-Day with you?"

"I may see him during the day."

"Huh. And you're okay with that?"

"I told him I didn't care. You know how I feel about Valentine's Day."

"I know how you felt about it in the past. But now you have Glen! Don't you want to spend the evening with him?"

"We see each other all the time. It's no big deal, Shell. Really."

"You're so unromantic."

"I'm plenty romantic. I'm just not a fan of made up holidays designed to sell flowers, chocolate, and jewelry."

"Watch it! I count on people buying jewelry for Valentine's Day. And what have you got against flowers and chocolate?"

"Nothing. It's just Valentine's Day and I don't have a great history if you recall."*

"Right. I forgot about that."

Guin wished that she could. Though she had long forgiven Birdy for what he had put her through.

"Anyway, I'll ask Steve about tonight, and let me know

---

* See Book 7, *A Perilous Proposal.*

if you want to come to the barbeque."

They ended the call and Guin rang Glen.

"I was just thinking about you," he said.

"What were you thinking?"

"That I missed you."

"Aw. Though it's not like we haven't seen each other in days."

"I know. It's just that we've been spending so much time together that when you're not around it feels…"

"It feels what?"

"Like a part of me is missing."

"I know how you feel."

"Do you?"

Guin thought for a minute.

"I do."

"So maybe we should…"

But Guin wasn't ready to have that conversation. At least not right now.

"Hey, are you free tonight?" she asked, changing the subject. "I need to write a review of the Asian place that just opened, Bamboo. I did take out from there the other night, but I should go there. I asked Shelly and Steve to join us. Can you make it?"

"Free Asian food? Count me in."

Guin smiled.

"Excellent. You want to come here and we can drive over together? Or you can meet me there. Up to you."

"I'll come to you."

"Okay. I'll text you what time as soon as I've heard back from Shelly. She just needed to double-check with Steve."

Guin heard back from Shelly an hour later. She and Steve were in. What time? Guin suggested they meet at the restaurant at seven and asked Shelly to make the reservation. That way the restaurant wouldn't be expecting her.

Guin was having a late lunch when she received an email from Owen. She opened it and began to read. She read it again and then called him. He answered right away. They spoke for several minutes. As soon as she hung up, Guin texted Ginny, telling her to call ASAP.

CHAPTER 28

Guin was back in her office, working, when she saw Ginny's name flash up on her phone.

"What's so urgent?" Ginny asked.

"Are you sitting down?"

"I am."

"Are you driving?"

"No, I'm at the office."

"Okay. You're not going to believe what I just found out."

"I'm on the edge of my seat."

"Ludwig Belem is really Willem Budge."

"Come again?"

"Ludwig Belem, the critic for *Art World*, is in fact Willem Budge, the painter who sued Farley Bishop for plagiarism."

"I know who Ludwig Belem and Willem Budge are, Guinivere. What do you mean they're the same?

"I mean they're the same person."

"And you know this how?"

"My brother-in-law, Owen, who runs a gallery in Chelsea, told me. I sent him the obit of Ludwig Belem that I found on *Art World*'s website and asked him if he knew that Belem had been an artist and if he'd ever come across Belem's artwork. He didn't know anything about Belem being an artist, but he did some digging and discovered that Ludwig Belem was Willem Budge!"

"How does he know that?"

"Owen was an art student in New York when the lawsuit was going on and knew both Bishop and Budge. Not personally, but he had seen them and their work. And he said the photo in the obit was of Budge."

"It could just be that Belem resembled Budge."

"I thought that too. And so did Owen, at first. So he sent the obit to one of his former instructors who knew everyone in the New York contemporary art world back then. And his instructor said that the man in the photo was Willem Budge."

"So maybe *Art World* used the wrong photo."

"They didn't. Owen's instructor knows the editor. He said the photo was from Belem's personnel file. I'm telling you, they're the same guy. Even their names are the same. Okay, not the same but anagrams. This is huge, Ginny!"

"But why change his name and hide his past?"

"I don't know. Maybe he wanted a fresh start. The point is, if Belem really is Budge then…"

"You just said that he was."

"You know what I mean. Anyway, the point is, if Owen's former instructor realized that Belem was Budge, it's likely Bishop did too and…"

Ginny stopped her.

"Farley didn't kill him."

"I know he's a friend, but you have to…"

"I've known Farley Bishop for years," said Ginny, cutting Guin off again. "Is he cantankerous? Yes. Is he a killer? No."

Guin knew better than to argue with her boss.

"I'm not saying he killed Belem—or Budge. I'm just saying we should talk to him. Find out if he knew they were the same."

Guin paused. *Did Detective Romero know that Belem was Budge? Should she ask her? Though if she didn't know, Guin was giving her another reason that Bishop might have wanted to send Belem down the stairs.*

"You should talk to Joel. See if he can reach Bishop. Tell him it's urgent that we speak with him."

"I'll ask Joel but…"

"I understand Bishop may not want to talk to me because I'm a reporter. But maybe he'll talk to you."

"I run a newspaper, Guinivere. I doubt Farley will talk to me either."

"But you're his friend. What if Joel tells him that anything he says to us would be off the record?"

"I doubt that that will make a difference."

"Would you at least ask Joel to reach out to him? Have him tell Bishop we just want to help."

Ginny sighed.

"I'll ask but…"

"Thank you."

"Don't thank me yet."

"Okay. By the way, I should have the Shell Museum story for you very soon."

"Excellent. And the restaurant review?"

"Next week."

"Okay. I need to go."

They ended the call, and Guin called Catering by Caroline. She really needed to speak to Carla, find out what the young woman had seen.

As luck would have it, Caroline was in. Guin asked her if she had gotten in touch with Carla. But Caroline said that she hadn't. She'd been too busy, and Carla hadn't been in.

"Will she be in later?" Guin remembered Caroline saying that Carla was supposed to work that weekend.

"Hold on. Let me check with Michelle."

Guin waited.

"According to Michelle, she's on the schedule for tonight."

"Do you know when she'll be there?"

"In an hour or so."

"Could you ask her to call me? My number's on the card I gave you. But I can give it to you now if it's easier."

"It's going to be crazy later."

"Please? I promise not to take much of her time."

"Fine. Give me your number. But I can't promise you she'll call."

"I understand."

Guin gave the caterer her number.

"And you say Carla should be there in an hour or so?"

"She should be, along with the rest of tonight's crew."

If only Guin lived closer. Though if she left now, she could get to the caterer's in just over an hour. If she didn't hit traffic.

"I just remembered. I have an appointment in Naples later," Guin lied. "Why don't I just stop by?"

"I don't know," said Caroline.

"I won't be long."

"Well, if you're going to be in Naples… But I told you, we're going to be busy. And I can only spare her for a few minutes. And if she doesn't want to talk to you…"

"Got it. I won't press."

"All right. I need to go," said the caterer.

"Okay. See you soon."

Guin grabbed her bag and her keys and hurried to her Mini, praying traffic wouldn't be too bad. Ninety minutes later, she was parked in front of the caterer's.

There was no one in the front of the shop, but Guin could hear a lot of activity in the back.

"Hello?" she called.

A few minutes later, a woman wearing an apron came out.

"Can I help you?"

"Is Carla here?"

"Who's asking?"

"Sorry. My name's Guinivere Jones. I spoke with Caroline a little while ago. I'm a reporter and…"

Just then Caroline came through the curtain separating the front of the shop from the back.

"Ms. Jones," said the caterer.

Guin greeted her and then asked if Carla was there.

"She is," said the caterer. "But we're all rather busy."

"I just need a few minutes of her time."

The caterer saw the look on Guin's face.

"I'll go speak with her. Wait here."

Guin watched as the caterer went back through the curtain. Guin was tempted to follow her. She was curious to see what was going on back there. There was a lot of noise, and something smelled delicious. No doubt they were preparing for tonight's event.

A few minutes later, the good-looking young man Guin had seen at the Baker Museum emerged from the back. *What was his name again? Was it Mario? No, Mariano.*

"Can I help you?" he asked Guin.

Guin smiled at him.

"It's Mariano, yes?"

The young man didn't return the smile.

"I remember you from the Baker Museum. I was actually hoping to speak with Carla. Is she available?"

"Carla's busy."

Was he protecting her?

"I just wanted to ask her a few questions about that evening, about the man she found on the stairs."

Mariano's expression remained stony.

"I'm not a cop," she continued. "I'm a reporter. But I promise not to use Carla's name. I just want to know what she saw that evening. Please. A man's been accused of murder, but I don't think he did it. And I need Carla's help. Tell her anything she says to me can be off the record. I won't use her name."

Guin knew she was rambling and sounded a bit desperate, but Carla was her best hope for clearing Bishop—or proving that he had done it.

"I can tell you what Carla saw. I was with her."

"You were? You can? What did you see?"

"You promise not to mention our names?"

"I promise."

Mariano looked like he was thinking it over. Then he told Guin what they had seen.

"We were coming up the stairs when we heard a crash. Carla was in front of me. We thought one of the servers had dropped some glasses or plates, but..."

"But it was the man in the wheelchair."

Mariano nodded.

"Did you see him fall?"

"No."

"What about Carla? Did she see him?"

"No. We were too far down."

"But you were the first to find him."

"When we heard the crash, we hurried up the stairs."

"And that's when you saw Mr. Belem lying there, on the landing."

Mariano nodded.

"Carla screamed. She knew right away something was wrong."

"Did you see anyone on the stairs? Anyone rush by you?"

"No. There was no one. Just him and the wheelchair."

"What about at the top of the stairs?"

"After Carla screamed, there were lots of people there."

"So neither of you actually saw what happened?"

"We just saw the body."

Guin wondered if Mariano was telling her the truth.

Though why would he lie? Unless he was protecting someone.

"What about the other servers? Did any of them see something?"

"You would have to ask them."

Was Mariano being difficult on purpose or did he really not know? Guin felt sure one of the servers must have seen something. After all, the outdoor kitchen was right by the stairs.

"Please, Mariano. A man's life is at stake. If you or one of your coworkers knows something about what happened that evening…"

Guin hated to beg but… It seemed to work.

"Talk to Elena."

"Is she here?"

"She's in back."

"Would you ask her to come out?"

"I will ask her. But she is very busy."

"Please," said Guin. "Tell her it will only take a minute."

Mariano went back to the kitchen. Ten minutes went by, and Guin was starting to think he had blown off her request. Or else Elena didn't wish to speak with her. She was tempted to go to the back, but she didn't want to cause a scene.

She was about to leave when an older woman in a server's uniform came out. Guin recognized her from the reception.

"Elena?"

The woman studied Guin.

"Mariano said you wanted to talk to me."

"I did. I do. I wanted to ask you about that evening at the Baker Museum, about what happened to the man in the wheelchair."

Elena didn't say anything.

"I know that Carla and Mariano found him. But Mariano said they didn't see him fall. What about you? Did you see him fall?"

"He was fine when I saw him."

"When was that? Was it near the end of the evening? Was he by the stairs? Where were you?"

Guin realized she was asking a lot of questions very quickly. But she sensed she didn't have much time.

"I was in the kitchen."

"What were you doing there?"

"Putting things away."

"And Mr. Belem, the man in the wheelchair, was nearby?"

Elena nodded.

"Was anyone with him?"

"He was talking to a man."

"What man? Can you describe him?"

"He was tall and skinny with gray hair."

That could describe several men who were there that evening, including Farley Bishop. Guin pulled out her phone and pulled up a picture of the artist.

"Was this the man you saw with Mr. Belem?" Guin showed Elena the photo.

"That's him."

"Do you know what they were saying?"

Elena shook her head.

"Did you see Mr. Belem talking with anyone else?"

"Just the lady."

"The lady?"

"The one in charge."

"You mean Alexandra Barnes, the curator?" Guin pulled up a photo of the curator and showed it to Elena.

"*Sí*. Her."

"Was this before or after you saw Mr. Belem with the man?"

"After."

"Did you happen to hear what they were saying?"

"No. But the lady wasn't happy."

"How do you know that?"

"She looked angry."

Could Alexandra Barnes have pushed Ludwig Belem down the stairs? But why?

"Then what happened?"

"I went inside."

"So you were inside when Mr. Belem went down the stairs?"

Elena nodded.

Guin frowned. She had hit another dead end. Though… maybe another server had seen what had happened. However, Mariano had told Guin to talk to Elena. Still, it was worth a shot.

"Elena, was anyone else with you outside in the outdoor kitchen, another server?"

"Just Juliana."

"Did she go inside with you?"

"No, she stayed outside."

So Juliana could have been there when it happened.

"Is she here? Can I speak with her?"

"She left."

"What do you mean?"

"She no longer works here."

"Where did she go?"

Elena didn't answer.

"Please, Elena. It's important I speak with her. A man's life is at stake. Do you know where I can find her? Is she here in Naples? I promise I won't tell her you were the one who told me where to find her."

Elena hesitated.

"Please?"

"She went to work with her cousin."

"Where?"

"Some new restaurant."

"Here in Naples?"

Elena nodded.

Guin was about to ask her the name of the restaurant, but someone from the kitchen was calling Elena's name.

"I need to go," she told Guin.

Before Guin could stop her, Elena hurried to the back.

Guin thought about following her. She needed the name of that restaurant. But she didn't think going to the back and hassling Elena was a good idea. She could always call the caterer's tomorrow and ask to speak with her then.

Guin pulled out her phone and checked the time. She should get back to Sanibel.

CHAPTER 29

Guin was about to get in her car when she heard her phone buzzing. It was Ginny. She swiped to answer. Joel had spoken with Bishop, and the artist had agreed to meet with Guin tomorrow at five in Bennett Emerson's office. Hallelujah!

Good thing Guin didn't have any plans. Though if she had, she would have canceled them.

She thanked Ginny, and Ginny told her to thank Joel.

Guin then got in her car and drove home. As she drove, she thought about what Elena had said. She had told Guin she had seen Bishop and Alexandra Barnes with Belem not long before he took a tumble. Had anyone else seen them? The detective mentioned multiple eyewitnesses. Had one of the guests seen something?

Guin tried to recall who had been out on the terrace when she had returned. She didn't know most of the people who had attended the event. Though she distinctly remembered seeing Sid and Martha Sachs and Bob Axelrod there. Had one of them seen something? She would reach out to them as soon as she got home, assuming she could find their contact info.

She parked the Mini and hurried inside, making a beeline for her office and her computer. She opened her browser and did a search for Sid and Martha Sachs in Naples. There were multiple results, all listing an address in Old Naples.

That had to be them. She found a phone number and decided to try it.

The phone rang several times.

"Hello?" said a female voice.

"Is this Martha Sachs?"

"It is, but I don't accept phone solicitations. So if…"

"Mrs. Sachs, it's Guinivere Jones with the *Sanibel-Captiva Sun-Times*. We met at the preview for the Farley Bishop exhibit at the Baker Museum last Friday."

No response.

"The model for Titania?"

"Oh, of course!" said Mrs. Sachs. "I remember you! Such an amazing likeness."

"Do you have a minute, Mrs. Sachs? I could really use your help with a story I'm working on."

"About the museum?"

"In a way. It's about the man who fell down the stairs."

"Dreadful that."

"By any chance, did you see what happened?"

"No, we were on the other side of the terrace."

"So you didn't see anyone with Mr. Belem over by the outdoor kitchen?"

"We were chatting with Bob. Or I was. And my back was to that part of the terrace. You should ask Sid. He was facing that way."

"Is he there?"

"He's at the club."

"Do you know when he'll be back?"

"He should be back soon. Though we have dinner plans."

"Could you ask him to call me later?"

"You don't want to talk to Sid after he's had a couple of drinks."

"What about tomorrow?"

"He's playing golf."

"Well, could you ask him to call me when he has a free minute? I'd really like to speak with him."

"Give me your number, and I'll have him call you."

"Thank you." Guin gave Mrs. Sachs her phone number. "Do you happen to know if any of the other guests saw anything?"

"I'm afraid I don't."

"Okay. Well, thank you for your time. And please have Mr. Sachs call me as soon as he's able."

"I'll give him the message."

Guin was giving the cats their dinner when she felt her phone vibrating in her back pocket. She took it out. It was Owen.

"Hey," she said. "Thanks again for the intel."

"It was really Barry." Barry was Owen's former instructor. "That's actually why I'm calling. Barry just phoned me with a juicy bit of gossip."

"Oh?"

"Apparently Belem was seeing someone, a gallery owner."

"And that's juicy because?"

"It was a conflict of interest. Belem reviewed several shows at the gallery. Never had a bad word to say about any of them."

"And you, or Barry, think that's because Belem was dating the owner of the gallery?"

"Sure looks that way."

"Maybe Belem just liked the art."

Owen snorted.

"Please. Liking one show, okay. But three?"

He had a point.

"So how does Barry know all this?"

"He heard it from a reliable source, someone who knew Marcus and Belem."

"Marcus?"

"He owns the gallery. It's actually just a couple of blocks from mine."

"You know him, Marcus, that is?"

"Not well."

"But you know him."

"I do."

"And do other people know about Marcus and Belem?"

"Doubtful. I mean, maybe a few. They must have been keeping their relationship on the qt. If word had gotten out, it could have ruined Belem's career. Marcus's too."

"You think Marcus knew about Belem's secret identity?"

"You mean that he was Willem Budge?"

"That's exactly what I mean."

"No idea. Maybe?"

"How would you feel about asking him?"

"Uh…"

"I need to know if Belem, or Budge, was still carrying a grudge against Farley Bishop. And Belem's paramour would be the perfect person to ask."

"I don't know, Guin."

"Please? You said you knew him."

"Not well enough to ask him a bunch of personal questions."

"Pretty please? You can't just stop over there, say hi, mention you heard about Belem and wanted to express your condolences, and then casually ask him a couple of questions about his dead lover?"

"I guess I could do that. There's actually a new exhibit opening over there. The reception's tomorrow evening. I had planned on stopping by."

"Perfect. Go there and see if you can get a minute alone with Marcus. Though maybe the reception's not the best place. There could be a lot of people there. Maybe go over there tomorrow morning when the gallery opens?"

"I take it you're eager to find out what Marcus knows about Belem."

"I am. Frankly, I'm a bit surprised that Marcus isn't here."

"I don't think they were married. And as I said, their relationship was kind of a secret. Plus Marcus has a new exhibit opening. Anyway, if it's that important to you, I'll go over there in the morning and see what I can find out."

"Thank you, Owen! You're the best!"

"Don't thank me yet. Hey, Lance is calling me. I should go."

"Give him my love."

"I will."

Glen collected Guin a little before seven. They arrived at the restaurant ten minutes later to find Shelly and Steve already there.

"Yoohoo!" said Shelly. "We're over here!"

Not that Guin couldn't see them. It was a small place.

Guin saw that Shelly's drink was half empty. How long had they been there?

"You been here long?"

"We decided to get here early and have a drink. I needed one after the afternoon I had."

"Oh, what's up?"

"You know that show I auditioned for?"

"You mean *Making It*?"

"That's the one!"

"What happened?"

"They canceled it."

"What?! But I thought you were a finalist."

"I was. But the network decided not to renew it. So…"

"I'm sorry, Shell. I know how much you were looking forward to it."

"*C'est la vie.*" She took a sip of her drink, which was hot pink.

"What are you drinking?"

"It's called a Pink Dragon. Don't ask me what's in it."

"Is it good?"

"Very."

Guin saw that Steve had a beer.

A server came over and asked Guin and Glen what they wanted to drink. Glen ordered a beer, and Guin thought about getting a cocktail but ordered a club soda with lime instead. She was working.

"So, what have you been up to?" Shelly asked her.

"Working." But Guin didn't want to discuss work tonight. At least hers. She turned to Steve.

"How are you, Steve? You still enjoying being a consultant?"

"It's all right."

"He likes it," said Shelly. "He just hates all the traveling."

"You've been doing a lot of traveling?"

Steve nodded.

"The nature of the beast. But I'd rather not talk about work if you don't mind. Shelly's not the only one who's had a tough day. Hey, Shelly told me about your trip to Paris. Sounds like you guys had a good time."

"We did," they answered at the same time. They looked at each other and chuckled.

"I'm telling you," Shelly said to her husband. "They're like two peas in a pod." She turned to Glen. "So how come you didn't propose? Isn't that what people in love do when they go to Paris?"

"Don't answer that," Guin told Glen. She turned to Shelly. "Really, Shell. Come, let's decide what to order. Get whatever you like."

They studied their menus and ordered four different appetizers and four different main dishes, all of which they would share. It was a lot of food, but the paper was paying, or would reimburse Guin, and they would take any leftovers home.

"I hope it's good," said Shelly. "We could use a good Asian place on the island."

"There's that hibachi place," said Steve. "And they serve sushi at Timbers."

"Yes, but I miss having Chinese food."

"Me too," said Guin. "Back when I was living in New York, there was a Chinese place on practically every block. In fact, when I was first working there, I would order food from this one place so often that the food would arrive, like, five minutes after I ordered it."

"Wow! Really?" said Shelly. "That's amazing. They must have been psychic."

"Or else they saw my phone number and figured I wanted what I always got."

Steve and Glen smiled.

A few minutes later, their appetizers arrived, and they dug in.

They finished eating forty minutes later. That was the thing about Asian food, or an Asian restaurant that was geared to takeout, the food came out fast. They had eaten the usual things one got: egg rolls, dumplings, barbequed ribs, and sushi to start, followed by a noodle dish, a stir fry, a curry, and a moo shu dish. All of it had been good though not spectacular. But the restaurant had just opened, and Guin had high hopes for it. Just eating there brought back fond memories. And the owner, who had come over to chat with them, said they planned on adding delivery service.

For dessert they had ordered a piece of mango cheesecake and green tea ice cream—they were too full to get more, and the restaurant had a limited dessert menu—

and received fortune cookies gratis.

Shelly immediately opened her cookie and frowned when she read her fortune.

"What does it say?" asked Guin.

"Don't pursue happiness—create it."

"That doesn't sound so bad."

"But what does it mean?"

"I think it means you should make your own happiness, which you do by creating jewelry."

Shelly didn't look convinced.

"What does your say?" she asked her husband.

"You will travel many places."

"Ain't that the truth. What about you, Glen?"

He opened his fortune cookie.

"Change is inevitable. Don't resist it."

"You expecting something to change?" Shelly asked him.

He didn't reply.

"Okay, your turn," Shelly said to Guin.

Guin opened her fortune cookie.

"Huh," she said.

"What?" said Shelly.

"I got the same fortune as Glen."

She looked over at him, but he seemed distracted.

"Is there something we should know?" Shelly asked the two of them.

"Actually," said Guin.

Shelly leaned in.

"Yes?"

"So… my mother has a friend whose husband works for the *New York Times*. He's in charge of the Business section. She practically ordered me to write to him and…"

"Oh my God!" said Shelly. "Did you get a job at the *New York Times* and didn't tell me?!"

"Down, girl. I just wrote to him."

"Did he write you back?"

"He did. This afternoon." She turned to Glen. "I meant to tell you."

"What did he say?!" asked Shelly.

"Not much. We're going to talk this coming week."

"That's so awesome, Guin! I can totally see you working for the *Times*. Though… does that mean you'd have to move back to New York?"

"I'm not going anywhere. I haven't even talked to the guy."

"He's totally going to want to hire you."

"I don't even know if they're looking. Anyway, let's get a check."

She signaled to their server and got the check. A few minutes later, they were standing in the parking lot, saying their goodbyes.

"So, you coming to our Valentine's Day barbeque on Sunday?" Shelly asked Guin. "I know you're working," she said to Glen.

Guin didn't really want to go to the barbeque, but she felt cornered.

"Who's going to be there?"

"You know, the usual suspects."

That meant Steve's fishing buddies and some of their couple friends. Which didn't excite Guin. Not that there was anything wrong with Steve's fishing buddies or their friends. But it wasn't how Guin wanted to spend Valentine's Day. Frankly, she'd rather spend it at home with the cats watching some bad rom-com.

"I wish you would come with me to the event in Naples," said Glen. "It'll be fun."

"That's right," said Shelly. "Guin said you were photographing some singles party."

"It's at this new wine bar. Looks really nice, and the food's supposed to be good too." He turned to Guin. "Come with me. It's only for a couple of hours."

"You should go," said Shelly. "Even though we'll miss having you at the barbeque."

Guin felt everyone looking at her.

"Fine. I'll go. But we're taking two cars. I don't want to be stuck there."

"Deal," said Glen. "Though maybe you won't want to leave so quickly."

Guin gave him a look.

"Yes, just how I want to spend Valentine's Day, with a bunch of drunk, horny singles."

"We're going," said Shelly. "Let me know how the party was and what the *Times* guy says."

Guin said that she would, and they said goodnight.

CHAPTER 30

"Is everything okay?" Guin asked Glen as they drove back to her place.

"Everything's fine. Why?"

"You seemed a bit distracted at the restaurant."

"Sorry. I just have a lot on my mind."

"Care to share?"

"It's just work stuff."

Guin knew not to push him.

"Speaking of work, I have news to share."

"About the *New York Times*?"

"No, about Ludwig Belem." Glen waited for her to go on. "Ludwig Belem, cantankerous critic for *Art World* is, in fact… drum roll, please… petulant painter Willem Budge, the man who sued Farley Bishop for plagiarism!"

"How do you know that?"

Guin filled him in.

"Wow," he said when she was done.

"But wait, there's more! Belem was conducting a secret affair with a gallery owner. And Owen's going to go over there tomorrow morning and speak with the guy."

"You think the gallery owner knew about Belem?"

"That's what I'm hoping to find out. That and if Belem still carried a grudge against Farley Bishop. And I went back to the caterer's this afternoon and spoke with a couple of the servers who worked at the Baker that evening. One of them, Elena, saw Bishop with Belem just before he fell."

"Did she see Bishop push him?"

"No, she went inside just before it happened. And, get this, she said she saw Alexandra Barnes with Belem too. After she saw Bishop."

"You don't think Ms. Barnes pushed him, do you?"

"I don't know what to think. But I should look into Ms. Barnes."

They arrived at Guin's and went inside.

"You want something to drink?" she asked Glen.

"You have any herbal tea?"

"I do. Come take a look."

He took out the box of chamomile and asked Guin if she wanted some.

"Sure," she said.

She boiled water in the electric kettle and poured it over the tea bags when it was ready.

"I did get another lead," she told Glen as they sipped their tea. "The server I spoke with, Elena, said that she had been with someone, another server, out on the terrace, who stayed behind when she went inside. The only problem is the woman no longer works for Caroline. Apparently, she quit right after. Works at some restaurant now. Elena didn't give me the name."

Glen continued to sip his tea and listen.

"I also spoke with Martha Sachs. She and her husband were on the terrace when it happened. She said she didn't see anything, but she thought her husband might have. Unfortunately, he wasn't there when I called, but she said he'd ring me back. And Ginny called. Joel somehow convinced Bishop to see me. I'm meeting with him at Bennett Emerson's office tomorrow at five. And…"

Glen put down his tea and told Guin to put down her mug. Then he took Guin's hand.

"That's enough work talk. Come."

"Where are you taking me?"

Yet Guin knew where he was taking her.

"Someplace where you can forget about work."

"And how do you propose to make me forget about work?" she asked him.

"I have a few ideas."

He gave her a wicked smile, and Guin followed him into the bedroom.

Guin was antsy the next morning. Glen had left. And she was anxiously waiting for Owen to call or text her. So when her phone rang at a little past nine-thirty, she grabbed it, hoping it was Owen. But it was Craig.

"Hey," she said. "You back from fishing already?"

"Just got back to the dock."

"How was it?"

"You really want to know?"

"You catch anything?"

"Got some grouper, a couple of snook, and a sheepshead."

"Is that good?"

"It's not bad. But that's not why I'm calling. Thought you'd want to know. They released the preliminary autopsy report."

Guin was about to ask how Craig knew that. But no doubt one of his buddies had told him.

"And? Anything interesting?"

"They're still waiting on the toxicology report, but…" Guin heard talking in the background.

"But what?" she said.

"Sorry. Al was asking me something. Belem had cancer."

"What kind of cancer."

"Lung."

"How bad?"

"Really bad. Stage four."

"Stage four? Was he terminal?"

"Hard to know without speaking to his doctor. But stage four isn't good."

Craig knew all about cancer, having had cancer of the prostate. Fortunately, they had caught it early, and he was okay now.

"You think Belem knew?" But he must have known—and been in a lot of pain. Maybe that was why he seemed so angry. She would be angry too if she had cancer, especially stage four.

"You learn anything else?"

"That's it."

"Okay. Thanks for letting me know about the autopsy report. Let me know if you hear anything else."

"Will do."

They ended the call, and Guin sat back in her chair. So, Belem had stage four lung cancer. No wonder he looked sickly. Why had he come to Naples if he was so ill? Was it because of Farley Bishop?

Guin thought about texting Owen. Surely, Marcus would know if Belem was on death's door. Or maybe not. Belem could have been keeping his cancer a secret. Well, there was only one way to find out.

She opened her texting app and began to type.

"Hey, Owen. You go to see Marcus yet? If not, when you do go, could you ask him if he knew Belem had cancer and that it was serious? Thanks!"

She hit send and looked out at the lake. A great egret flew by and landed on a tree branch. She watched it for a minute and then turned back to her computer. Her meeting with Farley Bishop wasn't for a while. But she had plenty to keep her busy until she had to leave, Ginny having sent her more articles to work on.

A little after three, Guin left for the museum. She hadn't heard from Owen and wondered what was up. Had he not made it over to the gallery? She thought about texting him again, but she would wait. He was probably busy.

There was traffic leaving Sanibel and on Route 41 going to Naples. But she had anticipated that and arrived at the Artis-Naples campus a little before five. She parked by the administrative building and headed inside.

She gave her name to the security guard and was allowed upstairs. Bennett Emerson's door was closed, but she could see a light on. And she could hear classical music playing.

She knocked on the door.

"Yes?" came the director's voice.

"It's Guinivere Jones, Mr. Emerson."

"Are you alone?" called the director.

Guin looked around. There was no one in the hallway.

"I am."

A minute later the door opened a crack. It was Bennett Emerson. He looked to the right and then to the left.

"You may come in," he said, satisfied that Guin was indeed alone.

"Thank you," she said.

She stepped inside the director's office and saw Farley Bishop seated in one of the chairs. He didn't look happy to see her.

"Mr. Bishop," she said. "Thank you for agreeing to see me."

He continued to frown.

Bennett Emerson took a seat at his desk and looked up at Guin.

"Won't you have a seat?"

Guin sat in the one empty chair.

"So, what did you want to ask Farley?"

"Uh," she said, wondering if she should reply to the director or to the painter. She looked over at Bishop and then back at the director. "I suppose I want to know if Mr. Bishop pushed Mr. Belem down the terrace stairs."

Guin looked over at the artist to see his reaction. He was still frowning.

"He did not," said the director.

"If you don't mind, I'd like to hear from Mr. Bishop."

She turned to look at the artist.

"I didn't push that pompous ass down the stairs. Though I'd…"

The director cut him off with a look. Then he turned back to Guin.

"There you have it, Ms. Jones. He didn't do it."

Now it was Guin's turn to frown.

"Then why did the police arrest him?"

"The police made a mistake."

"What about the evidence?"

Though all Guin knew about were the fingerprints.

"All circumstantial," said the director.

"And the eyewitnesses?"

"No one actually saw Farley push him."

Guin wondered if that was still true.

"As I said, the police made a mistake. Which is why they released him."

"I thought they released him because he posted bail."

The director tutted.

"You wouldn't happen to know who paid his bail, would you?"

"I did."

"You did?"

"Farley would have done the same for me."

Guin looked over at the painter. He was still frowning. She was convinced that was his default expression.

"Has he been staying with you?"

"That's really none of your business."

Guin turned to Bishop.

"Do you have a lawyer?"

The director answered for him.

"The best that money can buy."

"Who did he hire?"

"Jack Pomerantz."

Guin had never heard of him.

"Best defense attorney in Southwest Florida," said the director. "He's on the board here. Big fan of Farley's work."

Guin looked over at Bishop again. He continued to frown.

"And Mr. Pomerantz is convinced that Mr. Bishop is innocent?"

"He is. As is everyone here at the museum."

Well, of course he'd say that. The museum's reputation was at stake. You couldn't have artists shoving art critics, especially ones in wheelchairs, down stairs.

Guin turned back to Bishop.

"Did you know Ludwig Belem?"

"You don't need to answer that, Farley," said the director.

"Let me ask another question," said Guin. "Did you know that Ludwig Belem was actually a painter named Willem Budge?"

"Don't answer her, Farley!"

Now it was Guin's turn to frown. However, much to her surprise, Bishop answered.

"It's going to come out soon enough, Ben." He turned to Guin. "I didn't know it was him. Not at first. I hadn't seen Budge in over twenty years, and he had changed."

"But you knew it was him."

"He came over and introduced himself."

"What did he say to you?"

"He asked me if I remembered him."

"And did you?"

"I did not. I had never seen Ludwig Belem before. Though I knew the name."

"Then what?"

"He asked me if I was sure I didn't remember him. And I told him I was sure we had never met. He smirked at that and then said that I surely remembered his paintings, the ones I copied. That's when I knew."

"What did you say when he told you that?"

"I told him to get out, and then he…"

"I must counsel you, Farley…" It was the director again.

Guin ignored him.

"And then he what?"

"He told me he was there to review my work and that he would leave when he was good and ready."

"Did he say anything else to you?"

Guin saw the director shaking his head.

"Did he tell you he had cancer?" Guin asked Bishop.

"No," Bishop replied. "He had cancer?"

"Stage four lung."

Bishop frowned.

"What were you discussing with Belem by the terrace stairs? A server saw you speaking with him."

The director was shaking his head again. Bishop saw him and told Guin that he didn't remember. But Guin sensed he was lying.

The director stood up.

"I'm sorry, Ms. Jones. But that's all the time we have."

Guin stayed seated and stared at him. She had only been there a few minutes. And she had more questions.

"Ms. Jones?" said the director. Clearly, that was her cue to leave.

Guin got up.

"Thank you both for your time."

The director waited for her to leave and then shut the door behind her. Guin paused outside the director's office, listening at the door. But the director had turned up the music. She waited a few more seconds, then she made her way to the stairs.

Guin had hoped that Bishop would offer some sort of proof that he hadn't done it, that he could prove he had been nowhere near the terrace stairs when Belem fell. But he hadn't. And without proof or an alibi… Well, it didn't look good for him. Then another thought occurred to Guin. What if he was covering for someone?

CHAPTER 31

The next morning Guin turned on her phone and found a text from Glen wishing her a happy Valentine's Day with a GIF of a giant heart with the words *I love you*. She smiled and wrote him back, sending him a similar GIF. Then she got dressed and headed to the farmers market.

It wasn't yet eight, when the farmers market technically opened. However, the BIG ARTS parking lot, where Guin usually parked, was nearly full. Not a huge surprise. People liked to get to the market on the early side.

Guin made a beeline for Jean-Luc's booth, where there was already a line. Jake and Jo were there. Did that mean that Jean-Luc had fired the new people?

Finally, it was her turn.

"Good morning!" she said to Jake and Jo.

Jake smiled back at her.

"Happy Valentine's Day! What can I get you this morning?"

"Hm," said Guin, looking over the breakfast pastries. "I'll have an almond croissant, a *pain au chocolat*, and a regular croissant."

"Anything else? Maybe a baguette? Jo made them."

Guin looked at the baguettes. They did look good.

"Sure. Why not?"

Jake smiled and bagged Guin's pastries and baguette.

"What happened to the new people?" Guin asked. "Did Jean-Luc fire them?"

"No, they're working at the shop today. I think they were a bit overwhelmed by the market."

Guin could understand. The market was nonstop from the time it opened, actually before it opened, until it closed at two. Even busier than Jean-Luc's café.

"So, how much do I owe you?"

Jake told her, and Guin paid.

"You guys doing anything special for V-Day?" she asked him as he handed Guin her change.

"Nah, just hanging out."

Guin sensed the man behind her was growing impatient, so she told Jake she hoped he and Jo had a good one and moved on.

Guin made her way around the rest of the market, purchasing a small container of tropical fruit, some cheese, and some fresh pasta. When she got home, she made herself coffee. While it was brewing, she cut the three breakfast pastries in half, saving the other halves for tomorrow or the next day, and scrambled some eggs.

She normally didn't eat a big breakfast, or any breakfast. But Sunday was an exception. She slid the eggs onto a plate with the breakfast pastries and read the *New York Times* on her phone as she ate.

She paid particular attention to the Business section. She wanted to be prepared for her call with Bill Hendricks.

When she was done, she washed her plate, fork, and knife and put them in the drying rack. She had missed her early morning beach walk, and she had work to do. But it was so nice outside. And it was Sunday.

She brushed her teeth and then grabbed her phone and headed out.

The beach was crowded. Well, more crowded than it was when Guin was usually there, at seven a.m. She saw families and groups of women scanning the shore for shells as well as several men with fishing poles. Guin wished them all luck.

She walked past the sign for Beach Access #7 and then turned around.

She was feeling a bit grungy by the time she got home, so she went to take a shower. When she got out, she found a text from her brother, wishing her a happy Valentine's Day and asking how she was. Instead of texting him back, she called him. He picked up right away.

"Good morning," she said. "You're up early."

"It's not that early."

"Well, early for you."

"I'm up early."

"Not usually on the weekend. Anyway, thanks for the text. You and Owen have anything special planned for Valentine's Day?"

"We're having brunch with friends."

"That's it?"

"And Owen's cooking us dinner later. Speaking of my husband, I hear you two have been plotting together."

"I wouldn't say plotting. He's just helping me out with something. Though speaking of Owen, I was supposed to hear from him yesterday. Is he okay?"

"He's fine. Just crazy busy. You know how Saturdays are. Should I bug him for you?"

"You don't have to do that."

"It's my pleasure. So, what's up with you?"

"Not much. Just working."

"You and Glen doing anything special for V-Day?"

"He's dragging me to a singles party in Naples."

"Excuse me? I didn't take him for a swinger."

"It's not that kind of party. Glen's helping out a photographer friend, shooting the party for him. It's at some new wine bar. Glen asked me to go with him."

"Well, have fun."

"I'm sure I won't."

Lance chuckled.

"Hey, speaking of Naples, you talk to Mom?"

"Recently? She and Philip are supposed to fly down tomorrow. Are they not?"

"No, they're still flying down there. And she wants me and Lance to visit. But before we get tickets, I wanted to make sure you'd be around."

"When are you thinking of coming down?"

"The first weekend of March."

"That's the weekend of the Shell Show."

"Does that mean you won't be able to see us?"

"The show ends Saturday, and it's not like I have to be there the whole time. You should go."

"To the Shell Show? No, thank you. So, you'll be able to come to Naples?"

"You could always come here."

"Whatever. The point is, we'll get to see you, yes?"

"You will."

"Okay. I'll buy us tickets."

"You planning to stay with Mom and Philip?"

"That's the plan."

"You know you're welcome to stay here."

"I'd love to, but you know how Mom is."

Guin did know.

"Well, I'll be happy to see you and Owen wherever."

"Oh, and Mom said you had an interview with the *New York Times* this week. Good luck!"

Guin shook her head. No doubt Beryl had told her.

"It's not an interview. I'm just chatting with the guy. He's the husband of one of mom's friends. Probably just doing it as a courtesy."

"Well, whatever the reason, I'm sure you'll blow him away."

"Thanks for the vote of confidence, but I'm not even sure I want to work for the *Times*."

"What?! You used to dream of working there."

"That was a long time ago."

"Not that long ago."

"I don't want to work there if it means I have to move back to New York."

"What's wrong with New York? You don't have to live in Manhattan, you know. You could get a place in Brooklyn, near me and Owen."

"Too expensive."

"You could always go back to Connecticut."

"No, thank you."

"Hey, I've got to dash. Have fun tonight at the party. And let me know how it goes with the *Times* guy."

"I'll try, and I will."

"Good. Love you."

"Love you too."

Guin went to her office and pulled up the Sunday *Times* crossword on her computer. She was filling it out when she came across a clue for a six-letter word for an art repository. It had to be *MUSEUM*. That got her thinking about the Baker again and about Alexandra Barnes.

Other than her being a curator and working at the Broad in LA before coming to Naples, Guin knew nothing about her. Time to do a little research. She abandoned the Sunday *Times* crossword and went to the Baker's website. She found a lengthy biography of Bennett Emerson and a much shorter one for Alexandra Barnes.

Well, that was interesting. They had both worked at the Art Institute of Chicago. Had they been there at the same time?

Guin opened her browser and typed *Alexandra Barnes* into the search box. The screen began to fill, and Guin realized she should have added the word *curator* to narrow things down. She quickly added it and reran the search.

There were dozens of articles mentioning Alexandra Barnes or rather the exhibits she had curated or been involved with over the years. Had Ludwig Belem written about one of the exhibits she had curated? She scrolled back up and typed *Alexandra Barnes Ludwig Belem* into the search box.

Again, the screen began to fill. She saw an article from *Art World* and clicked on the link. It was a review of a Cy Twombly exhibit at the Art Institute of Chicago from 2009 by none other than Ludwig Belem. Guin began to read.

While Belem claimed to be an admirer of Twombly's work, he took issue with the exhibit, wondering why the curator in charge, one Alexandra Barnes, had chosen certain paintings. He also took issue with how the exhibit had been organized. Guin found Belem's criticisms a bit nitpicky.

She returned to the search results to see if Belem had critiqued any other exhibits Ms. Barnes had curated and found a review of an exhibit at the Broad titled *Mythos*, which had featured works from over a dozen contemporary artists. Belem had praised the concept and some of the works, but he had again taken the curator, one Alexandra Barnes, to task, questioning why she had chosen certain artists and paintings, implying that he would have done a better job.

Did he have some kind of personal grudge against her?

This review was from 2016, seven years after the Twombly show. So maybe it was just a coincidence. Guin looked to see if Belem had written about any other exhibits Ms. Barnes had curated and found one more. It was pretty recent, from just before Ms. Barnes had left the Broad.

Guin read it and frowned. It was more scathing than the others. And Belem actually wrote that he thought the Broad could and should do much better and might want to think about hiring a curator who was more in touch with the current contemporary art scene. Ouch.

Guin wondered if Belem's critique had had something to do with Alexandra Barnes leaving the Broad. Had the Broad taken Belem's advice and fired her? They wouldn't fire someone over a couple of bad reviews, would they? Though *Art World* did carry a lot of weight in the art world. Still.

What about Ms. Barnes? Did she have a grudge against Ludwig Belem? Even if he didn't get her fired, he had suggested it and had criticized her judgment. If someone had attacked her like that, Guin would have been pissed. More than pissed, furious. But enough to shove her attacker down a flight of stairs if given the chance?

Guin decided to do another search.

She typed *Alexandra Barnes Broad firing* into the search box, not really expecting to find anything. But lo and behold, the screen began to fill. Among the links was an article from the *Los Angeles Times* with the headline "Broad and curator part ways." Guin clicked on the link and began to read. When she was done, she sat back in her chair, staring at her computer screen.

She leaned forward and read the article one more time. Could the article be right? But why mention it if it wasn't true? She did another search to see if anyone else mentioned the link and found another article, this one older, mentioning it. Though really, when Guin thought about it, it wasn't that hard to believe. She wondered if Ginny knew. Well, there was only one way to find out. Guin picked up her phone and called her.

"Happy Valentine's Day!" said her boss.

"For some," said Guin.

"You wake up on the wrong side of the bed this morning?"

"You know I'm not a fan of Valentine's Day."

"Even after Paris? Where's Glen?"

"At his place. He shot a wedding yesterday. And he has another shoot tonight."

"No wonder you're in a bad mood."

"I'm not in a bad mood. I just don't like Valentine's Day. You don't celebrate it, do you?"

"Of course we do. It's one of my favorite holidays."

"It is?" This was news to Guin.

"I'm just messing with you. I loathe it. But it's great for advertising. However, I'm guessing you didn't call to discuss Valentine's Day."

"I did not. I called to ask you a question."

"Shoot."

"Did you know that Alexandra Barnes was Farley Bishop's daughter?"

"Excuse me?"

"I take it you didn't know."

"I did not. How do you know? Did your brother-in-law's former art instructor tell you?"

Guin ignored the snark.

"No. I read it in an article."

"You read it in an article?"

"A piece I found in the *Los Angeles Times* mentioned it in passing. I couldn't believe it, so I did a search. And she's definitely his daughter. I mean, why print something like that if it wasn't true? And you saw them together, Gin. She looks just like him. Well, a much younger female version of him." Guin had subconsciously noticed the resemblance before but had dismissed it. "And Bishop said his daughter's name was Sasha, which is a nickname for Alexandra. And… you really didn't know?"

"I knew he had a daughter, but he never mentioned her."

"Really?"

"If he did, I don't remember. I certainly would have remembered him mentioning that his daughter worked at the Baker."

She had a point.

"As far as I knew, he hadn't seen her in years."

"Maybe he hadn't until recently. She grew up in LA and worked at the Art Institute of Chicago and then the Broad. By the way, did you know that Bennett Emerson also worked at the Art Institute and that he had been a student of Bishop's?"

"He had?"

"Well, sort of. He studied with him in New York before deciding to become a curator."

Guin left out the part about Emerson crashing at Bishop's studio and being the cause, or one of them, of Bishop's wife leaving. However, now that she thought about it, had Bennett Emerson known that Alexandra Barnes was Farley Bishop's daughter? He must have.

"Guin? You still there?"

"Sorry. What was I saying?"

"You were saying that Alexandra Barnes was Farley's daughter and that Bennett Emerson had been a student of Farley's."

"Right. Yes. Pretty amazing, huh? Though why keep it a secret? I mean Ms. Barnes being Bishop's daughter."

"I'm not that surprised."

"Really? Why?"

"Maybe she resented him? He left when she was little and…"

"Technically, her mother was the one who left."

"Just work with me. So, her mother leaves and tells little Alexandra that her father doesn't love her. And she grows up hating him."

"We don't know that. After all, she clearly loves art, especially contemporary art. And she arranged that whole exhibit of his work. Well, technically, Bennett Emerson arranged it, but Ms. Barnes organized it. And she did a great job. Clearly, not the work of someone who hated the artist."

Ginny sighed.

"Fine. Maybe she didn't hate him. Or maybe she just wanted to succeed on her own merits. Who knows why people do things?"

That was true.

"Well, she may or may not have hated her father, but I doubt she had any love for Ludwig Belem."

"What makes you say that?"

"You should read the things he wrote about her. They were scathing. He even suggested that the Broad should fire her. And she left the Broad shortly after his article appeared. But the article I read didn't say whether she had been fired, just that they had parted ways."

"You don't say."

"And another thing. I spoke with one of the servers who was there. She said she saw Ms. Barnes with Belem over by the outdoor kitchen not long before he fell or was pushed."

"You don't really think she could have sent him toppling down those stairs, do you?"

Guin tried to picture the scene. Although she was probably in her fifties, Alexandra Barnes was a tall, athletic-looking woman. And she had an axe to grind against Ludwig Belem.

"It's no more unbelievable than Bishop pushing him."

"Just don't go accusing anyone of murder without the facts to back it up. We don't want the paper getting sued."

"I would never do that. You know that."

"Just so we're clear."

"Crystal."

"Good. I need to go. Enjoy the rest of your Valentine's Day."

Guin made a face as Ginny ended the call.

CHAPTER 32

Guin wanted someone else to bounce her theory off of. Was she crazy to think Alexandra Barnes could have pushed Ludwig Belem down the terrace stairs? She had motive and opportunity. Yet the police had arrested Farley Bishop.

She picked up her phone and called Glen.

"Good morning," he said. "I wish you were here."

"I wish you were here." Though if he had been, Guin might not have stumbled across her big discovery. "How was the wedding?"

"It was good."

"Everyone behave?"

"They did. It was a pretty mild affair."

Guin was glad to hear it.

"So, there's something I need to tell you. And I need you to tell me if I'm crazy or not."

"Okay," he said, sounding a bit concerned.

Then she told him about Alexandra Barnes and her theory.

"Wow," he said when Guin was through.

"Right?"

"So you really think she could have pushed him down the stairs?"

"I don't know. I mean, she could have. But Ginny's right. I shouldn't go accusing her without any proof."

"Maybe you should talk to Detective Romero again."

"You really think she'd reveal something? I didn't get much out of her the last time."

"You don't know unless you try. Maybe if you asked nicely… or told her what you knew…"

She didn't have anything to lose.

"Okay. I'll reach out to her tomorrow. So, what's the dress code for tonight?"

"Wear whatever you want."

"Could you be a bit more specific?"

"It's a singles party at a wine bar."

"I'm not looking to get laid."

"You're not?"

"Just by you. Okay, I'll figure something out. What time should I meet you there? I know you said the party started at six."

"Just come with me. If you're having a miserable time, you can get a car service to take you back to my place. But I doubt I'll be there past eight."

"You don't have to stay till it's over?"

"No, I just have to get pictures of the place and show people enjoying themselves. Then I'm out of there."

"Fine. I'll go with you. What time should I get to your place?"

"Be here at four."

"Okay."

Guin was reading when her phone started to buzz. She looked at the Caller ID. Whoever it was had a 239 number, the area code for Lee and Collier counties. But she didn't recognize it. She swiped to answer anyway.

"Guin Jones."

"Ms. Jones, it's Martha Sachs. I'm sorry it took so long to get back to you. We've had quite the busy weekend."

"That's all right. Thank you so much for getting back to

me. Did you speak with your husband?"

"I did."

"And did he recall seeing Mr. Belem on the terrace?"

"He did."

"Was he with anyone? Mr. Belem, that is."

"Sid said he saw him talking to Alexandra."

"Alexandra Barnes?"

"That's right. They were having some kind of row."

"They were arguing? Did he hear what they were saying?"

"They were too far away, and Sid doesn't hear that well."

"How does he know they were arguing?"

"He could just tell. He said you don't need to hear to tell when two people are arguing."

That was true.

"Did he see anyone else with Mr. Belem?"

"Bennett went over there."

"To Mr. Belem and Ms. Barnes?"

"That's right."

"Anyone else? Did he happen to see Mr. Bishop with Mr. Belem?"

"Sorry, he was there too."

"So Mr. Sachs saw all three of them, Mr. Bishop, Mr. Emerson, and Ms. Barnes, with Mr. Belem on the terrace?"

"That's what he told me and that detective."

"But you didn't see anything?"

"I was facing the other way and was busy chatting with Bob Axelrod."

"Did Mr. Sachs say when this was? Was this right before Mr. Belem went down the stairs or earlier?"

"I don't know. I didn't ask."

"Is Mr. Sachs there? Could you ask him? It's important."

"Hold on. I'll see if he's free. Sid? Can you come here, please?" Guin thought she heard someone yell back. "I have Ms. Jones on the phone. She has a question for you." More indistinct shouting. "It will only take a minute."

"Yes?" It was a man's voice. He sounded grumpy.

"Mr. Sachs?"

"Yes?"

"Hi, Mr. Sachs. I just had a quick question about that evening at the Baker. Your wife says that you saw Ms. Barnes, Mr. Emerson, and Mr. Bishop all speaking with Ludwig Belem, the man in the wheelchair, out on the terrace. Is that correct?"

"That's right. Looked like they were getting into it."

"Getting into it as in arguing?"

"Sure looked that way."

"Do you remember when this was? Was it just before Mr. Belem was found on the stairs?"

"I don't recall what time it was."

"But it was definitely after Glen and I said goodbye to the two of you."

"Yes."

"And did either of you see Mr. Bishop or Mr. Emerson or Ms. Barnes between the time they met with Mr. Belem and you heard Carla scream?"

"Carla?" said Mrs. Sachs.

"She's the young woman who found him. She worked for the caterer."

"Oh, yes. Poor thing. Now that I think about it, Alexandra was with us when we heard the young woman scream. She had come over to have a word with Bob."

"How long had she been with you before you heard the scream?"

"I don't know. A few minutes?"

Well, unless she had super speed like the Flash or could turn invisible, it was unlikely Alexandra Barnes had been the one who pushed Belem down the stairs. Though Guin still couldn't completely rule her out.

"What about Mr. Bishop and Mr. Emerson? Did either of

you see them before the scream, other than with Mr. Belem?"

"I saw Bennett just after we heard Carla scream," said Mrs. Sachs. "He was by the stairs. He must have heard her and rushed over."

"What about Mr. Bishop?"

"I don't recall seeing him."

"What about you, Mr. Sachs?"

"Hm?"

"I asked if you saw Mr. Bishop on the terrace just before Carla screamed?"

"Didn't see him. Can I go now? I'm missing the game."

"Yes. Thank you for your help."

"Forgive Sid's rudeness," said Mrs. Sachs.

"I understand," said Guin. "Is he a big football fan?"

"He is."

"Well, I'll let you go too. Thank you again for talking to me."

"I still can't believe Farley pushed that man."

"Maybe he didn't."

"But the police…"

"Aren't always right. Anyway, I should go. Good day, Mrs. Sachs."

Guin ended the call and looked out the window. She was starting to formulate another idea about who could have pushed Ludwig Belem down the stairs. But right now, she needed to get ready for the Valentine's Day party.

She was in her closet when she heard her phone. She rushed to get it. It was Owen. Finally! She quickly swiped to answer.

"Owen!"

"Sorry for not calling. Yesterday was crazy at the gallery."

"You sell a lot of art?"

"As a matter of fact, we did."

"Good for you! So I take it you didn't get over to see Marcus."

"I did see him, at the reception. He wasn't there when I went over in the morning."

"And? You find out anything?"

"Not much, I'm afraid. It was rather crowded over there, and he didn't want people to overhear us."

"But you learned something?"

"I did. I went over to pay my condolences, as you suggested. Marcus thanked me but said they had broken up."

"When did they break up?"

"Marcus said a few weeks ago. It was rather sudden. Belem just announced he was done."

"Belem broke up with *him*?"

"That's what Marcus said."

"Did Belem give a reason?"

"I didn't ask."

"Did Marcus know Belem was dead?"

"He did. He said he got a call from someone at the Collier County Sheriff's Office. He was Belem's emergency contact. Belem hadn't changed it."

"Oof. Did he know that Belem had cancer?"

"I didn't ask. It felt weird. Sorry."

"Did you ask him if he knew that Belem was Budge?"

"Not exactly. I asked him if he knew an artist named Willem Budge."

"And?"

"He said he'd heard of him but didn't know him."

"You believe him?"

"Why would he lie?"

Guin could think of a couple of reasons.

"You learn anything else?"

"No, sorry. As I said, it was busy over there. And I don't think Marcus wanted to talk about his ex."

"I understand. Well, thanks for trying."

"Hey, did Lance tell you?"

"Tell me what?"

"That we're coming down there in a few weeks."

"Yes, he told me. I'm so glad you two can make it! Apparently, my mother is good for something. By the way, you're welcome to stay here."

"Thanks, but Carol will be upset if we don't stay with her and Philip."

"At least I'll get to see the two of you."

"And I'm planning on going to the Baker to see the exhibit."

"Great! You'll love it. Hey, I need to go. But thanks for calling."

"No problem. You have plans for Valentine's Day?"

"I'm going to a singles party. Don't ask. Okay, talk to you and Lance soon. Bye!"

CHAPTER 33

Guin arrived at Glen's place a little after four. She hadn't been able to decide what to wear, finally throwing on a pair of jeans and a funky light blue top. She was about to ring the doorbell but stopped. Instead, she reached into her bag and pulled out the key Glen had given her and let herself in.

"Hello?" she called.

"Hey!" said Glen, coming out to greet her. "You used your key!"

"Though every ounce of me wanted to ring the doorbell."

"But you didn't."

Glen eyed her.

"You look great."

"Thanks. So do you. And we match."

Glen was dressed in a pair of form-fitting jeans and a pale blue button-down shirt that was open at the neck.

"I just need to grab my equipment and we can go."

As they drove to Naples, Guin told him about her call with the Sachses and Owen.

"So you think Bennett Emerson could have pushed him?" asked Glen.

"He was right there by the stairs. And he and Bishop do kind of look alike from a distance. Well, if you saw them from behind, and it was dark. Maybe someone confused them."

"But what's his motive?"

Guin frowned.

They arrived at the wine bar a little before five-thirty. Glen found a spot to park nearby, and they headed inside. The restaurant was located in downtown Naples on a side street. It was an attractive looking place, though a bit on the dark side. What a reviewer would call cozy. There was a large bar in the center surrounded by barstools and small high-top tables. Along the walls were booths. In between was a scattering of regular tables.

Guin wondered how many people could fit and if the place would feel claustrophobic when full. Well, she would soon find out.

"I should go find the event coordinator," said Glen. "You want to have a seat and get a drink?"

"Sure."

Guin went over to the bar and took a seat. There were two bartenders, a man and a woman.

"What can I get you?" asked the female bartender.

"What do you recommend?"

"I'll get you tonight's special menu."

The bartender returned less than a minute later with a pink menu, which she placed in front of Guin. There were a half-dozen drinks listed, all of them in shades of pink. Guin thought about getting a Cosmo, but this was a wine bar. She should have a glass of wine.

"I'll have a glass of rosé."

"Plain or sparkling?"

Guin thought for a minute.

"You know what? Make it sparkling."

The bartender smiled.

"Sparkling it is."

She went to get Guin's sparkling rosé, and Guin looked around. There were people bustling around the place, no doubt finishing getting everything ready for the party, which would be starting soon.

"Juliana!" called the other bartender. "More glasses, *por favor*!"

Guin immediately whipped around to see who the other bartender was talking to. What were the chances it was the same Juliana who had worked at the Baker event? Slim to none, Guin thought.

The room was dimly lit, but Guin swore that she recognized the young woman. Though she only got a glimpse of her as Juliana disappeared into the back, no doubt to get more glasses.

"Excuse me," Guin said to the bartender.

He stopped what he was doing and looked over at her.

"The woman you were just talking to, Juliana, has she worked here long?"

"The place just opened. None of us has been here long."

Duh. Guin knew that.

"Do you know where she worked before? She looks familiar."

"Maybe she just has one of those faces."

"I know where I saw her!" said Guin, trying to see if she was right. "It was at a party at the Baker Museum. She served me a drink." Not true, but close enough.

The bartender eyed Guin suspiciously.

"Here's your sparkling rosé," said the other bartender, placing the glass in front of Guin.

"Thank you," said Guin. She took a sip, keeping an eye out for Juliana. Finally, she reappeared, carrying a box of clean glasses, which she placed on the bar.

"Thanks," said the bartender.

Juliana looked to be heading back to the kitchen, but Guin stopped her.

"Excuse me," she called. "Didn't I see you at the Baker Museum last Friday?"

Juliana froze, and her eyes grew wide.

Guin got up and approached her.

"I'm not a cop," she said, keeping her voice soft. "I just want to ask you a couple of questions. I'm a friend of the man who was accused of killing the man in the wheelchair."

Juliana didn't move. She looked terrified.

"I spoke with Elena. She said you were in the outdoor kitchen when it happened."

The male bartender came over.

"Is everything okay?" he asked Juliana. "Is this lady bothering you?"

Guin turned to him.

"I just wanted to ask Juliana a few questions."

"What kind of questions?"

"Juliana may have been a witness to a murder at the Baker Museum last Friday."

The bartender looked at Guin.

"What are you talking about?"

"You must have read about it or seen it on the news."

"I try not to watch the news."

Guin didn't blame him.

"You say someone was murdered?"

Guin nodded.

"An art critic."

"What's that got to do with Juliana?"

"She was there. And I think she saw what happened."

The bartender turned to Juliana and asked her something in Spanish. Guin was pretty sure it was, "Were you there?"

Juliana, still looking frightened, nodded.

"Did you see what happened?" asked the bartender, in English, no doubt for Guin's benefit, and then in Spanish.

Juliana replied to the bartender in Spanish. The two went back and forth. Guin didn't understand what they were saying. Finally, they stopped.

"You a cop?" the bartender asked her.

"No, I'm a friend of the artist," Guin replied. "The man who was accused of killing the critic." She didn't want to tell them that she was a reporter for fear of scaring them off. "He says he didn't do it, and I want to believe him." Guin looked at Juliana. "But Juliana may be the only person who knows what really happened."

The bartender conversed with Juliana again in Spanish. Then he turned back to Guin.

"You won't report her to the police or to ICE?" ICE stood for Immigration and Customs Enforcement.

"Absolutely not. I told you, I'm not a cop. Does she not have a green card?"

"She applied, but it takes a long time."

Okay. So that's why Juliana was hesitant to say anything. She was worried about being deported.

Guin looked at Juliana.

"Please. Do you know what happened, how the man in the wheelchair came to fall down the terrace stairs?"

Juliana looked at the bartender. He nodded. Juliana turned back to Guin and began speaking in rapid Spanish.

"I don't understand," Guin said to the bartender.

"She said she was in the kitchen, putting things away. The man in the wheelchair was arguing with a lady."

"Was she tall with dark hair?" Guin asked Juliana.

Juliana nodded.

It must be Alexandra Barnes.

"Then what happened?"

Juliana spoke in Spanish again.

"She said *el jefe*, the chief, came over."

"You mean Bennett Emerson, the director of the museum, tall man with gray hair?"

Juliana nodded.

"Then what?"

More Spanish. The bartender translated.

"She said another man came over."

"What man?"

"Juliana said he looked like the first man but older."

She must mean Farley Bishop. Just to be sure, Guin took out her phone.

"Are these the people you saw with the man in the wheelchair?" she asked Juliana, showing her their photos.

Juliana nodded.

"What were they doing?"

Juliana replied in Spanish.

"She said they were arguing."

"Does she know what they were arguing about?"

Juliana shook her head. Guin sensed that Juliana understood English but probably didn't speak it well or was shy.

"Then what?"

More Spanish.

"She said the lady left."

"What about the director, *el jefe*, and the other man?"

Juliana spoke in Spanish again.

"She said the other man went down the stairs."

"And the director, *el jefe*?"

Guin waited for the bartender to translate.

"He stayed a bit longer, then he left too."

"Did he go down the stairs?"

Juliana said something in Spanish to the bartender.

"No. She said he went to talk on his phone."

"And the man in the wheelchair? He was alone?"

Guin was confused.

Juliana was saying something to the bartender.

"She said he asked her for a glass of water and took some pills."

Could Belem have poisoned himself? She wished she could see the toxicology report. But it probably wouldn't be out for days.

Juliana was still talking.

"A few minutes later," the bartender translated, "he rolled himself over to the stairs. Then he shouted something that sounded like, 'Farley, don't!' and went over."

Guin stared.

"He rolled down the stairs on his own?" she asked Juliana.

Juliana nodded. Then she began speaking in Spanish again.

"Juliana didn't understand until it was too late. Then Carla screamed. And she got scared and ran."

"So you didn't talk to the police? But why did you run?" Though Guin thought she knew.

Juliana was speaking in Spanish again. Once again, the bartender translated.

"She was afraid the police would think she pushed the man. She knows she should not have run, but she was scared."

Guin honestly couldn't blame Juliana for running. But she would need to talk to the police.

Just then Glen came over.

"Everything all right over here?" he asked Guin.

"Yes," said Guin. "Juliana here just solved the mystery of who killed Ludwig Belem."

"She did?" Glen looked confused. And Guin saw Juliana looking nervous again. Did she think Glen was a cop? He was carrying a camera.

Guin turned to Juliana and the bartender.

"This is my friend, Glen, he's a photographer. He's here to take pictures of the party."

That seemed to calm Juliana down a bit.

Guin turned back to Glen.

"Juliana was working at the Baker that evening. She was in the outdoor kitchen when Ludwig Belem fell and saw what happened."

"So, who pushed him?"

"He pushed himself."

"He pushed himself?"

"He rolled his wheelchair to the top of the stairs, apparently shouted 'Farley, don't!'—no doubt hoping someone would hear him and think Bishop pushed him—and then pushed himself over."

"Wow. That's twisted. So he deliberately tried to frame Bishop."

"Sounds like it. And it would have worked, if not for Juliana here."

"She going to talk to Detective Romero?"

At the mention of Detective Romero, Juliana looked frightened again.

"The detective is a nice woman," Guin told her. "She's not going to deport you." However, Guin couldn't be sure about that. She would need to speak to the detective and feel her out before having Juliana talk to her.

"Hey, I need to go," said Glen. "The party's about to start. You good?"

"I'm good."

He gave her a kiss and told her he'd check on her later.

Guin turned to see that Juliana had gone and the bartender had returned to the bar. She went over to him.

"Did Juliana leave?"

"No, she went back to the kitchen."

Guin breathed a sigh of relief.

"I'm Guin, by the way. And I didn't catch your name."

"Carlos."

"You and Juliana…?"

"She's my cousin."

"Ah." That's right. Elena had said Juliana was going to work with a cousin. She must have meant Carlos.

"Thank you for translating. I'm afraid my Spanish isn't very good."

He shrugged.

"I know Juliana doesn't want to talk to the police, but she should tell them what she saw. An innocent man's been accused of murder. I know the detective in charge."

"Detective Romero."

"You know her?"

"No, your friend said her name."

Right.

"I can talk to her, explain the situation. I'm sure she'd understand."

Carlos didn't look so certain.

"Could you at least talk to Juliana, tell her it's important that she speak with the detective? As I said, I'll talk to her first. I won't mention Juliana's name. If you like, I can call you after I've spoken with her."

Carlos looked like he was thinking about it.

"Could I get your number? That way I can text you after I've spoken with her."

Carlos hesitated and then gave it to her.

"Thank you." She dug in her bag. "Here's Detective Romero's card," she said, handing it to Carlos. "Just in case."

"Okay everyone!" boomed a male voice from across the room. Guin turned and looked over. He must be the man in charge of the event. Glen was standing next to him. "Showtime!" said the man.

The door to the wine bar opened, and a crowd of noisy singles made their way inside. Guin reached for her sparkling rosé and took a healthy sip. It was warm and flat. Super. She signaled to the bartender and ordered another one. She had a feeling it was going to be a long night.

CHAPTER 34

Guin had tried to remain inconspicuous in the corner of the bar, but two men and a woman had hit on her. And she had had enough. She searched for Glen, wondering how he was supposed to take good pictures in such a dark, crowded space. She finally found him by the kissing booth.

The kissing booth had been the brainchild of the event coordinator. Couples could go there to kiss. Though the couple in there now was doing way more than kissing.

Guin went up to Glen and gently touched him on his arm.

"Yes?" he said. "Oh, it's you."

"You have a minute?"

"Sure."

Guin looked over at the couple who were making out.

"How much do you think they've had to drink?"

"Probably too much. So, what's up? You having a good time?"

Guin gave him a look.

"I'll take that as a no."

"I'm going."

"So soon?"

"We've been here nearly two hours."

"Yes, but the party didn't start until…" He saw the look Guin was giving him and didn't finish the sentence. "I should be able to get out of here soon."

"How soon?"

"Let me go speak with the event coordinator. He should be around here somewhere. Don't go anywhere."

Guin looked over at the kissing booth. There was another couple waiting for their turn. Looked like they were getting restless. Guin saw the man who was waiting tap the man who had his tongue down his partner's throat. The tongue jockey looked up at the man who had tapped him and grinned. Then he and his partner got up and moved away and the new couple took a seat and began to kiss. Guin didn't think of herself as a prude, but she was a bit grossed out. These people hardly knew each other.

Finally, Glen came back.

"Sorry, but he wants me to stay."

"I understand, but I need to go."

"You can't wait another thirty minutes?"

"No."

Glen sighed.

"I'm sorry. I didn't realize it would be like this."

"You didn't?" It had been exactly as Guin had expected, which was why she hadn't wanted to go with him. "Anyway, you stay. You have a job to do. But I'm getting a ride. I'll see you back at your place."

"You sure I can't convince you to stay?"

"Positive. I've already been hit on three times. And I can't deal with the music. How can people even hear each other?"

"What?" said Glen.

"Exactly."

Guin got out her phone and ordered a car.

"Twenty minutes?!"

"Everything okay?" asked Glen, seeing Guin's scowl.

"It says a car won't be here for another twenty minutes."

"See, you should stay. I promise, no more than thirty minutes. Then we're out of here."

Guin continued to scowl.

"Fine. But I'm going for a walk."

The event coordinator came over to have a word with Glen. Glen told him just a second.

"Thirty minutes," he said to Guin.

"Yeah, yeah, yeah," she replied. Then she headed out the door.

The cool night air felt good. Guin closed her eyes and inhaled, slowly breathing out through her mouth. Already she felt better. She heard a low grumble and realized it was her stomach. She hadn't eaten anything at the party.

She glanced over at 5th Avenue South. There was no shortage of restaurants there, all of them likely to be full of people celebrating Valentine's Day. And she wasn't looking for an expensive, sit-down meal. She just needed a nibble.

She began to walk down the avenue, not sure where she was going, when she passed a store selling gelato. Her stomach let out another growl. Guin went inside.

She knew she should really eat something more nutritious, but the different flavors of gelati looked so good. And the line was short.

"What can I get you?" asked the young woman behind the counter when it was Guin's turn.

Guin looked at the different cup sizes.

"I'll have a small cup of pistachio and hazelnut." *Nuts were healthy, right?*

Guin watched as the young woman scooped the gelato into a cup. Her stomach started to gurgle again. Guin told it to shush.

She took a seat against the wall after she had paid and dipped her spoon into the creamy mixture, making sure to get both flavors. She closed her eyes as the gelato melted on her tongue.

She took another bite, savoring the sweet, nutty goodness. Soon, she was feeling much better. She was also feeling thirsty. She purchased a small bottle of water and took a sip. A few minutes later, the gelato was gone. Time to take a walk.

Fifth Avenue South was alive with activity, so different from Sanibel on a Sunday evening. Though it was Valentine's Day. She headed down towards the water, doubting Glen would really be only thirty minutes. She glanced at the different restaurants, galleries, and shops she passed.

She got to the end of the avenue and decided it might not be wise to actually go onto the beach. She didn't want to get all sandy. She turned around and headed up the other side of 5th Avenue South. She was nearly back where she had started when she felt her phone vibrating in her back pocket. She pulled it out. It was Glen. He was done and wanted to know where she was.

"I'll meet you outside the wine bar," she wrote him back.

He was standing there when she arrived.

"Where'd you go?" he asked her.

"I took a walk along Fifth Avenue South."

"You want to get some food?"

"I had some gelato. But if you want to get something…"

"It's okay. I have food at home."

"But it'll take us around an hour to get there."

"I'll live. Let's go."

□

Guin woke up Monday morning to find Glen not in bed again. Had he left without telling her? She looked at the time. It was after seven. Though they hadn't gone to sleep until close to midnight.

She got up and headed to the kitchen. There was a fresh pot of coffee but no note. So he must be there. She helped herself and took her mug out to the lanai. Glen was there, looking out onto the canal.

"You okay?" she asked him.

"Just couldn't sleep."

"Any particular reason?"

He turned to look at her.

"Nothing you need to worry about." Which, of course, made Guin worry.

"If something's up, you can tell me."

"I know," he said.

"I should head back to Sanibel soon."

"You going to call Detective Romero, tell her about Juliana?"

"I was planning to. Do you think I shouldn't?"

"No, you should. But I'd leave Juliana's name out of it."

"I was planning to."

They were quiet for a minute.

"You sure you don't want to tell me what's bothering you?"

"Who says something's bothering me?"

"You've been distracted lately. And you said you couldn't sleep."

He reached out and clasped Guin's hand.

"It's sweet of you to be concerned, but I'm fine."

Guin frowned. She felt as though Glen was blocking her out, just like Art had done when she had started to grow suspicious of him. But she didn't say anything.

"Okay. I'm going to get dressed and go."

"You don't have to," he said.

"I know. But I've got a lot to do today. And my parents are flying in."

"Right. I forgot about that."

"I hope you didn't forget about Wednesday."

"Got it on my calendar."

"Good."

Guin gave him a kiss on his forehead and then went to the bedroom to get dressed.

As Guin drove back to Sanibel she wondered what was bothering Glen. She didn't really think he was cheating on her. But something was definitely up. Why wouldn't he say?

She pulled into her driveway, got out, locked the Mini, and went inside. Immediately, she was assailed by Fauna and Spot. She cleaned their bowls and gave them fresh food and water. Then she headed into the bedroom to take a shower.

She was eager to call Detective Romero but decided to phone Craig first. Though he was probably out fishing. She called him anyway and was surprised when he answered.

"What's up?"

"You out fishing?"

"Nope. Home. Waiting for the AC guy."

"Your AC not working?"

"Just having it checked."

"Ah."

"So, what's up?"

Guin told him about her encounter with Juliana.

"You think I should tell Detective Romero?"

"You think this Juliana's telling the truth?"

"I do. Why would she lie?"

"To protect herself."

"I doubt she pushed Belem down the stairs. What motive did she have?"

"Maybe he hit on her."

"He's gay."

"Maybe he threatened to report her."

"How would he know she was undocumented?"

"Fine. Let's assume she's telling the truth. She should talk to the police."

"I know. But she's worried they'll arrest or deport her."

"The police don't deport people."

"Try telling her that. So you think I should call the detective?"

"Yes."

"Another thing, can you ask your source about the toxicology report?"

"You wondering about those pills he took?"

"I am. They may have just been pain meds but…"

"You think he poisoned himself?"

"It's possible. Maybe he was worried the stairs wouldn't kill him."

"You really think he was that sick?"

"Mentally or physically? You said he had stage four lung cancer. Maybe he was terminal. Maybe he knew he was going to die and saw an opportunity to get back at the man he felt was responsible for ruining his life."

"That's pretty sick if true."

"I know. Anyway, can you check to see if the medical examiner found anything?"

"I'll do my best."

"Thanks."

They ended the call, and Guin called Detective Romero's cell phone. As luck would have it, the detective answered.

"Romero."

"Detective Romero, this is Guin Jones. I have important news about the Ludwig Belem case."

Guin thought she heard the detective sigh.

"Yes?"

"I spoke with an eyewitness who saw Ludwig Belem by the stairs that evening. She heard him call Bishop's name and then roll his wheelchair down the stairs."

"What is this eyewitness's name?"

"I'm not at liberty to say."

"Yet you want me to believe her story."

"She's telling the truth."

"And you know this because…?"

"I need you to trust me. It's a bit of a delicate situation. She's waiting for her green card and…"

"Let me guess: She doesn't want to talk to the police

because she's worried we'll turn her over to ICE."

"Something like that."

Another sigh.

"Tell her to call me."

"You won't turn her over to ICE or arrest her for withholding evidence?"

"Not if she comes forward and can prove her story."

"Great. I'll have her call you. Thank you, Detective."

Guin got off the phone feeling relieved. She immediately texted Carlos. No reply. Should she also leave a message for him at the wine bar? Couldn't hurt. Though it was too early to call over there. In the meantime, she was eager to speak with Farley Bishop. But how to reach him?

She knew that Bennett Emerson knew how to reach him and probably Alexandra Barnes did too. Would they be at the museum today? The museum was closed, but hopefully the administrative offices were open.

Guin called the main number for the museum. A recorded message let callers know that the museum was closed. But Guin was able to access the directory. Unfortunately, Bennett Emerson's voicemail box was full. She called back and tried Alexandra Barnes's extension. Her voicemail box was full too. Guin frowned. Then she remembered, the curator had two people that worked with her. But she didn't remember their names.

She went to the Baker Museum's website and searched for a directory. Success! She scanned the list. There was an assistant curator named Kara Bartek. Could that be the young woman Guin had met? There was an email for her but no phone number. But now that she had Kara's name, she could go through the phone directory.

She called the main number again and pressed the number for the museum directory. She started to type Kara's name and got a hit. The phone rang, and a woman picked up.

"This is Kara."

"Hi, Kara. My name's Guinivere Jones. I'm a reporter with the *Sanibel-Captiva Sun-Times*. We met the other day. I'm trying to reach Alexandra Barnes, but her mailbox is full. Do you know how I can reach her? It's important that I speak with her. Actually, I'm trying reach her fa—." Guin stopped herself. She had no idea if Kara knew that Farley Bishop was the curator's father. "I'm trying to reach Farley Bishop. As I said, it's very important that I speak with them."

"I'm sorry, Ms. Jones. Alex won't be in until tomorrow."

"What about Farley Bishop? Do you know how I can reach him?"

"I'm sorry, I don't."

Guin wondered if Kara was telling her the truth. The young woman was probably told to play dumb when it came to Bishop, especially with reporters.

"All right. Can you give her a message? Tell her that I have proof that Farley Bishop didn't kill that critic."

"You do?"

"I do. Tell her that and that I'd like to arrange a meeting with her and Mr. Bishop and Mr. Emerson. For as soon as possible."

"Give me your number."

Guin gave it to her, and Kara promised to deliver the message. Then Guin phoned Ginny.

CHAPTER 35

Ginny crowed when she heard the news. She had always believed that Farley Bishop was innocent. Though she agreed it wouldn't be wise to publish anything just yet. They would wait until Bishop had been officially cleared. But Ginny was sure Bishop would be vindicated.

That afternoon, Kara called to let Guin know that Ms. Barnes, Mr. Emerson, and Mr. Bishop could meet with her in Mr. Emerson's office the following day at nine a.m. Did that work for her? Guin said that it did.

A little before five, Guin called over to the wine bar, not having heard back from Carlos. Had he given her a fake number? Neither Carlos nor Juliana was working that evening, but the woman who answered said she'd give Carlos the message. Guin would text him tomorrow if she hadn't heard back from him.

Shortly after she had hung up, Craig called. According to his source, the pills Belem had taken were opioids, no doubt to help with the pain from his cancer.

Well, that was good news. Sort of. At least no one could be accused of poisoning him. Still, what kind of pain must he have been in to kill himself like that—and to blame Bishop? Guin suspected something had been eating away at Belem long before the cancer. She wished she could ask Marcus about him. But she felt it would be inappropriate.

□

Guin had set her alarm for six-thirty, even though she was normally up then. She just didn't want to risk oversleeping when she had an important meeting in North Naples. She took a quick shower, keeping her hair dry, put on a skirt and blouse, fed and watered the cats, and made herself some coffee and toast. She ate and drank quickly. Then she went to brush her teeth. At seven-thirty, she was out the door.

She arrived at the administrative building with eight minutes to spare. She checked her face in the rearview mirror, took a deep breath, released it, and got out of the car.

There was a guard in the lobby. Guin told him she had an appointment with Alexandra Barnes and the director, and he let her go upstairs.

The door to Bennett Emerson's office was ajar. She knocked and then poked her head in. The director, the curator, and Farley Bishop were all there.

"Do come in, Ms. Jones," said the director. He was smiling. A good sign. "Won't you have a seat?"

Guin sat.

"Kara said you had good news," said the curator.

"I do," said Guin. She looked over at Bishop. "I know you didn't kill Ludwig Belem."

"You have proof?" said the director.

"I spoke with an eyewitness." The director opened his mouth. No doubt to ask who the eyewitness was. But Guin cut him off. "I'm not at liberty to say who, but she saw the whole thing."

"It was that server," Ms. Barnes said to the director. "The one who disappeared. She was in the outdoor kitchen."

Guin tried to keep a poker face.

"Has she spoken with the police?" asked the director.

"Not yet. But she will, soon." Or so Guin hoped.

"So, who killed him?" asked the curator.

"He killed himself," Guin replied.

"He killed himself?" said the director. "But I heard him shout Farley's name."

"He shouted it to make it seem as though Mr. Bishop had pushed him," Guin explained.

"I don't understand," said the director. "Why? And why kill himself?"

"He had stage four lung cancer. It was likely terminal. And I suspect he was in a lot of pain."

"Are you saying he knew he was going to die and decided to frame Farley?"

"That's exactly what I'm saying."

"I told you I didn't do it," grumbled Bishop.

"I'm sorry I doubted you, Farley."

"Did you really think Mr. Bishop pushed Mr. Belem—or should I say, Willem Budge—down the stairs?" Guin asked the director.

"You don't know the awful things he said to us," he replied. "He threatened to ruin our careers."

"He already tried to sabotage mine," said the curator. "And nearly succeeded. Just because I was Farley's daughter."

That's awful, thought Guin. *What kind of person does that?* Though she knew the answer. Someone who was in a lot of pain.

"And this eyewitness… You said she hasn't gone to the police yet. But you believe that she will?" asked the director.

"I do. In fact, I've already spoken with Detective Romero about her."

That seemed to mollify the director.

Guin then turned to Farley Bishop.

"Now that we've cleared that up, there's something I've been wanting to ask you. Actually, two things."

He waited for her to go on.

"Where were you when Belem went down the stairs?"

"Yes, where were you?" asked the curator.

"I was having a smoke. Things had gotten a bit heated upstairs with Willem and rather than shove him down the stairs—yes, I thought about it—I went downstairs by the loading dock to have a cigarette."

"I thought you had stopped," said the director, while the curator said, "You know you're not supposed to smoke."

"That's why I didn't tell the two of you."

"Did anyone see you?" Guin asked.

"One of the guards, but I swore him to secrecy."

The curator rolled her eyes.

"What's your other question?" asked Bishop.

"Why did you want to paint me? And who's the little girl in the painting, the one in the last room?"

Guin realized that was two questions, but Bishop didn't say anything. He looked wistful.

"The little girl was my sister, Jean."

"Was?"

"She died when she was six."

"I'm sorry," said Guin. "What happened?"

"She got polio when I was four. Our parents sent me away, to keep me safe. By the time I was allowed to return home, they had buried her."

The room was very quiet.

"Jean had hair just like yours. Same coloring too. My parents were always saying that Jean was the light of their lives. They kept a picture of her on the mantle. When I asked them what had happened to her, they told me the fairies had taken her. Jean loved fairy tales and would dress up like a fairy. I used to tell them that I would find the fairies that took her and bring her back."

Guin felt herself choking up. Now she knew why Bishop had wanted to paint her and had her dress that way.

"Thank you for telling me," Guin said to him. Then she got up. "I should go."

She paused at the door and then let herself out.

Guin still hadn't heard back from Carlos. So she called the wine bar again that evening. This time, he was there. Guin told him about her conversation with Detective Romero, and he said that he would call the detective and make an appointment to see her with Juliana.

That evening, Guin slept fitfully. She would be speaking with Bill Hendricks the next morning, and she was nervous. Though she didn't know why. Well, she did, but she didn't want to admit it.

She had been reading the Business section every day and making notes. However, she doubted Hendricks would be quizzing her.

She got up in the morning and went for a walk. It was chilly out, probably in the fifties, and she went back inside to get a lightweight down jacket. Then she headed down to the beach.

Despite the cool weather, there were a dozen or so people out looking for shells. Guin was still cold, but she hoped she would warm up. She walked briskly, her eyes cast downward, and yelped when a wave of cold water washed over her feet. Maybe this hadn't been such a good idea.

She was about to turn around when she saw something white with brown spots rolling in the surf. She winced as she ran into the water. The water was freezing, though she told herself it wasn't that cold.

She reached for the object just as the tide was about to take it back out to sea.

"Gotcha!" she said.

Still standing in the cold water, she held up her find, not believing her eyes. It was a junonia shell. And it looked to be intact.

"Thank you!" she said to the sea.

She quickly rinsed the shell to get the sand out of it and held it up again. This was definitely a sign, she thought. But a sign of what? Another wave crashed over her calves. Guin was losing sensation in her toes. Time to get out of the water and head home.

She took a quick pic of the junonia and then pocketed her prize.

As soon as she got home, she took a warm shower. Then she made herself a pot of coffee and some scrambled eggs. She needed caffeine and protein. Finally, it was time to call Bill Hendricks. Guin entered his number into her phone and waited while his phone rang.

He answered after four rings.

"Hendricks."

"Good morning, Mr. Hendricks. This is Guinivere Jones."

□

Guin arrived at Glen's at four-thirty. He had asked her to get there early as he had something to discuss with her. She was about to ring his doorbell when she remembered she had the key. This would take some getting used to. She let herself in and called Glen's name. He emerged from his office, a smile on his face.

"You look very nice," she said to him.

"So do you," he replied.

Guin smiled. She had spent extra time getting ready for their dinner with her parents and was wearing one of her favorite dresses. And miraculously, her hair was behaving.

"How did your talk with Bill Hendricks go? Do you want something to drink?"

"Do you have an open bottle of wine?" she replied. "I could use a glass."

"Coming right up."

She followed him to the kitchen.

"Red or white?" he asked.

"I'll take white if you have it."

"As it happens, I have a lovely sauvignon blanc chilling."

Glen poured them each a glass.

"Cheers," he said, holding up his glass.

"Cheers," said Guin, clinking her glass against his.

They each took a sip.

"This is good," she said.

"I'm glad you like it. So, how'd the interview go?"

"First of all, it wasn't an interview. It was more of a get-to-know-you session."

"So, how did the get-to-know-you session go?"

"Good! He wants me to come up to New York for an actual interview."

"That's wonderful, Guin! See, I told you they'd want you!"

"No one's offered me a job yet, but Bill was very encouraging. He actually knew who I was and was familiar with my work."

"See."

"Yeah, yeah, yeah. Still, there's no guarantee they're going to offer me anything. And I'm not sure I'd take it if they do."

"What?! Are you crazy? If the *New York Times* offered you a job, you wouldn't take it?"

"Not if it paid nothing and I had to move to New York."

"I doubt they pay nothing."

"You know what I mean."

"Well, I'm excited for you. When do you go to New York?"

"I still need to work that out. But soon I think. So, you had something you wanted to tell me?"

Glen put down his wineglass.

"I've been offered a job."

"A *job* job, not a freelance gig?"

"A *job* job."

"Where?"

"In New York."

"*New York* New York?"

"*New York* New York."

"Doing what?"

"Remember that early morning phone call I received, the one that freaked you out?"

"I was not freaked out." Though she had been.

"It was my friend Raj, who I used to work with. He created an app that helps you find and hire photographers for various occasions. Kind of like Zocdoc or Uber. He says I gave him the idea."

"Didn't you say Raj was in London?"

"He is. He launched the app—it's really a business—over there. It's been doing brilliantly, and now he wants to take it stateside. And he wants me to get it up and running here."

"In New York."

"He wants to start in New York and then expand from there."

Guin took another sip of her wine.

"What did you tell him?"

"I told him I needed to think about it."

"Do you want to do it?"

"It's a great opportunity. A once in a lifetime opportunity really."

That meant he wanted to do it. But Guin could sense a but.

"But it would mean being in New York for at least six months. Though I would fly back here as often as I could to check on my folks," he quickly added.

Guin noted that he didn't mention flying back to see her.

"Have you told them about the job?"

"Not yet. I wanted to discuss it with you first."

"I guess I should be flattered." However, she was hurt that he hadn't mentioned flying back to see her. This was Detective O'Loughlin all over again.

"So what do you think I should do?"

"I think it sounds like an amazing opportunity. You should go for it. Though I'll miss you."

Glen stared at her. Then realization dawned.

"You don't understand. I want you to come with me."

Now it was Guin's turn to stare.

"You do?"

"How can you say that? I'm not going to New York for six months without you. I couldn't stand it."

"But… what about my job, and my house, and the cats?"

"We'd take the cats with us, of course. And you can rent out your house or find a house sitter. And as for your job, it sounds like you might have a new one soon."

"Whoa there, partner. I don't even have an official interview yet."

"But you will. And I know they'll want you."

"And what happens after six months? What if they want you to stay or they want you to go someplace else?"

"We'll tackle that six months from now. Right now, I just want to know if you'd be willing to go with me."

"You're asking me to make a pretty big commitment."

"I know, and that's why…" Glen got down on one knee and pulled out a small black velvet box. He opened it. Inside was a diamond ring. Guin could feel her heart hammering against her chest and covered her mouth.

"Guinivere Ann Jones, will you marry me?"

Guin began to cry. She had no idea why she was crying. It just snuck up on her. And now her nose was running. Ugh. She saw Glen's look of concern and wiped her nose and her eyes.

"Do you mean it?" she said.

"Of course I mean it," he replied.

"Okay."

"Okay?"

"Okay," she said, smiling down at him.

"Okay, you'll marry me?"

"You need me to say it?"

"I do."

"Yes, Glen Anderson, I will marry you."

He let out a whoop and then picked Guin up and twirled her around.

"Put me down," she said.

They were both grinning.

"I can't believe you said yes."

"Did you want me to say no?"

"No. I just…" He kissed her and then let her go. "I've been wanting to ask you since Paris."

"You wanted to ask me to marry you in Paris? Why didn't you?"

"I was afraid you'd say no. That I was just asking you because it was Paris and I had gotten carried away."

He had a point. It's probably what she would have said.

"So, you going to try on the ring?"

"You already gave me a ring." Guin held up her hand with the sapphire and diamond promise ring.

"Well, now you have two rings from me. Is that a problem?"

Guin was going to say something but changed her mind.

"Not at all."

"Here, let me," he said, taking the ring out of the box and slipping it on Guin's other ring finger. "It's perfect. Just like you."

Guin looked at him skeptically.

"How much wine did you have before I got here?"

"Just a glass."

Guin looked down at her hand. She had to admit, the ring was very nice. When had Glen purchased it? She looked at her watch. "We should go. My parents will kill me if we're late."

They got in Glen's BMW and headed down to Naples.

"So, you going to tell your mother and stepfather the big news?"

"Which big news? You mean the interview at the *New York Times*, your new job, or that we're now officially engaged?"

"All of it," said Glen.

"Hm…"

"You don't want to tell them?"

"How about we wait until dessert?"

"You really think you can hold out that long?"

"Probably not," she laughed. "So, you're sure about all of this—me, the job, everything?"

"As sure as I've been about anything. I love you, Guinivere Jones."

"And I love you."

And in that moment, as the sun was starting to set, Guin had never felt happier.

EPILOGUE

Guin had insisted that the wedding be on Sanibel. It was a small, private, low-key affair a few weeks after Glen had proposed, when Guin's brother and Owen were down. She and Glen had gone to City Hall to obtain a marriage license a few days before. Now it was time for the ceremony.

It was being held in her backyard and would be attended only by close friends and family. Afterward, there would be a buffet dinner catered by Bailey's.

Among those attending were Ginny and Joel, Steve and Shelly, Craig and Betty, Lenny, Sam Elliott, who had insisted on photographing the wedding for free, Glen's best friend from high school, and Raj, who had flown in with his wife.

Shelly and Guin's mother had insisted that Guin purchase a new dress for the occasion, even though Guin had said that she was fine wearing something she already had. But she had to admit she loved the pale blue maxi dress they had found in Naples. And Shelly had made Guin a crown of dried flowers to wear on her head and had lent her the veil she had worn at her own wedding, which she had attached to the crown. So now Guin had something old (Glen's grandmother's ring), something new (her crown), something borrowed (the veil), and something blue (the dress).

It had been a team effort turning Guin's backyard into a wedding venue, and Guin had been delighted with the result.

Now here she was, walking down the makeshift aisle with her stepfather. They had decided not to hire musicians, using recorded music instead, which was fine by Guin.

Owen had wanted to conduct the ceremony, but as he wasn't notarized in Florida, a state requirement, they had hired KC Kellerman to officiate. Guin owed her.*

The ceremony had gone smoothly so far. And Guin breathed a sigh of relief when no one had objected—or taken a shot at her.* As KC told Glen he could now kiss the bride, Guin smiled. Someone whooped as he did. Probably Lance. Then it was time to eat.

They didn't take an official honeymoon. That would have to wait. Instead, they went to New York for a long weekend: Guin for her second interview at the *Times* and Glen to sign leases on office space and an apartment, both of which the company would pay for.

Guin was uneasy about moving to New York, even temporarily. Though her mother and brother and old friends were thrilled. Maybe it wouldn't be so bad. Just in case it was, she was keeping her house on Sanibel. And Ginny had said her job would be waiting for her.

The cats, of course, as Glen had promised, would be going with them to New York. No way was Guin leaving them behind. And Jimbo and Sally, her Sanibel neighbors, would be looking after her place, as would Sadie and Sam, who lived next door. Sam even said he had bought an extra camera to point at her house. (He was obsessed with security.)

Guin still didn't know if she had a new job when they got back to Sanibel. Bill had warned her the *Times* often moved slowly. But if that didn't pan out, Lance had said that Guin

---

* Read Book 7, *A Perilous Proposal.*

could come work for him as a copywriter. And she could always freelance again.

Now as Guin stood on the beach, watching the sun go down, she wondered where she would be six months or a year from now. Would she be in New York or right back here on Sanibel? She had no idea.

Before she knew it, the sun had slipped into the sea, accompanied by a burst of light. It was a green flash! Another sign. She smiled to herself and then turned around and headed home.

Acknowledgments

First, thank you for reading this book. If you enjoyed it, and I hope you did, please consider reviewing and/or rating it on Amazon and/or Goodreads.

Similarly, a huge thank you to all of you who follow the Sanibel Island Mysteries page on Facebook and left me encouraging comments or emailed me after the hurricane, letting me know you cared. You guys got me through a very rough time when I wasn't sure if I would ever write again—or be able to write about Sanibel.

Moving right along… Thank you Kenny for believing in me and telling me I could do this. Thank you Amanda Walter and Robin Muth, my invaluable first readers, who have been with me from early on in my journey, for your comments and corrections. Thank you Mom, aka Sue Lonoff de Cuevas, who taught writing at Harvard, for ensuring that there were no embarrassing grammar or style errors.

And because you can judge a book by its cover, thank you Rita Sri Harningsih for doing a great job on the jacket. Similarly, my thanks to Jason Anderson (no relation to Glen) of Polgarus Studio for making my books look as good on the inside as they do on the outside.

Lastly, a special thank you to Courtney McNeil, the director and chief curator of the Baker Museum in Naples, as well as the staff there, for answering my many questions about the museum. Though I am a member of the museum and have been to the Baker many times, I now know a lot more about the museum thanks to them.

About the Sanibel Island Mystery series

To learn more about the Sanibel Island Mystery series, visit https://SanibelIslandMysteries.com and follow the Sanibel Island Mysteries Facebook page, https://www.facebook.com/SanibelIslandMysteries/.

Made in the USA
Columbia, SC
16 December 2024

49712997R00195